THE THREE DEATHS OF WILLA STANNARD

A THRILLER

KATE ROBARDS

CROOKED
LANE

NEW YORK

Published in the United States by Crooked Lane Books, an imprint of The Quick Brown Fox & Company LLC.

Crooked Lane Books and its logo are trademarks of The Quick Brown Fox & Company LLC.

Library of Congress Catalog-in-Publication data available upon request.

ISBN (hardcover): 978-1-63910-347-8
ISBN (ebook): 978-1-63910-348-5

Cover design by Kara Klontz

Printed in the United States.

www.crookedlanebooks.com

Crooked Lane Books
34 West 27th St., 10th Floor
New York, NY 10001

First Edition: June 2023

10 9 8 7 6 5 4 3 2 1

THE THREE DEATHS OF WILLA STANNARD

PROLOGUE

Willa

Now

I F WILLA STANNARD were on air to break the news of her death, she'd report that the police lights sliced through the night. Carved through the darkness. Fragmented the neighborhood. Anything to give a dead-end story a sense of urgency.

It was a hard habit to break, the urge to compose stories the moment there was any quiet. Willa couldn't escape the hum of words in her mind. She'd string together effortlessly eloquent sentences that were always sharper than the ones the production assistants drafted.

It wouldn't even be a story worth reporting, not at first. Until the responding officer set off the police scanner airwaves with a recognizable name, a story about a woman dead in her bathtub wouldn't make it onto the air. Chicago was too big, with too many deaths, for it to matter.

She knew that in the broadcast news business, she wasn't ideal. She was unlikable. Her unflinching honesty, deadpan observations, and naked ambition never contributed well to on-air ratings. When she was still on the evening news, older women had been her worst-performing demographic.

But tomorrow, when her former colleague, a charming brunette with controlled sadness in her eyes, broke the story that it was Willa who had been found in a bathtub by the chocolate factory, she knew it would be the fifty-five-plus group who would mourn her death most.

She sank deeper into the tepid water. She had practiced for this moment. Role-played the instant when his arms would hold her underwater. She'd waited too long, grown too comfortable with her own death, to fight anymore. Since she was a little girl, breathing in the scent of fresh-picked poppies and baby's breath, fighting to ignore the hot pain in her ribs from the heel of his boot, she'd known he'd kill her.

Her arm hairs prickled, crying for a shot of hot water. She swiped at her forearm to smooth out the hairs and marveled at the spray of red her wrist left behind in the water. She sank lower until her ears submerged and she heard an insistent, dull buzz, the way a motorboat sounds when you're swimming. It reminded her of the rattle of cicadas at night.

*　*　*

Later, after all this, people would tell stories about her. There would be vague memories, myths, and speculations. They'd wonder if her on-air breakdown was the beginning of her downfall. They'd feel a special privilege to have witnessed it, like the morbid curiosity that causes gapers' blocks in traffic. And they'd be right, mostly. But they wouldn't know what came first.

1

Sawyer

"I T'S ONLY THREE minutes, but it should be the hardest three minutes of your day!"

My legs burn as I pedal sprints. I shout the countdown into my sweaty headset and hold on to a relentless smile as the class grabs their towels, white but glowing blue in the strobing black light, to mop their foreheads.

"Namaste, ladies. See you at this time next week," I call as I step off my platform.

As the room clears, I turn off the scattered flickering electric candles. I pause below the ceiling-mounted fan to take a few deep breaths. I need to update my playlist to fit the aggressive arc of class better. I grab my water bottle and squint as my eyes adjust to the blinding-white lockers outside the studio.

It's always jarring to step into the bright afternoon sun after an otherworldly candlelit ride with a pack of cultishly obsessive women. Their sweaty glamour and energy are addictive; they're the best medicine for avoiding the cruelly located frozen yogurt shop next door to the studio. The line extends down the sidewalk, even past summer's peak. Two teenagers in Catholic school uniforms perch on a giant planter that spills over with tiny flowers as they pick raspberries from their yogurts. I ache for a taste, but I'd rather have approval from the women who take my class, who don't try to conceal their disappointment when they find out their spin instructor weighs more than them. Where's the motivation when you're already the skinniest person in the room?

Within walking distance of the studio, just north of Lake Street, maple trees canopy the entrance to the courtyard of my three-story apartment building. My legs feel wobbly from the ride, and the walk, and the final climb to the third floor. As I round the corner to 3F, I stop when I see two police officers stationed in front of my door.

One steps forward with a puffy hand extended. "Officer Mallory Curry." With a firm shake, she introduces herself. "I'm the commanding officer of the crime scene investigation unit. This is Officer Jonah Lackey. Are you Sawyer Stannard?"

I nod.

"May we come in?" Officer Curry tips her head toward the door.

"Tell me," I whisper.

The officers exchange glances.

"Is Willa Stannard your sister?"

I nod again.

"Ms. Stannard," Curry starts, "I'm sorry to let you know that Willa is dead. We tried to contact your mother, but she wasn't at her residence. We'd like to speak with you about what happened, but we'd prefer to do so indoors. May we come in?"

My heartbeat thuds in my ears as her words come into focus.

"Are you serious?"

"Ms. Stannard, I wouldn't joke about this."

The unsteady feeling of vertigo hits me. I feel my vision turn to a shadowy brown and start to darken to black at the edges, like a burnt photograph. The sweat blanketing my body turns alternately icy and hot, and a sharp wave of nausea bubbles in my throat. I clamp my hand over my mouth and fumble in my bag for my keys. The young cop—already I forget his name and think of him only as *the uniform*—says something and puts his hand on my sweaty shoulder for a moment before the lady gives a sharp shake of her head and his hand drops.

Inside, I stumble to the couch and bow my head. My shoes sink into the rubbery foam of a yoga mat that stretches the length of the living room. When I raise my head, Officer Curry speaks.

"I am sorry for your loss, Ms. Stannard. You must have many questions. I will answer them to the extent that I can, but I also have a few questions for you."

"Wait. Wait," I say, pawing through my bag for my phone. "This is a mistake. She just called me." My fingers tremble as I struggle to unlock my phone. "She left a message. I didn't even listen yet."

I hold the phone to my ear and strain to make sense of the words. I play a voice mail from Willa once, twice, three times while the officers watch me intently, their eyes unreadable.

"She said it's important. I have to call her back."

"Ms. Stannard . . ."

"Wait!" My voice is high and frantic. I hit redial and listen as Willa's poised, throaty voice instructs me to leave a message, that she'll return my call.

I stare at the list of recent calls. The red text that announces Willa's missed call mocks me. A chill spreads through my body.

"Was it a car accident?" I picture Willa's sleek black car crumpled on the side of the expressway, causing one of those epic rush-hour backups where drivers forget how angry the crawl of traffic made them as they slow to gape at the wreckage.

"Willa was found by her landlord this morning when he arrived to inquire on the status of her rent payment. She was found in her bathtub, and at this time, all indications point to suicide."

My head snaps up. Is this a cruel joke? "No. No, there must be a mistake. She'd never commit—" I can't choke it out. Suicide? Never. She's too perfect to even consider it.

"She left a note, which I'd like you to read. And it appears that she began the process of giving away belongings." Curry's voice is gruff, no-nonsense, but as she looks over her thick-framed glasses, her eyes turn almost motherly. "Sawyer, the scene suggests this is a suicide. Do you know if Willa ever spoke about wanting to harm herself? Was she depressed?"

"No, never. Wait—the bathtub? What happened?"

Without hesitating, Officer Curry says, "It appears that she cut her wrists. Now, I believe that we're dealing with a nonsuspicious death, but we always take steps to rule out foul play before classifying a death as a suicide."

I try to make sense of what she's saying. "You said she left a note?"

With a brisk nod, she motions to the uniform, who darts his hand into his pocket and retrieves a piece of paper. He steps forward and hands it to me.

"It's a photocopy, obviously." He smiles apologetically, and I cringe. He's too young to have this responsibility. Then again, what responsibility is this? The worst has already happened; he's only along for the ride.

The copy captures a discreet watermarked monogram announcing Willa's initials. Her handwriting is sharp and narrow but legible: *Sawyer, I'm sorry. I wish I was brave enough not to do it. I know you'll never forgive me.*

I hold the note with a shaky hand. Willa is blunt. Too honest, too direct. But she is a writer too—an award-winning journalist. She cares more about the truth than people's feelings, but wouldn't she have given more of an explanation in her last written note?

"What can you tell me about your sister?" Officer Curry prompts. "Did you have a close relationship with her?"

I press my lips together while I study the photocopy. Overly terse and stained in the corner, the note is at odds with Willa's perfectionism. *She has more books than she has friends*, I think about saying. She interrupts too much. She tells you what to do. She's not all that likable, or maybe it's just that she doesn't like that I'm too aimless and unmotivated for her.

"We get along. We just don't talk very often anymore," I concede. I measure my voice, trying to make it slow and deliberate. "But still, I know her. I know she would never kill herself."

My voice breaks and betrays me. I think of the way Willa used to stutter when we were kids, how the frustration would frame her face as she tried to gain her composure. I think of the exercises she would do in front of the mirror to calm her nerves, and how they worked so well she got a job in front of a TV camera. I take a deep breath to steady the room.

"This is wrong. Are there any signs of an intruder?"

"There are no signs of a break-in, but we took Willa's clothes for testing. I have the DNA unit looking into the case. I'm treating this as a high-profile death."

Curry pauses and glances at her partner. I see then that his eyes are sharper than I imagined; they track around the room, shrewdly taking in everything from the galley kitchen to the arched doorways to the nonworking fireplace. Curry turns back to study me.

"Please take another look at the note," she says, "and tell me what comes to mind when you read it. Did Willa do something to hurt or offend you?"

Again I look at her words. "What comes to mind . . . is that this note is a fake."

Officer Curry's eyebrows disappear below her shaggy salt-and-pepper bangs, but she doesn't take her eyes off me to glance at her partner this time.

"Willa didn't like me enough to use her last words apologizing to me. God, she never apologized for anything in her life. She never thought she did anything wrong. Believe me when I say it's out of character for her to say sorry for anything. Ever."

"When was the last time you saw Willa?"

"Months. Maybe Christmas. She worked a lot, and my schedule can get kind of unconventional. Lots of evening classes. I know she moved out of her condo, but I've never even been to her new apartment."

Officer Curry stuffs her large hands into the pockets of her navy police jacket, which in the late-summer heat is a starched and sturdy reminder of her position.

"Look, Ms. Stannard. Given the presence of the note and the way Willa started to clear out her belongings, I don't suspect foul play is involved. We will keep you informed of the investigation as it progresses." From her pocket, she pulls a thick ivory business card. "Contact me if you think of anything that may be relevant to the case."

Curry starts toward the door while the uniform follows so close he clips her heels.

"And Sawyer?" she says with her hand on the doorknob. "I can't keep this from the media. Given Willa's . . . celebrity in the area, I am certain that her death will be on the news. I'm sorry you'll have to see that."

As they exit the apartment, the uniform closes the door so softly I don't hear it latch. The room falls silent, quiet enough for me to hear the insistent screaming of the Ruizes' baby next door.

I replay the officers' words, turning them over in my leaden mind. Did she say, *Willa died*, *Your sister is dead*, or *Willa's dead*? I try to reconstruct it, but already I can't remember. All I know is that she didn't offer a euphemism, like *Your sister has passed*.

I recall that the officer said they couldn't contact our mother. It dawns on me that this task, informing a mother of her daughter's death, now falls to me. The realization sends a surge of bile up my throat, and I clamp a shaking hand over my mouth to keep it in.

Once more, I hit redial on my phone, willing my sister to answer. I hold my breath as it rings, feeling superstitious. A part of me believes she'll answer, despite what the officers said. For months she's let my calls go to voice mail, but still I pray that she'll pick up, that it was all a misunderstanding.

There's a mechanical click, and once again she tells me to leave a message. This time I do, because I can't shake the superstition.

I stand at the window and stare past the courtyard, watching the officers climb into their police car. My heart clenches as they drive off without lights or sirens. There is no emergency. There is nothing to hurry about anymore.

Willa Stannard, former reporter for KZTV, passes away unexpectedly

Posted 5:17 A.M., September 4, 2018, by Kenton Lowell, KZTV

CHICAGO—Willa Stannard, KZTV's former reporter, died Thursday in an apparent suicide. She was thirty-three.

A representative from the Chicago Police Department told KZTV that officers responded to a death investigation at the 3000 block of North Marion Street in the Fulton River District at 2:50 P.M. on Monday and identified Stannard.

Stannard was a valued reporter for the KZTV station from 2007 to 2016 until she left to pursue an opportunity at a progressive local newspaper, *TruthShout*.

Best known for her tenacity and passion for objective reporting, Stannard was a hardworking and determined journalist. In 2013, she won the Steele Award for best investigative journalism for an undercover article about substandard care at hospices. Her coverage on doctors treating patients despite malpractice charges earned her a nomination for the Morrow Media Award in 2014.

Stannard faced public scrutiny when she suffered from an on-air panic attack during an evening newscast in December 2015. She left her position as anchor host midprogram, leaving an underprepared junior colleague to complete the remainder of the live newscast. Her actions gained national attention with mental health professionals and self-help gurus. Stannard retreated from broadcast journalism but continued to write under a pseudonym at *TruthShout.*

Stannard is survived by her mother, Claudia Stannard, and her sister, Sawyer Stannard.

2

Sawyer

THE CLOYING SCENT of roses and carnations, all white, pure, fills the room.

The ceiling is too low, and the track lighting shines too bright, but it seems as if all the pretty women clogging the room applied their makeup knowing that the shadows would drag down their under-eye circles. It's a congested circus of glowing TV personalities and shaggy-haired writers who've attempted to dress their best in wrinkled brown suits. You could call them Willa's former colleagues, but mostly they're here to be near a modicum of leftover fame and scandal. I can almost hear them scratching notes to use in an article later. They all have that hungry, focused look Willa used to get when she drafted a story in her mind, taking in all the details.

When the doors to the parlor open, the onlookers hang back and eye my mother and me before descending for a look. Momma's uneven sigh warbles through the room as she approaches first. She starts to sob with gasping, erratic whines. Her anguish rolls through the room and sets off all the pretty women, who bow their heads delicately and dab at the corners of their eyes. A few of the hardened reporters stare at me, willing me to comfort my mother. It's Willa's ex Leo, the cuffs of his dress shirt rolled to his slender fore-arms, who gently tugs on Claudia's arm and steers her to the rows of folding chairs padded with a nubby blush fabric.

I walk to the casket slowly, unsteady in heels on the faded, lumpy carpet. I peer in and feel my forehead furrow.

It isn't Willa.

No, Willa has an icy-blond pixie cut that swoops down over her left eye. She always wears smoky-eye makeup and plucks her brows until they have just the right arch to convey her permanent skepticism.

But that's not who lies in the billowy folds of the casket. This woman is nearly a skeleton; she is ravaged, like a junkie, and bony, not the willowy beauty Willa is. Her hair has faded to its natural color, leaving her roots the color of smoked walnuts.

I study the woman before me. Willa is cool and reserved and always replies to emails within twenty-four hours. Pressed, lint-free. Exacting. She never neglects to do any-thing. This isn't her.

True, I haven't seen her in months. I told Officer Curry I saw her last Christmas, but that wasn't right, I realized later. It's been more than a year, at least. She started to dis-tance herself from me and Momma, and like everything else Willa did, she was good at it. She didn't spend the holidays with us, she didn't return our phone calls, and she didn't seem bothered by any of it. At first, I didn't know it was intentional, her distance. Was that a warning sign? Guilt feels like a hard lump in my chest. Why did I give up on her so easily?

On wobbly feet, I find a seat in the first row. Hushed murmurs fill the room as the mourners get their chance to file past Willa.

"Is it just me, or is her nose different than it used to be?"

"Definitely had some work done."

"I knew that hair color didn't come from nature."

I don't have a plump aunt to squeeze my hand reassuringly, no grandmother to show dignified sorrow, no weathered grandpa to shake his head at everything, proving that the younger generation has it all wrong. It's only Momma.

And now she sobs. Messy, angry tears. Showy tears to prove she hurts the most. Embarrassing tears when all the other women are so demure in their grief. I feel guilty for judging her, but I can't stop my mind from churning disloyal thoughts.

The priest has heavy jowls and a military buzz cut. His rimless glasses disappear into the ruddy apples of his cheeks. Willa would have towered over him.

"We gather here today to celebrate the life of Willa Josephine Stannard, who has returned to her home with God, our Father."

Suddenly I remember the way Willa would squeeze my hand in church. The muscles in her thin arm would tense as she gripped my hand as hard as she could. So hard I thought the delicate bones would crack and break right there in the pew. During every hymn, every forced interaction with our neighbors, I'd look around to see if any other pair of siblings had thick, corded forearm muscles to indicate that they did the same thing. All I saw were limp hands, and so I loved the pain she caused me. It was our secret.

The priest invites guests to give a eulogy because I've refused to do it. I met with the funeral director; I selected the programs and the pallbearers, the casket and the clothes Willa would be buried in; but I knew I couldn't deliver her eulogy. She spoke for me for years when I was a late talker. I can't find my voice now either.

At the priest's invitation, Brooke Conroy is on her feet instantly. Her toned thighs strain against her fitted black skirt. She smooths wrinkles as she takes the priest's spot at the podium adjacent to Willa. She smells like lavender and honey. Before Willa's panic attack went viral, the most scandalous thing to happen at the station was an intern posting a cell phone video of Brooke biting into a juicy nectarine and licking her lips lasciviously.

"My name is Brooke Conroy, and I'm Willa's coworker, and more importantly, her friend. Willa and I worked together at KZTV until she retired from broadcast journalism. I offer my deepest condolences to Willa's family and friends and also the public, who welcomed her into their home nightly . . ." Her brown hair is impossibly glossy under the radiant lights.

"Willa's story is one we need to address publicly," she continues, "because it's about privacy in a time when all-access prevails. We are in a time when twenty-four seven access is customary, and Willa fought against that, ultimately sacrificing her life for privacy and fairness. I saw firsthand her frustration at not being taken seriously as a journalist in a male-dominated industry. She was concerned about being pigeonholed as one type of reporter."

My fists are clenched and sweaty as I listen to Brooke. I need to say something. Willa deserves more. But how can I sum up her life? It's too big a task. She was too many things for me to summarize her in front of these people who didn't really know her.

All I can think about is the way Willa set herself apart. How can I say that to the room without it sounding like Willa was standoffish? It wasn't like that, anyway; she didn't do it to be distant. She did it to rebel. She refused to see *Titanic*, she railed against social media, and I caught her scowling at babies more than once. She was smart and responsible, but sometimes it seemed she was born indignant. I'm not sure if Willa always wanted her choices or if she chose them to defy everyone else.

Brooke raises a manicured hand to gently stroke the white rose pinned to the lapel of her shirt. "I wear this rose today to commemorate my friend and a friend to many. To bring awareness to the fight for justice for women in journalism. And to remind everyone that, while we live our lives in the spotlight, we too are entitled to retreat into solitude. Thank you, and God bless."

As Brooke takes her seat, I concentrate on keeping my posture upright. The more overt my mother's grief becomes, the more inconspicuous I want my grief to be.

My mother leans across the chairs, and her large breasts threaten to spill out of her black blouse. Her face is a mottled red, and her hair is limp and wavy. Years of exposure to lily pollen as a florist have stained her fingertips a yellowish brown.

"That Brooke Conroy is really beautiful," Claudia says as her feverish eyes tame in admiration. "She sent the Sentiments of Serenity spray to the left of the casket. It's our most expensive arrangement. Don't you think it's so tasteful?" Her blond eyebrows have thinned and paled so much as she's aged that they can't express her emotions anymore, so she relies on exaggerated eye movements.

Beside her, too wide to fit on a single mourner's chair, is her boyfriend, Oz. Buffered by an extra seat, he trains his deep-set eyes ahead stoically when I glance at him, avoiding my stare. It's no secret I dislike him. My mother says I don't understand him because he never smiles, but I haven't trusted him since I found out he's been fired by landlords for stealing from apartments he visited on the pretense of doing paint jobs and maintenance. I hope it's clear to onlookers that this petty criminal is not my father, though he sits in the first row of seats, designated for those allowed to grieve the hardest.

I level my gaze ahead as the priest returns to the front, waves a censer over the casket, and recites a prayer. He peers at Willa through his smudged glasses and lifts a limp hand to snake a rosary through her fingers. Then he ushers us from the room so he can be the last person to look into Willa's unfamiliar face before she's lowered into the ground.

I think again of the way my bones would crackle when she squeezed my hand in church. I can't reconcile the feeling of her hot hand in mine with the image of the priest's dry, chalky palm stroking her skin for the final time.

*   *   *

The faded floral carpet extends into the vestibule. Clumps of women with CrossFit and Bar Method bodies huddle together with obligatory displays of grief.

"—just happy she didn't do it on the air."

"Well, she did commit *career* suicide on air."

Their words inflame my cheeks. Conflict feels like a swollen lump in my chest, burning bright and radiating into my stomach. Harmony is my religion, but I feel combative for my sister. I cast an accusing glance their way, and they have the decency to quit tittering and look contrite.

Across the room, Leo stands by a hissing coffeepot with two people I recognize as Willa's college friends.

"I'm sorry to interrupt," I say as I approach.

"Sawyer." Leo pulls me into an awkward embrace. "I can't tell you how sorry I am."

Behind his glasses, his dark eyes sag with mourning. He doted on Willa when they were together. She dominated their relationship and heaped the burden of her perfectionism on his shoulders. Now he'll carry the weight of her casket to the waiting hearse.

"You remember Remy and Noah?"

They murmur condolences with downcast eyes. They look like the kind of people who relish conversations filled with sarcasm, the more esoteric the better. They make me

want to be more bubbly and cheerful than usual to counteract their trained cynicism. But not today.

I turn to Leo. "This doesn't seem real. You knew her
best, right? How did this happen?" I can't keep the note of
accusation out of my voice.

His slight shoulders slump inward. "Used to know her,
maybe. Not anymore. We've been broken up for more than
a year."

"But did you ever talk to her still? Did she seem
depressed?" I ask, thinking of the way the cops asked me the
same question in my apartment just a few days ago. I don't
know if it would be better or worse if Leo knew and I didn't.

"She hadn't been herself for a long time."

"Did you know?" I ask, turning to Remy and Noah.

"Know? Of course we didn't know Willa was suicidal,"
Remy snaps. She presses her berry lips together until they're
a thin gash.

Noah shoves his hands in his pockets, bunching the
baggy folds of his oversize sweater.

"Willa begged off plans most weekends," Noah offers.
"She was out of town on a work assignment whenever we
invited her to hang out."

His hair looks unwashed and greasy, like he's a rebel-
lious teenager instead of a man in his thirties. I can't imagine Willa spending time with him or Remy, whose eyes
simmer like unlit coals above the smooth plane of her flat,
porcelain cheeks. Willa always said she preferred solitude,
and now I know why.

"Had you seen her recently, at least?"

My voice, desperate, is too loud over the din in the
room. A few people glance my way, and I notice for the first
time that the police officer from the other day is standing
beside a brass-plated sign with Willa's birth and death dates.
It's been a week since she died, but only days since we found
out.

Across the room, Momma, unsteady in her low heels, approaches Officer Curry with a look on her face that is simultaneously aggressive and repentant. She would demand answers, but she is terrified of upsetting anyone. She'll probably just end up begging the officer to reassure her that everything will be okay.

"It's an intrusion to peer at someone's grief. A violation," Remy says.

I dart my gaze away from my mother to see that Remy's attention has followed her across the room, on her way to quiz the officer. I feel my cheeks flame. *It's my grief too*, I want to say.

Leo's hand is on my arm. "I saw her a few months ago, Sawyer," he says, bringing me back to the moment. The hot lights, the tinkle of inappropriate laughter, the smell of bitter roasted coffee in the air assault me. "Let's meet and I can tell you about my last moments with her. If that would help."

Last. That word. He's already filed it away, neat and final.

"I'd like that."

If I can piece together Willa's final months, maybe I'll understand why I'm standing here with these hypocrites and sightseers as my sister lies in the next room, an hour away from being lowered into the ground.

* * *

Officer Curry is wearing her dress blues today, but her hair looks just as tousled as it did that afternoon in my apartment. Her face is impassive as she approaches, her gaze direct yet somber.

"Ms. Stannard, may I have a word?"

We step to the side, out of earshot of Remy, Noah, and Leo.

"Quite a turnout," she comments. She stands stoically at my side as we both turn to look around the crowded foyer. She seems comfortable in the silence, while I fight the urge to become too chatty to fill the quiet in our corner.

"As you know, my unit has been combing Willa's apartment for any signs of foul play. Evidence collected from her apartment returned a few items that my investigation unit is looking into right now. We did find trace amounts of DNA on the sheets, a few unsourced fibers, and what tests show to be dog hair in her bedroom.

"What I don't want is for you to put unwarranted weight on these items," she continues. "They may not be indicators of foul play in any way. I want to be clear when I say I still believe we're dealing with a classic case of suicide here. But we're going to leave no stone unturned."

My mind reels. "You found DNA? Whose?"

"We don't know the answer to that yet. We ran it through the system, and it returned no hits. It might be a dead end. It could easily be from a boyfriend or visitor."

"So it's . . ."

"It's semen. From an unknown male," Curry confirms.

I tear my eyes away from the room to look at her. At this moment, I feel authenticity radiate from her, and I know I can trust her to find out what happened to Willa. She doesn't talk to me in the patronizing, honeyed way that all the women in my fitness classes do; she seems steadfast, reliable.

Curry meets my gaze without turning her head. "Sawyer, please don't get your hopes up just yet."

When unwashed sheets and dog hair in Willa's meticulous apartment are all I have to go on, it is hard to feel buoyed, but I feel a niggling lightness in my chest that whispers it might not be a suicide after all.

3

Willa

One month before

"ON THIS DAY, we not only look back to remember our beautiful daughter, but we look ahead to the day when we may find peace and closure," Grace said, composed and careful. She turned to Willa. "How's that?"

"If you use that quote, be sure to use mine too." Jack tapped a wrench against his palm, unaware of how menacing he looked in the shadowy, leaking boathouse. "My wife doesn't want to point fingers, but I do. There are so many people to blame. I blame the deranged sicko for breaking into my home to steal my daughter. I blame the police for the countless mistakes they made as they botched the investigation. I blame—"

"Jack, I don't disagree, but the moment I quote you speaking about who's to blame, that finger pointing is going to turn right to you and Grace," Willa said quietly.

She shifted in a nylon lawn chair, a twin to the striped one Grace sat on next to her. Swollen raindrops plunked overhead on the tin roof of the old boathouse where Willa had insisted they meet. Investigative reporting, she'd found, was a delicate balance between creating trust and disrupting it. So today, on the anniversary of Grace and Jack's baby's kidnapping, Willa had suggested they talk in the spot where so many speculated little Melody had had her final moments.

"Jack, stop," Grace chided. "I'm sorry, dear."

"No, this is good. Emotion is good," Willa assured them. "So, in the nearly thirty years since Melody went missing, there have been many theories, few suspects, and no new evidence. Short of a confession, you may never know who did this. What would you say if you could speak to the person who took Melody?"

"You didn't . . ." Jack took a few lumbering steps past the docked pontoon boat and stopped short of the curtain of rainfall sliding off the boathouse's roof.

"Jack, what are you—"

He waved Grace off with an impatient swat. "I thought you might have invited him here. Stewed up some drama for the book." Jack turned away to mask the bitterness that flowed so freely from him. "He's not coming, right?"

"What would you say to him if I had asked him to come here today?" Willa prodded.

"I'd say he doesn't deserve to live after the pain he's caused my family."

Willa looked past Jack to the quiet gravel road beyond their modest cottage. She shivered, maybe from the rain, maybe from the conjured image of Abel Bowen's lurching, hollow-eyed figure appearing on the private drive.

She'd spent so many hours with both men—the accused and the victim interchangeable—that she knew someone wouldn't survive if she had staged a confrontation.

"That's a good quote." Willa cleared her throat with a rattling cough left behind from an unshakable cold. "I call that an inciting quote. It jams together guilt and anger and the threat of chaos. It's the type of quote that elicits a confession."

Hope flooded Grace's eyes while fury simmered in Jack's.

"Do you know something that we don't know?"

CHAPTER

4

Sawyer

MY EARS THROB from the music as it floods through the headphones. Sweaty hair whips through the air, and sometimes I throw my head so hard the earbuds fall out. Mostly I move in place, since the floor is cluttered with laundry baskets and the box to the IKEA dresser I never got around to building. In the dark I thrash my arms and head as hard as I can. More than anything, I want an overhead fan to circulate the hot air in my tiny prewar bedroom.

A sour smell rises from my sheets and settles in the room like a dense fog. The past few nights I've woken with my shirt clinging to my damp chest, my hair matted in a nest on my sweaty forehead, and an ache in my ears after falling asleep wearing earbuds. I wear them to drown out the whispers of Willa's ghost.

Last night, I swore I could hear her as I drifted to sleep.

Growing up, our twin beds had a narrow aisle between them, barely big enough to walk through. It was so easy to whisper in the dark. I told Willa everything—every smile or snub from boys in my class, every secret from notes passed at recess, every song I heard on the radio.

And Willa listened. She laughed. She offered tantaliz-
ing peeks into her day, little crumbs I'd turn over in my
mind endlessly as I tried to puzzle out what it was like to be
a teenage girl. I'd talk her ear off if she let me. She was
always the first one to say good-night. More than once, she
awoke to find me cuddled in her bed, even though only a
foot or two separated us in our beds.

I am nearly thirty now, but last night, I wanted nothing
more than to cuddle beside her, breathing in the faint citrus
smell of her shampoo. I needed so badly to hear her whisper
to me in the hazy twilight before sleep set in that I conjured
her throaty voice in my empty room.

The earbud tumbles out again, and I hear the insistent
wail of the neighbor's baby, the Euclid Avenue traffic that
never seems to stop, and someone's surround-sound speakers shouting an action scene in a movie. The normal sounds
of a normal night. But without music to drown it all out, it's
quiet enough to remember that it's anything but normal
now.

The persistent ding of social media posts bulldogs
through the music, reducing the volume every time someone offers condolences or, worse, *likes* a post about Willa's
death. Facebook is full of self-pitying obituaries mourning
the poster's loss, not my sister, and I get chills every time I
see a posthumous photo of Willa on Instagram. Social
media leaked the news of her death before I could figure out
how to tell Momma, so I only had to imagine the way she
dropped to her knees and howled when the manager at the
florist shop asked her about her daughter's suicide.

My chest heaves as I place my hands on the wall and
extend my leg into a runner's stretch for a cooldown.

Music keeps me from replaying conversations in my
head, repeating each exchange until it reaches elevated
importance. Willa called it memory hoarding, but it's not
that I try to remember every detail. It's a chance to see where

I could have been more assertive and apologize less. I have plenty of things to be sorry for in real life: I'm constantly running late; I can be careless, though I prefer to call it scattered; I'm the kind of person who's perpetually screwing up and always admitting it.

But I can't break the habit of apologizing, even when I redraw conversations in my mind.

"Kelly? I'm sorry, but could I have a minute of your time? I might need some time off work for a little while. It won't be long, and I can help find a replacement instructor. I don't want to cause any inconvenience."

God, I can almost hear the questioning lilt in my voice when I talked to the lead instructor. I feel sick thinking of how the insecurity bubbled in my chest as she eyed me, drenched in sweat after leading a class just minutes before. I hoped she thought my makeup was smeared because of the sauna-like studio, not because I started to cry during the thick hill of resistance training. I'd shouted my normal self-help maxims: "Eyes closed, hearts open! Be honest about who you are trying to be!" The tears started to flow, and I tried to keep the choke out of my voice as we pushed through the arms and the sprint and the stretch. All I could think of was the morbid mantra running through my mind on an endless loop: *Willa, dead, suicide. Willa, dead, suicide.* I pumped my legs in beat to the words. By the time I flicked the lights on after the room emptied, I knew I couldn't offer inspiration when I couldn't think about anything but Willa.

Kelly didn't want to give me any time off, I could tell. Her eyes said there were a dozen girls or more, all skinnier, more *inspirational*, waiting to be an instructor at our location. They said that if you take time off, you won't get afternoon classes in the future. But in the end, she agreed and promised her support, even though her face betrayed her words.

My galley kitchen teems with unwashed pots and pans, now dating back to before the funeral. The smell of baked-on egg and spinach settles in the hot air and makes my stomach turn. I haven't eaten much today, but I exercised twice. It didn't help; I still feel the fluttery anxiousness I've felt since I heard about Willa two weeks ago.

I notice that the small pine table—forever imprinted with the indentations of an old grocery list, written before I realized how soft the wood was—still has two place mats set out. I wonder if the hawk-eyed policeman noticed them and assumed I had a regular dinner guest. The truth is, I haven't had a friend over in months, and it's been even longer since I've had a boyfriend. But I read a book that said it was important to act "as if" when you wanted something. So I've been acting as if I live with a man ever since. It's not just the extra place mat. It's an empty drawer. It's space for his toothbrush and room to hang his coat in the tiny hallway closet. Suddenly I feel foolish and hope desperately that the officers don't assume I have a boyfriend and ask to speak to him for any reason.

I run my finger over the ghostly grocery list carved into the tabletop, rubbing *zucchini* mindlessly, and it hits me that Willa will never meet a future boyfriend of mine. She would have grilled him. She would have insulted him in such a way that he didn't realize it until he had to ask me later, in private. She would have made it clear she was smarter than him and that he wasn't good enough for me. She would have been all bluster, though, because she would have been happy for me, in the end.

I shake my head to clear it of the scene I conjured so easily: an imaginary boyfriend intimidated by a dead sister. I tear my hand away from the table and turn to the refrigerator.

Light from the fridge—now stocked only with water bottles and week-old vegetables—floods the kitchen as I grab a drink. The headphones are still draped over my neck; the tinny sound of the song is interrupted by the phone ringing. I pop one earbud in my ear.

"Momma." I take a long swig of water because I know she didn't call to have a conversation. She called to talk and doesn't care if I respond.

"So I called the insurance company today, and they said they might not pay out the death benefits, even though I'm listed as the beneficiary." Claudia is always in the middle of a thought when she calls. "They won't pay out if the suicide happened within two years of when Willa took out the policy. There's fine print I don't understand, of course, but that's the gist of it. So I need to figure out when Willa started paying for her insurance. Can you take a look at her paperwork for me?"

"Doesn't the insurance company have details about her policy start date?"

"Sawyer," Claudia moans, "you can't trust them. Of course they're going to avoid paying out her life insurance if possible."

"Not everyone is trying to take advantage of you, Momma," I sigh.

I hear the familiar hitch in my mother's throat that tells me she's about to cry. She's too sensitive, reactive as a beaten dog, and breaks down at the first indication of a disagreement. I'm surprised she could interact with the insurance company at all; she's usually wiped out the moment she feels pressured or intimidated.

"Fine," I cede. "I'll take a look."

"Oh, thank you, baby. You know, I can't sleep. Haven't slept for days. I want to help, but I can't stop thinking about what's going to happen."

Her words echo how I feel, but suddenly I feel combative instead of consoling.

"Nothing's going to happen," I say. "Willa died, and that's what happened. Now there's nothing more that's going to happen."

It feels good to say something with such certainty, even if my words are bleak.

"There's a lot more that could happen, as far as insurance is concerned. Our best hope is that her death is considered an accident, though Oz says he doubts that will happen."

My skin prickles as if a wave of electricity shuddered through my body.

"That's what this is about, then? I get it now. Oz wants the insurance money. It was bad enough that you brought him to the funeral when all he does is take advantage of you." I swat the light switch, and the kitchen floods with fluorescent light. "I would never pretend to assume how a mother would act when one of her daughters dies. But your behavior is shameful."

Her tears flow into the earpiece of the phone, and muffled, gasping cries echo into the kitchen.

"Sawyer, baby, I'm sorry. Oz is here for me when I need someone. He's not trying to take Willa's insurance money, only to help me get what's due to me. Tell me you still love me," Claudia begs.

I stand over the sink and turn on the tap, watching the water run ineffectually over the crust of old food. I picture them having limp, wet sex that results in my mother mopping up tears and tending to urinary tract infections. They've already been together four, going on five, years. My heart thuds loudly in my chest, screaming of my weakened state and how I hate conflict, just like my mother. I lower the faucet handle to shut off the water. I'll wash the dishes tomorrow.

"I don't want to argue," I concede. "I'm not myself right now. I'm going to Willa's tomorrow afternoon to start going through her stuff. I'll set aside the insurance paperwork for you."

"That's my girl. Don't ever leave me, baby. You're all I've got."

"I know. I'm sorry. Bye, Momma."

At the kitchen entrance, I flick off the lights again, knowing I'm too wiped out to clean. As the fluorescents flicker off, my mind places Willa at the sink, dutifully washing the dirty dishes. She'd never let them pile up like that. I wonder what she'd say if she were here.

I think of my old cubicle buddy, Emily, from the short time I worked in sales after college. Located in a twelve-story midrise overlooking a Mediterranean restaurant and a Dunkin' Donuts, the office was full of skinny, judgmental girls. Emily was the only person who spoke to me after I made the fatal misstep of arriving on my first day in a cheap suit from the juniors department.

Emily and I went to an after-work happy hour once a month. It only took one drink for Emily to open up about her brother, who'd died of an overdose when she was a teenager. It took two drinks for her anger to come out, and three for the unrestricted guilt to pour through.

As my eyes readjust to the absence of light, I wonder if I'll become untethered about Willa just like Emily was about her dead brother. If anger will bubble to the surface to mask the culpability I feel for not saving Willa.

5

Willa

Five years before

WILLA WONDERED IF it was her job to save Sawyer.
She stood beside a row of more than a dozen porta potties with a sunny smile pasted on her face and her arms held just slightly away from her body to avoid unsightly sweat stains on her blue dress. She pretended not to know that Sawyer was taking this long because she was purging everything she'd eaten from the vendors at the Taste. Admission might have been free, but at the price of food tickets, Willa was surprised Sawyer could afford to waste money like that.

It was hot like only July in Chicago can be. The sky was swelling with the promise of fat raindrops that would sizzle on the pavement. Willa invited Sawyer to meet her after her on-location segment covering the third day of the Taste of Chicago. It was a breezy piece, but it was cause to celebrate: those three minutes of coverage represented Willa's last stint as a beat reporter. The offer to become a news desk anchor had arrived late last week, and along with it, a substantial pay raise. Willa had wasted no time accepting the offer.

She hated reporting from the field. KZTV didn't care about burrowing into a story and finding an unexpected angle. The producers wanted you to read from the teleprompter while looking good near a charred building or in a snowstorm. Now that she was in front of the camera, she wouldn't win any awards for her investigative articles like she had earlier in her career.

She shifted her weight, trying to get more comfortable in her heels, and regretted her decision to ask Sawyer to meet her here. She should have invited Leo. They'd met recently when Willa was a panelist at a discussion about culture and media. During the event, the east-facing windows absorbed the morning sun and filtered a warm golden light into the posh hotel meeting room. The sun must have been in the eyes of a man in the second row, because he kept raising one hand to shield the light. On his other arm, he wore a cast. When the panel wrapped, he approached her with what Willa thought were intellectual, thoughtful questions. They talked until the hotel staff scurried into the room and began to pull the chairs from their tidy rows and stack them in the corners. Willa liked the way he grinned self-deprecatingly when he explained his broken wrist was courtesy of his overconfidence on Rollerblades. She gave him her phone number, and they'd been seeing each other ever since.

"Hey, aren't you that newsgirl?" asked a man in a Hawaiian shirt and khaki ball cap. He held a greasy ear of corn on the cob between his pudgy fingers, like so many others at the Taste.

She flashed him her on-air smile and nodded. "Yes, I am. You won't want to miss KZTV's evening news today. I'll reveal just how many slices of deep-dish pizza Lou Malnati's served up today." She winked, he laughed, and Willa cringed inwardly while maintaining the smile that paid her bills.

The door to the porta potty swung open, and Sawyer discreetly rubbed at her mouth as she walked to the hand-washing station. She was wiping her wet hands on her shorts when she approached Willa.

"Something wasn't sitting right with me. Seafood trucks might be a bad idea," she said with a wan smile. "Do you want to head over to the stage to check out the music act?"

Willa chewed on a response, wondering if she would ruin the day by suggesting Sawyer get help for her eating disorder. It ebbed and flowed; sometimes Sawyer seemed to have conquered it. Other times, Willa pretended to ignore it while wrestling with how much she should interfere with Sawyer's life.

Instead, Willa kept her mouth closed and reluctantly nodded. Some people might have thought that Willa voiced every opinion she had, but she held back so much. Her mind churned. She couldn't shake her feeling of responsibility, of feeling that she had failed her little sister.

They weaved their way through the walkways jammed with people. A loud rumble of thunder rolled over Grant Park, and the crowd sizzled with excitement. A woman with a halo of frizzy hair walked impossibly slow in front of Willa. Even in her three-inch heels, Willa couldn't slow her pace that much. Beside her, a man with a child on his shoulders blocked the view of the city skyline. As Willa steered Sawyer to pass them, the view opened to reveal silvery monoliths rising out of the late-afternoon haze. She caught Sawyer smiling at the cityscape with a dreamy expression.

"Have you thought more about moving to the city?" Willa asked, relieved to change the subject.

Sawyer shook her head and bumped into Willa as a group of teenagers jostled her, rushing to get lawn seats in the outdoor amphitheater.

"I don't know how I'd afford it. Besides, the family I'm working for now lives in the suburbs. And Momma needs someone around to help out around the house, anyway."

Willa was happy she was dolled up with her false eyelashes and stiff on-air dress; they reminded her she was always being observed and to mind her facial reactions. If she'd been alone with Sawyer, her face would have slid into its natural state—pinched and disapproving—more easily. She would have lectured Sawyer to start living her life for herself, not their mother.

She loved Sawyer, but she resented the way she flitted between interests when Willa tried so hard. Willa wasn't a sweatpants-and-Netflix type of girl. She'd learned to play chess, sanitized the fridge, and grew herbs on the windowsill. She was productive. Sawyer spent her time bouncing between boyfriends and following larks that she proudly announced would be her new career. She was insufferable, the way she submitted herself to something with a burst of energy but then gave up just as fast. Within the span of a single year, she was going to become a botanist, chef, photographer, calligrapher, and Willa's favorite, Hula-Hoop instructor. Where had she ended up? As a nanny with a mound of debt from the community college she'd attended, where she'd earned a generic degree in sales that she used for half a year before quitting that job too.

When Sawyer had announced she'd attend Willa's alma mater, Willa was pleased. Surprised, but pleased. But Sawyer didn't last more than a semester before she was back home with their mother in Hillside. Willa wondered what went through her mind the first night she found herself back in her twin bed crowned with the bedazzled headboard of a preteen.

When they were little, it hadn't mattered that Willa was an overachiever while Sawyer lagged behind. Big sisters were supposed to be larger-than-life. But their differences became more pronounced as they aged. It took effort to maintain their relationship now. Willa was becoming embarrassed by her successes when she spent time with Sawyer. She hadn't even told her the reason she asked her to meet her at the Taste. She didn't reveal her promotion yet, even though she was slotted to take over Tucker Byrne's seat at the news desk when he retired next week.

"Look!" Sawyer said, pointing ahead to a crowd gathered at Buckingham Fountain Plaza. "That should have been your story today."

Hundreds of people salsa danced in the plaza. The speakers blared loud, distorted notes, but the lively horns cut through the dizzying humidity and no one seemed to mind either. Couples swayed and exchanged positions with so much synchronicity it felt to Willa as if she and Sawyer had stepped into a hive. Legs and laughs and flashes of bright summer clothing moved forward and back.

"Who would have guessed so many people know how to salsa?" Willa said with a laugh.

Sawyer grabbed her wrist and began to shimmy. She barely cleared Willa's chest in her flat sandals. "Let's dance!"

She waved Willa's stiff arm and twirled around her. Willa gently shook her off. She was riding high after news of her promotion, but she'd never be carefree enough to dance in public.

A deeply tanned man in a sleeveless T-shirt eyed Sawyer as she danced. He looked to be just the type Sawyer dated: on the edge of handsome, dim-witted, and hopelessly broken. Sometimes Willa thought a man might prove to be the one thing Sawyer would stick to without giving up, but they always left her before she could find out. Sawyer emanated a type of desperate longing that repelled men, even the broken ones.

Heavy raindrops began to plop onto the bare arms of the dancers, slowly at first, then faster and more insistent. A murmur of exhilaration grew until it was hard to hear the fuzzy music. The dancers became more animated, legs moving faster to keep time with the rain.

Sawyer shrieked and laughed, catching eyes with the tanned man.

"Let's get a drink," he shouted at her, as if the rain made her hard of hearing.

As Sawyer glanced at Willa, her eyes so full of hope, Willa turned away, efficiently rummaging through her shoulder bag and unfurling a sturdy umbrella over her head.

She'd let Sawyer go, of course, but she couldn't fight the disappointment that settled over her. It was a familiar feeling. She spent more time feeling dull and disillusioned than she cared to admit. But she was good at hiding it. So she conjured her on-air smile once more and, with it, granted Sawyer permission to make poor decisions, even though Willa knew better.

6

Sawyer

PATCHY VINES OF ivy creep up the limestone walls of the Gothic Revival–era building where Leo works. The turn-of-the-century campus is more striking outside than inside; Leo's office affords no picturesque moments. He sits at a metal desk facing a floor-to-ceiling window with faded curtains that look to be as old as the building.

"Sawyer, thanks for coming. It's our free period now. I've got about an hour until my next class. Urbanization and Social Deviance."

"Right," I say, glancing at the stack of books on his desk. "You teach sociology?"

"And criminology. Associate professor right now, but I hope to drop the *associate* part in the next few years." He straightens his bony shoulders. "With the new title comes my own office. Which I desperately need, as you can see," he says, gesturing at an adjacent desk piled high with books and adorned with a Cubs pennant overhead.

"I thought email was supposed to replace all this paper," I say with a laugh, running my thumb along the crinkled edges of a tall stack of assignments on Leo's desk.

His precision leaks out as he nudges the papers back into a straight pile when I disrupt their alignment with the corner of his desk. I'm reminded of Willa's unyielding perfectionism, and an ache radiates through my chest.

"It turns out that students are pretty clever when it comes to blaming late assignments on technical glitches. Printed papers are the only way I can enforce truthfulness," he says, his voice taking on a steely teacher tone. He sends a vibrato through the metal desk when he drums his long, girlish fingers on the surface. "Let's get a coffee down in the courtyard before my officemate comes back," he suggests. "I couldn't live with myself if he overheard us and thought he could profit from details about Willa in some way."

As I follow him out of the office, it occurs to me that he's right: the most personal details of my sister's life, a life she tried to keep private despite public scrutiny from being an on-air personality in one of the biggest television markets in the nation, are a hot commodity right now. It won't be long before her former colleagues begin to troll her apartment building, scouring for loose-lipped neighbors or speculating that the weeds spidering through sidewalk cracks foretold her demise. It won't be long before they find me too, but I've made it harder by deleting my social media accounts.

In the hallway, ecclesiastical paintings dot the walls. It feels lavishly ornamental—nearly medieval—but shabby and depressing too. Leo looks like he fits in well.

A warm gust of wind blows a few early-to-fall leaves into the stairwell, where the marble steps are dull and bowed. Leo pays for our coffees, and we take a seat by an ornate fountain that dribbles water into a mucky sludge of last year's leaves.

"Willa preferred hers black," he says as he takes a seat.

I grip the paper cup harder and relish the burn of hot coffee as I fight back a fresh wave of tears.

"I feel like a cliché for saying this, but it doesn't make sense," I say. "She wouldn't have done this. I'm sure everyone who has had someone . . . die . . . in this way feels this way. But it's true. It isn't her." I gaze at a statue of a cloaked nun kneeling in prayer and watch as students file past, oblivious to her history or sacrifice. "She had ambition. Drive. This isn't her."

"I can see how you'd think that," Leo says carefully. "She was your big sister. She didn't want you to see her as anything other than perfect."

"She didn't want anyone to see her as anything other than perfect," I correct. "Did you know she used to stutter?"

Leo turns his head, listening. Waiting.

"It's true," I say. "When we were kids, she hated any situation where she had to speak publicly. She got teased. But she did these breathing exercises and recorded herself and worked at it all the time. Even after she thought I fell asleep at night, she'd get up and practice speeches in the mirror, in the dark. I didn't know then that Momma couldn't afford a therapist to help her. All I saw was her fierce determination. She was so strong, Leo."

"It's easy to romanticize her now that she's gone, but she wasn't perfect. Far from it," he says with a reedy, clipped voice. He shifts his weight, and his knees creak audibly.

"I know she wasn't perfect. But I'm saying she wouldn't have done this to herself."

Leo sets his coffee on the ground and leans forward, resting his elbows on his knees. "I'm not surprised she did this. She suffered a major career setback, took an entry-level role that was beneath her experience-wise, and effectively became a shut-in. She severed herself from everyone and everything.

"In the last couple months I was with her," he continues, "she started to drink often, and heavily. Your guard goes up when you see drinks hidden in sweaty paper bags. It wasn't like that with Willa. But in retrospect, it was enough that I should have said something. I did, but not enough to stop her."

He gazes at a bare ash tree, clearly dead, across the quad as he remembers. He wears the burden of guilt heavily. "It's easy to look back and think about what you could have done, could have said, if you only saw the signs. And I saw them. She complained of headaches, insomnia. She stopped her self-taught French lessons. She used to practice her French phrases while she blow-dried her hair in the morning. Then she stopped both—I never heard another *parlez-vous* or the sound of the blow dryer. All signs of depression, when you know what to look for."

I pull my eyes from the statue and the stream of students in front of the cathedral-like library. Leo is next to me, so I can't see his eyes. Somehow it makes it easier to talk to him this way, to say what I really want to say but can't when we're head-on. It reminds me of the way I'd wait until my mother was doing dishes, tethered to the sink with soapy hands, to ask my most uncomfortable questions. Even if he feels the same way about talking to me, I notice he still can't bring himself to voice the full truth: he refuses to use the word *suicide*.

"You really think she was depressed, then?"

Leo sighs and shifts on the concrete bench. His folded cuff shakes loose with the movement, and he bunches the fabric back up to his elbow, ignoring it when it collapses again a moment later. "At the risk of sounding dramatic, it was like a deep melancholy permeated her soul. But it wasn't sudden. It was as if it was lurking all along and she finally gave up the fight. She became cruel. It was why we broke up."

They'd been together a little over three years. When two people date that long in their late twenties and early thirties, it's easy to imagine their relationship is moving toward marriage. I'm not sure Willa ever thought that way, even though it must have been on her mind. I followed their relationship from afar via Leo's Facebook account, seeing all the glamorous dresses Willa wore to each of Leo's three sisters' lavish weddings.

We settle into silence. I think back to a time when I got drinks with Willa shortly after her breakup with Leo, more than a year ago. She'd quit her job at KZTV by then and, though I didn't know it at the time, put her condo up for sale. It was unusual for her to be social, even more for her to suggest we meet up at a bar. Sure, she drank a lot that night, but she and Leo had just ended their relationship.

She was more open than usual, talking a little too fast, gesturing a little too much. Acting more like me, really. She explained that she'd broken up with Leo. That he was a "private slob," as she put it, and she listed the most offensive qualities: he used expired acne cream from when he was a teenager, dousing his bathroom with the pervasive scent of retinol. She'd once found a hair wrapped in the bristles of his toothbrush that he didn't remove for three days, and he never bothered to clean his smudged glasses. I remember the way she wiped invisible lint off her shirt as she finished telling me of all his crimes, as if to distance herself from his slovenly ways. Mostly I remember the way she said my name in a conspiratorial way as she leaned over the sticky wooden bar table. Willa rarely used my name; it was a treat when she did. Nearly everyone I met liked to use my name liberally in conversation, since it was somewhat unique and there was no good way to shorten it. Willa uttered it only on special occasions.

As if to verify that Willa's version of their breakup is the truth, I turn to Leo and try to see if his glasses bear any telltale fingerprint smudges. Maybe it's the angle of the midday sun, but I can't see a thing, and somehow that makes me more uncertain than before.

"I won't accept that it's a suicide, or even that Willa was depressed. I think you're just constructing that narrative now to explain away the unexplainable. Maybe she drank more than she should have or was mean to you, but that doesn't mean she killed herself." My heart thunders at the force of my words. "I spoke with the police officer working her case at the funeral, and she said they found unidentified DNA on Willa's sheets."

"Sawyer, I think you're minimizing her depression. That DNA could be from anyone. A friend, a one-night stand, even a factory worker at whatever sweatshop manufactured her sheets."

Frustrated, I look away as Leo picks up his coffee again and takes generous swigs from the cooled cup.

"So you can just disregard the mystery DNA. Fine. What about the unsourced fibers and dog hairs found in her apartment?" I say, remembering Curry's revelation.

"Could be anything, really," he says, resigned. "I can think of dozens of historical cases where unknown fibers turned out to be nothing more than red herrings."

"I thought you teach criminology. I would think that you, of anyone, would see the significance of these clues."

"Clues to what, Sawyer? Maybe they're clues to how she lived her final days, but I doubt they're clues into her death. I think that's pretty cut-and-dried." He freezes. "Oh, sorry. I didn't mean to . . . I know how she died . . . her wrists. I didn't mean to imply . . ."

"It's okay. Forget it." I jam my thumbnail in my mouth and gnaw on it to mask the quivering hitch that overtakes my voice.

"If you're trying to piece together her final months, I'm not sure I can be of much help. We were broken up. But I did meet with her not too long ago. She reached out to me for some information for something she was working on. It was more like a business meeting than anything else. I met with her here on campus. She looked a little different but seemed really focused on her work. So that's probably how she was spending her last few months," Leo offers.

"What did you talk about?"

"Ah, investigation procedures?" He squints as he brings the memory into focus. "She wanted to know about missing persons cases specifically. I told her what I knew. There wasn't much more to it than that."

"It was for a story she was working on?"

"I assume so. I mean, why else would she be gathering information about that sort of thing?"

I nod slowly. If she was working on a story, it meant she still was still motivated to achieve something.

The afternoon sun glints off the stained-glass windows of the chapel across the courtyard. The students sprawled across the manicured lawn have thinned out. Leo checks his watch, adjusting the thick leather band on his bony wrist. I think about how little I know about him. I know he enjoys craft brews, goes on autumn bike tours, and launches model rockets with his nephew on the weekends. But I don't know why he and Willa were together when they seem so different.

They both have a quiet energy, and I remember that Willa once said they liked to debate for fun. Only Willa, with her love of precision and facts, could find enjoyment in that. Like Willa, Leo seems steadfast and pragmatic. Sitting on this campus, a relic from the turn of the twentieth century, I think Leo might be the type to protect the past and preserve tradition. Willa, always set in her perfectionist habits, placed high value on tradition, something that permeated the campus and seemed to seep into Leo too.

"I should get going." He gestures with his empty coffee cup at the wooden door leading out of the courtyard. He looks at me searchingly, almost needy in the desperate way his eyes reveal his compulsion to make everything okay. It reminds me of Momma. "I'd like to meet again to talk about Willa, but I'd like to talk about her life instead of her death."

A sudden sadness hits me, a prickling in my stomach and an ache in my heart. I could never put it into words, but I always thought it might be the same feeling that people call homesickness. More than distinct loneliness, it's a physical, tickling ache that spreads through my chest and makes me want to climb into the warm spot in Willa's bed like I used to do when we were little. The wicked burn of nostalgia.

Leo turns away, and in the late afternoon sun, I glimpse a greasy smudge on his eyeglasses. It doesn't feel any better to see that Willa might have been telling the truth.

7

Willa

Three years before

"THERE'S NOTHING TO SAY about it."

"Willa."

"What?"

"You've never not had something to say."

She tucked a strand of hair behind her ear as she looked up. Leo stood at the island in the kitchen with a plate of sliced apples. He crunched on one as he eyed her. He always said he felt like he wasn't allowed to snack on the couch, that the furniture was for looking, not living. Him keeping his distance was the only thing that kept her from crying; if he came any closer, she knew she couldn't keep up the steely wall she'd erected since leaving the studio.

"Well, I didn't speak when I was supposed to this evening. That's all."

"You had a panic attack on air. It's something."

"I'm humiliated, okay? There's not much more to say."

The loud crunch of a Yellow Delicious. "Try," he said, dragging the word out.

Willa inhaled deeply and felt the words rush from her. She'd been trying to write the explanation in her head since the four o'clock news ended, knowing she'd have to have a reason for what happened. "Kris had just reported on an earthquake in Indonesia. Six-point-four magnitude. Dozens killed. Then it was my turn for the national news." She looked down at her hands, rubbing her manicured nails along the suede piping on the couch. "My story was about an inmate awaiting execution in Georgia. Nothing special in the copy—he appealed, but there were no public dissents about his stay of execution. It should have taken less than a minute to report on the full story. But I couldn't do it."

"Was it the story that stopped you?"

"No, I don't think so. I don't know what it was."

For a moment they didn't speak; the only sound was Leo chomping on the apple. Willa leaned back, wishing that she owned the type of inviting couch she could sink into to disappear forever. But it had clean lines and no give, so she was just as exposed as she'd been all day.

The ceramic plate chinked as Leo placed it in the sink. She watched as he wiped his sticky fingers on her needlessly expensive dish towel, purchased more for aesthetics than actual dish drying.

"I felt like I couldn't get enough air. It was different from the way you feel short of breath when you climb too many stairs. It was more like there just was no air anymore," she said. "I started to feel really, really sweaty. You know how our news desk is backed up against the windows facing the street? Well, it just felt like the setting sun was beating in on me so hard that I started to boil. It was merciless.

"But that wasn't the worst of it. I couldn't breathe, and I was boiling to death, but that wasn't anything compared to how I felt inside. I don't know how to explain it. I just felt like I was going to die. Right then. Like maybe I was having a heart attack or something, I don't know. I felt sheer terror."

She quieted because she felt the telltale lump form in her throat, the one that warned tears were imminent. Her voice, normally low, throaty, almost husky—sensual—had an uncharacteristic tremor.

"What were you scared of?" Leo asked, edging closer now.

Willa swallowed, trying to force away the tears. "That's the exact question I've been dreading. It minimizes it. It makes it sound like there was something tangible that caused me to panic—on air, of all times. It wasn't anything I can point to," she said. "I have to face it. It took me eight years to build my reputation in journalism and twenty-five seconds of dead airtime to ruin it."

"Your career is not ruined."

"It is. It's over."

"KZTV is not going to fire you over this. It happens. Didn't it just happen to that guy on the national morning news a couple years ago?"

"He managed to shift back to his co-anchor. I didn't do that. I fled. I was scheduled to anchor the four, five, and six o'clock news. A panic attack is one thing, but walking off-camera is the kiss of death. Kris just sat there. Marisol, the showrunner, just stood there. The weather guy and the traffic girl just stood there. No one did anything but let me stare, panicked, into the camera as I faced what I thought to be my death. After, they all acted empathetic, but I could tell they were more triumphant than anything."

"You're being dramatic, Willa. You're embarrassed now, but it's going to be fine."

"Have you been online today? Have you seen what people are saying about me?"

She'd spent the walk to the El and the subway ride back to her condo deriding herself for choosing not to drive that day, hiding behind silent earbuds that afforded privacy in a city that refused to give it. It was something she did often: remove herself from the world but observe everyone else. It was soon enough after her meltdown that no one seemed to notice her, but they would tomorrow. And the day after. Chicago could provide anonymity until someone thrust themselves into the public eye on the most-watched evening news broadcast in the city.

"What can they even say? So you had a panic attack. It happened. Honestly, it's probably been culminating for years. That's how these things work. It snuck out at the most inopportune moment, yes, but it's probably the product of you being too critical of yourself for years. Now is not the time to fixate on this as a failure. It'll only be more likely to happen again."

"Oh, great, thanks, Leo. Now I not only have to worry about recovering from this ultimate humiliation, but I have to worry about it happening again."

"What about therapy?" he said.

Willa scoffed. "I refuse to see a shrink," she said, trying to minimize the profession, "even if it happens every day for the rest of my life."

Usually she found herself having a more caustic, harsher conversation in her head than with the person she was talking to. Words chugged through a calculated filter before exiting her mouth, but that didn't mean she was nice. Leo was different because he always got the unedited version of what she was thinking. He got the brunt of her acidic tongue. Maybe it was even worse than it should have been, since she spent so much time trying to keep it under wraps for everyone else.

Leo sat on a leather slingback chair and crossed his ankle over his knee. He leaned back to study her, and she felt sick. She'd been under a microscope since it happened. She didn't even want him to look at her. She stood to face the wall opposite Leo, where her journalism awards hung in meticulous straight rows.

It wasn't that long ago that she had been onstage accepting the Steele Award as the stage lights gleamed off its brushed platinum surface. Willa was an industry expert. Celebrated, praised, respected. It was what had catapulted her career and landed her a spot on the evening news in Chicago.

Now she'd be none of those things.

"It won't happen again. I didn't mean to worry you any more than you already are. Maybe we just need a distraction. Christmas is coming up. We could decorate."

"Are you kidding?"

"People decorate for Christmas, Willa. It's not that crazy of a suggestion."

She eyed the bookcase, stuffed with glossy hardcover books. Dim recessed lighting illuminated the titles on their spines. Could she stuff the shelves with hand-me-down holiday decorations just to "get in the spirit"? Slide in tchotchkes from her mother—ceramic snowmen with chipped noses, angels missing their mate, festive stuffed mice because someone decided that anything, even a disgusting rodent, could be made Christmasy? Tradition was something to be respected, but only when it explained the past, not when it was forced and commercialized.

"I don't want to uproot my life for a sense of false cheer. Seriously, Leo, this is the worst possible time to suggest it."

"Forget it. I just wanted to offer a distraction so you don't get into your head about this." He shifted, and the hand-dyed tobacco leather creaked under him. "When my parents were our age, they had two kids, and they never skipped a single tradition. They did everything."

"I despise when people use this word, but most use it incorrectly. But here goes: Leo, you are *literally* saying the worst possible things to me right now. I'm thirty. I don't have kids. I don't have a husband. What I had was my career. And now I don't have that. So don't try to distract me with fucking Christmas decorations and traditions. It only serves to remind me of what I gave up to be where I am, and now I just threw all that away."

They lapsed into silence. Thankfully. Willa kept her eyes on the plaque while wondering if she should have gone down a different path. She'd worked to be self-sufficient and successful. She'd built her hard edges on purpose. She'd tried to be the opposite of her mother, but she'd failed at that too.

She didn't want to drive Leo away. She liked that he didn't follow trends and didn't care what others thought. He was her escape from the inflated egos of the news media world she inhabited. Leo spent his evenings tinkering with an old CB radio and teaching himself to play a keyboard piano. He scoured thrift stores for puzzles and presented them proudly to Willa. They liked to laugh that taking on a used thousand-piece puzzle was the riskiest activity they did.

"I don't know what I was thinking," she conceded. It was easier to be vulnerable when she didn't have to look at Leo, who she knew would be giving her those weak puppy-dog eyes he got when she was too blunt. "I was never going to be comfortable on-screen. I stuttered as a kid, for God's sake. I tried to approach the job offer objectively, but I think the achievement it represented clouded my judgment. I thought if I took the responsibility seriously, it wouldn't matter if I wasn't good at improvising or if I wasn't all that likable. I should be behind the scenes. That's how it was when I was at my best."

"So what now?"

She turned around, and sure enough, Leo's eyes were wide and his brows creased in that way that had once seemed so kindhearted and indulgent—her antithesis, drawing her in—but now just made him look pathetic. Now when he looked at her like that, she felt her guard go up instead of lower.

"Now I face what I created."

8

Sawyer

T HOUGH SHE WAS a single mother, Claudia managed to raise us without ever driving a car. That wasn't a small feat; we didn't live in the city, where public transportation was ample. We lived fifteen miles from Chicago, in a single-story brick ranch in Hillside with a postage-stamp yard and neighbors who mostly kept to themselves.

When pressed, all she would say was that she once knew someone who died in a car accident and it scared her enough to keep her grounded. It was one of those tragically glamorous things about our mother. She wouldn't reveal who it was or what the circumstances were, which left us, as young girls, endlessly curious.

She left the house only to go to work at a nearby florist shop and, once a week, church and the post office. In exchange for an extra shift at the shop, Momma's coworker bought us two bags of groceries each week, so she rarely even went to the store.

Willa and I walked to school and bummed a ride from other parents, and later, friends, when we needed it. As with so many things, Willa and I reacted differently to the lack of transportation. As soon as she could, she bought a used car and took off to the farthest school in the state that would offer her a scholarship. I left, too, but only for a semester. I didn't like being so far from home. Even after college, I stayed close and moved to an apartment where I could walk to work.

It's why I don't mind the forty-minute walk from the university to my apartment in the Arts District. I wait for a quiet stretch of road after the Metra rushes by on its way to the western suburbs. I find Officer Curry's number in my phone's recent contacts and hit dial.

"Officer Mallory Curry. How can I help you?"

"Officer, hi. This is Sawyer Stannard. I'm calling to find out if there's been any progress made to identify the DNA you found in my sister's apartment."

"Ms. Stannard, hello. We haven't received the results of the test yet. When we do, we'll be sure to inform you," she says, her voice brusque, businesslike.

"How long does it normally take?"

"Up to a few weeks, depending on how backed up the facility is right now and how many other priority cases come in. This case, Ms. Stannard, is not listed as a priority right now."

"But it's already been, what, three weeks since she died? Doesn't the presence of the . . . the semen . . . doesn't that point to foul play? It could have been an intruder."

I pass mostly houses as I walk, and I've seen only a few lawn-care workers blowing stray leaves into the street, but still, I lower my voice as I speak into the phone. The homes have curb appeal and character in abundance. They vary from English Tudors to French Provincials to Dutch Colonials, and they've all been maintained to perfection, with sleek slate roofs and copper gutters gleaming in the setting sunlight.

"Not necessarily," Curry says. "Willa showed no signs of rape, and the apartment showed no signs of a break-in. I have no reason to believe that the presence of the semen was the result of a nonconsensual act. But this is a sudden, unattended death. We work it first as a homicide, then a suicide, then an accident, and finally as an unnatural occurrence."

"But what if she let the person in? What if she knew him?"

"What are you suggesting?"

I sigh noisily into the phone. "Have you looked into Oz? I'm not sure of his last name, but he's my mother's boyfriend. He does apartment maintenance and odd jobs. I think he's been fired by landlords before for stealing. He steals from my mother regularly, though she turns a blind eye to it. What if Willa let him in? What if he did it to benefit from the insurance money that my mother would get when Willa died?"

"We've looked into Oz. His real name is Lobosz. He was painting an apartment in Hillside when Willa died. The landlord vouched for him."

"I thought she died in the evening. Oz was on a painting job at night? Officer, please," I plead. I am near a school now, and the children dart and shriek and pulse with life on the playground. "He has a record. He could stand to gain from her death through his relationship with my mother. Someone was there. We know that much. Does he have a dog? Do you even know? It could have been him."

I picture him as I speak: his dark, coarse hair, his snub nose with flaring nostrils, his pockmarked skin. The way the cleft in his square chin deepens when Claudia cries, which is often. He is easy enough to cast a villain in my mind.

Curry exhales through her nose. When she speaks, her voice is clipped. "We're looking into that possibility, Ms. Stannard. But let me remind you, Lobosz—and your mother, and you—stand to gain nothing from Willa's death if it's ruled a suicide. So it doesn't make much sense to stage the crime scene as if it was a suicide. To pen a note and mention your name."

My heart starts to thrum in my chest as she reminds me of the note Willa left behind.

Sawyer, I'm sorry. I wish I was brave enough not to do it. I know you'll never forgive me.

"And," she continues, "Willa's closest contacts confirm that she was depressed. Leo Reed. Brooke Conroy, from KZTV." She hesitates. "Your mother."

"My mother told you that Willa was depressed?" I ask incredulously.

A group of three older women is standing in the front yard of a modern home. Their conversation can be heard from where I am—"open-concept" . . . "historic" . . . "a landmark"—and I don't want them to hear mine. Self-consciously, I bow my head.

Curry inhales and seems to hold her breath. She exhales slowly, and her voice is gentler when she speaks. "Have you been in her apartment yet?"

I feel my skin prickle with understanding before she continues. I know she's going to tell me something definitive, something irreversible.

"What is it?" I ask, my voice small. At least I'm past the noisy playground.

"The boxes in the closet all have Post-it notes on them. *Donate. Sell. Sawyer. Momma.* It's textbook behavior to purge personal possessions before suicide. Willa labeled everything for you. Even her cabinets were empty. She was prepared to die.

"It's likely that this case will be closed soon and ruled a suicide," she continues. "We can't waste resources if signs do not point to homicide. This is Chicago. We have no shortage of verified homicides. You understand, I'm sure. But something to be aware of, beyond the insurance troubles and the stigma and the questions you're facing now: when the case is closed, and if it is ruled a suicide, the note will be made public. I dislike it as much as you do. But it's unavoidable."

It feels like a punch to the gut. It's the most intrusive thing I can imagine. Forget the internet articles and the TV reports and the meddling insurance agents. That feels like nothing now. Knowing the whole world will see how vulnerable Willa was in her final moments is the most insulting part of this mess. Once the word *suicide* was breathed, Willa's reputation was ruined, but this is an indignity.

"I understand," I say. I don't. How could my sister's final words be published for the whole world to see? They are too personal, too private. She published hundreds of stories as a journalist. Isn't that enough words to give to the world?

"When the DNA results come in, I'll call you. Until then, perhaps you should visit Willa's apartment. Our techs are done gathering evidence. I know that nothing will help you understand why this happened, but seeing how she left things might help explain what she was thinking at the time."

When she hangs up, the street noise seems to reawaken. The mantra echoes through my mind on an endless loop again: *Willa, dead, suicide.* Cars fly down the street—it has a speed limit of twenty-five that is always ignored—and vibrant chatter from street-side cafés floats onto the sidewalk. I'm downtown, not far from home.

I think of my apartment, only a few blocks away. It's messy, but it feels homey and lived in, and it hums with life. I dread a trip to Willa's apartment. After she quit her job at KZTV, she downsized from her smug condo in River North to a small garden apartment in the Fulton River District. Her condo was always so meticulous that I suspected even the cleaning products under the sink would be organized and labeled. Her move to the basement apartment carried with it an air of embarrassment, so I didn't offer to visit or give a housewarming gift. I've never been to her "new apartment," not in the nearly three years she's been there.

It's time to stop avoiding it and see where she spent her final days.

9

Sawyer

I T'S FUNNY WHAT you hold on to when you have nothing else.

Our father is gone. That's all we know.

By the time I started preschool, the questions were endless: Who is my dad? Why doesn't he live with us? Is he ever coming back?

Does he miss me?

I still remember the day Momma sat us down, one daughter at each arm. I clutched my doll in my lap and breathed in the flowery-sweet smell of Momma. Her skin was still warm from gardening in the sun, and she had dirt caked on her knees like she did most summer days.

"He wasn't ready to be a father, and now he'll never get the chance," she said, her voice tight and quiet.

And that was it. She refused to give more details or answer any questions.

I think he died when we were young, but Willa thought he left us. It was our favorite debate. She hated how I imagined him as perfect: dying was the only thing he did wrong. She thought he left us for an easier life, an easier wife.

Then he could come back to us, I'd counter.

All we had of him was a single dog-eared photo with a handwritten date on the back. We'd stare at it and try to cherry-pick his best features and assign them to ourselves. *You have his chin, his cheekbones, his posture. I'll take his nose and thick hair.* A revolving door of masculine features we didn't mind being associated with our little-girl faces.

I thought Willa secretly wanted his features to be hers too, even though she was steadfast in her belief that he'd abandoned us. In my memory-hoarding mind, I still remember what she used to say: "He doesn't have the right to choose us again after he made the choice to leave us. He's an asshole for leaving us. But at least he's consistent."

I have so much more than a single photo to remind me of her. But if she was right and our father did leave us, then she became an asshole just like him. But she'd always be consistent.

*   *   *

The scent of chocolate from the cocoa-bean processor hangs heavy in the air. Passing by the Blommer factory, I become more uncertain that I have the right address. Overgrown grass and weeds sprout through fractures in the concrete. A few steps lead down to the door of Willa's garden apartment. Inside, a dim overhead light crackles, and a neighbor stomps erratically in the upstairs unit as if stamping out a wily silverfish.

It's all wrong; it isn't where a rigid perfectionist like Willa would live.

But she's there in the meticulous room. The furniture is a little too oversized, too modern, for the outdated space. Willa once forced our mother to sit on a sheet on that sleek gray couch when we visited her old condo and she hadn't changed out of her pollen-stained pants from the florist shop first.

I take a shaky breath as I gaze around the room at the remains of Willa's life. After what Officer Curry said about Willa supposedly packing up her possessions, I prepared myself to enter an empty apartment. But the apartment, though stark, is still stamped with Willa's personality. The shelves are filled with what have to be hundreds of books. I glance at the titles: *Deadly Duplicity. Heart Full of Lies. Fury and Sacrifice. Murder and Betrayal.* More true crime than travel books, that's for sure. Her acerbic voice rattles in my head, and I can almost hear her say that, just once, she'd like to hear the word *voracious* used to describe not only a reader, as she was often labeled, or an insatiable eater, but a listener. Now I know it's because she wanted someone to listen to her with the ravenous intensity that she used to devour these books.

Framed articles line the wall. Her best undercover exposés: investigating substandard hospice care, probing student safety at boarding schools, revealing doctors treating patients despite malpractice charges. It's a journalistic integrity hall of fame, immersive, risk-taking writing at its finest. Why wasn't this enough?

Unsure where to start, I continue down the hall and glance into the kitchen. Bigger than mine, but it looks unused. I fling open the fridge, thinking I'll start with a drink while getting settled. In the back of my mind I tell myself not to drink too much. I don't want to think about it, but I know I can't pee in the same bathroom where Willa died.

The door peels away from its suction, but there is no rattle of condiments in the door. The fridge is completely empty.

I feel tears claw at the back of my throat. This is what Officer Curry warned me of. Willa had cleaned out. She was ready to leave.

The door swings closed, and the empty insides seem to swallow up the possibility that this was an accident. No one staging a murder would think to empty out Willa's fridge and spritz Lysol in the vegetable crisper to polish it for the next occupant.

Beside the fridge, though, the recycling bin stinks with empty bottles, a touch of alcohol pooling in the bottom. It's sat untouched for three weeks, at least. Overhead, the neighbor barrels across the room like an express train, and it sets off an unsettling rattle within the glass bottles. Curry was right, and now it looks like Leo was right too, at least about her drinking habits. Seeing Willa's vice revealed reminds me of the time she heard my choking cough and walked in on me purging dinner.

This is going to be worse than I expected.

How did we get here? We grew up in the same house, with the same mother. Claudia was excessively tolerant, but we didn't push her like we could have. Yes, I got in trouble: for breaking Willa's watch, for giving the middle finger to passing cars for no good reason, for accepting a dare to climb the neighbor's rusty basketball hoop—a dare that landed me in the emergency room with eleven stitches in my knee. But that was the worst of it. Willa was different. As a teenager, she was tight-lipped and indignant. Our mother demanded unchallenged loyalty, and Willa refused to give it as she got older. And so I learned not to push our mother, to be the good one. I sought approval, and I got it.

We contrasted even as children. I was the pudgy little sister with rosacea-stained cheeks and a palpable, sticky yearning to be liked. Willa was tough, grit and fire. I was, and still am, scattered but warm, goofy, a little too insecure. Why did I think I was strong enough to do this myself?

Grudgingly, I turn the corner from the kitchen and step into the hallway. The carpet is matted and discolored in front of the bathroom door. I peer in, half expecting the room to radiate carnage. My sister died here, after all. I flick on the light and see that it's been scoured clean. I thought the grout might bear missed droplets of blood, but the old tiles and porcelain are as spotless as they could be at their age. The scent of bleach hangs in the bathroom and infects the apartment with the eye-watering sting of clean.

A half-empty shampoo bottle is perched in the corner of the tub, and a box of tampons sits on the counter near the sink. My chest tightens with a vise-grip ache. Seeing the tampons hurts more than the empty fridge because they point to Willa's everyday life, not her readying for death. Folded over the edge of the tub is a washcloth, dried to a stiff white flag of defeat.

Heading down the hallway, I brace myself to see her bedroom, the most personal, private room of the apartment.

But it's less intimate than the waiting room at the doctor's office. Even they have magazines. The bed is stripped of sheets, and her dresser is bare. No jewelry sits out, no piles of coins are stacked on the nightstand. No tufts of dust huddle in the corners. I look for signs that Oz may have been here, but the room reveals no secrets.

I move to her desk, a writer's mecca. It mirrors how she wanted to be seen: sleek and complicated. A single photo graces the polished desktop, the only one in her whole apartment. It's Willa, alone, in front of an overflowing flower bed. Age four, maybe five. I pick it up. She's looking into the camera with an uncharacteristic wide-eyed openness. It was taken before her eyes became an unknowable mask in every photo. Willa tended to be stoic, I think, in direct response to our mother's emotional outbursts. The more sensitive, reactant, and anxious Claudia became, the cooler Willa became. But in this picture she was just a little girl.

I sit down in her desk chair, and it's here that I feel her ghost settle over me. How many of her last hours, days, did she spend in this chair?

I push away the thought—and my guilt at the intrusion of poking through her belongings—as I lift the screen of her laptop. A cheery pink Post-it note is affixed to the corner of the screen. On it, a series of numbers and letters. Her password, I realize, and I frown as I type it in. I tell myself it's a convenience for Willa's life, not a preparation for her death.

The laptop whirs to a start, and I navigate to her email. The police have scoured it, I'm sure. Or I hope they have. There might be a clue to her state of mind in her recent messages.

Her email account is frustratingly organized. Bank statements and bills are filed neatly into folders. There's a folder labeled *Recent Purchases*, and it's full of receipts for podcasts bought on iTunes and books about the KonMari Method of organizing. Not exactly a woman on the verge of dying.

I can't help but feel conflicted as I search through her messages. I can't shake the feeling that she was too busy to willingly give up on life, even if the empty fridge and boxed-up belongings suggest otherwise.

An email dated a few days before Willa died sits in her inbox, waiting on a reply. As I click into it, I wonder if I have to be the one to set up an autoresponse to inform Willa's contacts that she's no longer responding to messages. It's morbid but also so practical that I shudder.

I scan the email quickly at first, then more closely:

Dear Christine,

We have no interest in speaking to you. While we appreciate your reference to "ethical journalism," my father has been misrepresented in sensationalized, inaccurate, insensitive reporting for nearly three decades. Media coverage has only intensified the trauma felt by our family.

*Please respect our wishes and do not contact us
again.*

Sincerely,

Edwin Vaughn

I scroll down to see the original email requesting an
interview. The messages are forwarded to the inbox from a
different email address bearing the name Christine Fleury.

Who is she, and why is Willa getting her emails?

I bring up a browser and Google the name. Dozens of
hits on the first page connect Christine Fleury with *Truth-
Shout*, the newspaper where Willa worked. I realize this
must be the pseudonym she adopted after she quit KZTV.

If she was using her pseudonym, was she working on an
undercover story for *TruthShout* when she died?

Could it be related to her death?

10

Sawyer

Noah's and Remy's sulky faces brush through my mind. Didn't they say Willa had been leaving town on work assignments most weekends? I hurriedly click through Willa's account to see if I can find more messages like this. I wonder if she had been working on a dangerous story, if she met a shady person while interviewing.

There are a few messages from a woman named Frenchie Bell, whom I know to be Willa's boss at *TruthShout*. Not her real name. *Francine*. Brassy hair, braying laugh, and ten years Willa's junior. I find Frenchie's phone number in an email signature and dial her on my cell.

"Frenchie," she calls out in a singsong voice.

"Um, hi, Frenchie. This is Sawyer Stannard, Willa's sister?"

Instantly I regret the call. I've opened myself up to patronizing platitudes and phony remembrances. But I know if I hang up, the aborted call from a grieving sister may make its way to the press. News of the death hasn't died away yet.

"Sawyer," she purrs, drawing out my name.

"I have a quick question for you. I don't have much time," I lie. "Was Willa working on an undercover story when she . . . when she passed?"

Frenchie inhales deeply. "An exposé? No, nothing like that. She hadn't filed any new bylines in months."

"Really? But—"

"God knows I'd have welcomed it," she interrupts. "It's why I hired her. Truth be told, she's been more of a freelance fact-checker, if anything. She's barely been on the payroll. Speaking of, I'll have our HR department send her final paycheck."

I cringe and end the call. If Willa wasn't working on a story for the newspaper, for what story was she requesting this interview? And why did she have to hide behind her pseudonym for it? I turn back to the laptop to keep searching. God, she paid for a lot of podcasts. I navigate to the sent folder.

A sick fascination spreads through me as I click through the messages. I'm a voyeur, but what am I looking for? Then I see it. It's addressed to Red Folio Literary Agency.

> Gemma, great to meet you at the writers' conference in Chicago last year. As promised, I mailed a copy of the book proposal about the Melody Wynne disappearance to your office. A formality at this stage, but I understand why you need it. Looking forward to working with you. W.

The now-familiar tingle of unrest worms its way through my body. The butterflies of uncertainty awake in my stomach as I hunch closer to the screen. If she was motivated enough to write a book, she wasn't depressed. There could still be foul play involved in her death.

I type *Melody Wynne* into the search engine and click on an article from the archives of a newspaper, the *Trowbridge Gazette*. It's dated August 7, 1992.

CHESHIRE, MI—Authorities are searching for an eighteen-month-old girl who went missing from her Lake Chicora home on Tuesday afternoon.

The mother of Melody Wynne said she last saw her daughter at approximately two o'clock in the afternoon in their lakeside cottage when she set her down for a nap. Grace Wynne went outside to garden on the east side of the house. When she went into the house to rouse her daughter from her nap at three o'clock, Melody was missing. The girl's mother made a 911 call to police at 3:06 P.M. to report that her daughter had been abducted, according to the emergency dispatcher.

"Please bring her home. She's my only baby. She's my everything. Please bring her back home to us," Grace Wynne said on Tuesday evening.

Authorities are centering their search on the Wynnes' house, the lake, and the surrounding woods. There is no sign of forced entry. The front and back doors of the house were left unlocked while the mother gardened in the yard. No ransom note was left behind. The local sheriff's department is conducting a thorough search of the area for any signs of Melody or her abductor.

Melody is a white female with blond hair and brown eyes. She is thirty-two inches tall and weighs twenty-five pounds.

During a news conference on Tuesday evening, authorities made a plea for information from the public.

"Our goal is to speak to everyone living on or near the lake. We will contact everyone living nearby to determine if they have any information that can help us find Melody. Please check nearby wooded areas and any outbuildings on your property. Call us if you see or hear anything unusual," said Trowbridge Township officer Corbin Campbell.

Parents Grace and Jack Wynne are praying for a safe return of their daughter.

"She's a beautiful baby. I'll do anything for her to come home. If anyone knows where she is, please call the sheriff. She could be anywhere by now," said Grace Wynne.

A one-thousand-dollar reward is being offered for any information leading to Melody Wynne's safe return. For anyone who may have information on Melody's disappearance, please call the Trowbridge County Sheriff's office.

I've gnawed off all the nails on my left hand by the time I finish the article. I keep my hand in my mouth as I try to smooth out the jagged edges. I think about the out-of-town trips Remy mentioned. If they weren't for a *TruthShout* article, they might have been in regard to this story.

I have to know why Willa spent her last months writing about a twenty-six-year-old cold case about a missing baby in Michigan. And why she never thought to tell anyone about it.

I write an email to Gemma at Red Folio Literary Agency explaining who I am and that I'd like a copy of the book proposal. The blinking cursor is intimidating as I figure out which words to use to inform her that my sister is dead. Willa was the writer, not me. The words feel like they've hit an oil slick in my mind. I can't grasp any that can convey what I want to say. Nothing can match how I feel about her death—the words all seem so weak and inadequate when I read them back. Finally, I settle for simplicity, sure that Gemma would have heard the news about Willa's death already anyway. I hit send, and within moments an autoresponse arrives in the inbox, informing me that Gemma is on maternity leave. *Of course it wouldn't be that easy*, I think wryly.

With a few swift clicks, I enter the browsing history and type in *map*. The last result is from nearly a year ago: the quickest route from her address to a rural town in Michigan. I open the link and cross-check the address with the name of the town in the article. Cheshire, Michigan, population 1,800. An unincorporated town where a good chunk of the residents live below the poverty line, I find when I search.

Why this story? Why the secrecy?

I hit print and make an impulsive choice to visit the family of the missing girl this weekend. It means more days off work. Another conversation with Kelly, the power-hungry spin tyrant.

I stand to stretch and wander into the front of the apartment, past the haunted bathroom and empty kitchen. Standing on my toes, I strain to peer out the window. At garden level, it looks out into the scruffy yard. The grass glitters with forgotten laundry coins reflecting the setting sun. The smell of chocolate from the cocoa-bean processors is more palpable than when I arrived. Time to catch the train back to Oak Park before darkness settles.

As I scan the street, a rusted-out truck catches my eye. Instantly I recognize the dark hair and Slavic complexion of the man in the driver's seat. Oz. Idling down the street as if he's patrolling the apartment. Or casing it.

My heart thrums in my chest as I duck below the window frame. Unease washes over me. The fluttery feeling of agitation hasn't left my chest since I heard about Willa's death.

I look down at the map in my hand. Cheshire, Michigan. Like the mysterious, redirection-happy Cheshire cat. I realize I am Alice: frustrated and lost, chasing my dead sister down a rabbit hole.

Cry of the Cicadas: The True Story of Melody Wynne's Disappearance

by Willa Stannard

Introduction

The summer that the cicadas came to Cheshire, eighteen-month-old Melody Wynne disappeared.

On August 4, 1992, Grace Wynne entered the lakeside bungalow she shared with her husband, Jack, after gardening in the yard and discovered that her daughter was missing.

When the responding officer arrived at the Wynne home, he was informed by Grace that the doors and windows were unlocked and no screens were damaged. There was no sign of forced entry to the house or even any disturbance near the open window of Melody's room. The grass in the yard was sun-scorched to a brittle white hay, affording no sign of an intruder's footprints leading up to the house.

The case of Melody's abduction was dead from the beginning: there were no signs of an intruder, no witnesses, no ransom demands, no trail of forensic evidence to follow, no confessions, and no solution. Police investigated a neighbor with a criminal background, a local man who expressed undue interest in the case, and later, the parents.

"Abduction by a stranger is remote. It's a slim chance we don't know who took her," Trowbridge

Township officer Corbin Campbell said to a local reporter the evening Melody was reported missing.

It was a case that changed the way people parented; it bred a pervasive fear of a ghostlike child abductor. A child is abducted every forty seconds in the United States. The majority of perpetrators are relatives, followed by acquaintances of the victim and, finally, strangers. While the Trowbridge County Sheriff's Office stated that it's a "slim chance" the perpetrator was not related to or known by Melody, no one has ever been apprehended in the case.

The case might have been dead before it even began—but was Melody Wynne dead as well?

11

Sawyer

O N THE DRIVE, I pass roadside stands selling blueberries and taxidermy shops operated out of living rooms. I pass a few churches, the kind with modest white siding and a reverent steeple. There's a sunflower field that beams at me as I pass, the flowers reveling in their late-summer glory. Mostly I pass signs for campgrounds and boating access.

Lake Chicora is in an untouched corner of the county, in the rural town of Cheshire. I wonder how many times Willa made this trip. Before I let Marion Street and the backdrop of the city fall away, I study Willa's vehicle manual with an intensity I haven't felt since I first learned to count carbs. The soft leather seats absorb the sound of my spoken self-reminders to use turn signals and drive in the center lane—all the things I recall from drivers' ed but never have to put into practice.

After I find myself passing a lighthouse beacon welcoming visitors to Michigan, I realize that the drive is a reprieve. Though I'm chasing Willa's footsteps, it doesn't feel as suffocating here as it does in Chicago.

When the paved road begins to curve, I keep driving straight, bumping Willa's car clumsily onto the gravel road. Dense woods choke the one-lane road. A sign says *Speed Limit: 5*, and I snicker at the impossible speed until I hit a deep groove that nearly sends the car into the bushes. I slow considerably. A puff of ashy dirt works its way through the air vent and gives me a coughing fit.

The road follows a meandering creek. Wildflowers reach for the car as I pass. Bright-red poppies, delicate Queen Anne's lace, and vibrant purple salvia wave at the car.

I haven't passed any visible houses yet, and I've driven for nearly a mile. I'm only a three-hour drive from the metropolis of Chicago, but the isolation feels as if I've ventured into rural Appalachia or the New Mexico hills. Lake Chicora, I learned as I Googled, is a destination passed over as the secret summer spot for rich Chicagoans. It's not a town with a beloved country diner or even a Dairy Queen to go on dates. The nearest burger joint is fifteen miles from the lake.

It's not until I pull up alongside a small house on the lake that I begin to second-guess my decision to come here. It's not the first time I've acted before I put real thought into something. The tiny house has weathered vinyl siding, a metal roof, and an enclosed porch facing the lake. Nearby, mildewed panels of wood rise from the water to form a forgotten boathouse.

The smell hits me first as I open the door. The air smells of stagnant lake water and fetid, rotting wood, made stronger by the absence of wind. Geese chatter with defiance as they gather on the banks of the uninhibited corner where the shallow creek meets the lake.

The snap of a screen door alerts me to the woman standing on the stoop.

"Christine?"

I turn. My stomach nose-dives to my feet. This must be Grace Wynne, the mother of the missing girl. She doesn't look like tragedy has marked her, but I feel humbled just seeing her.

"Oh. I'm sorry," she says, stepping into the yard, which is pockmarked by crabgrass and weeds. "I thought you were someone else."

"Mrs. Wynne?" That tentative note crawls into my voice at the end. I try to channel Willa's husky, self-assured tone. "I'm here on behalf of Christine Fleury. She had an accident, so I'm taking over work on the book for her." I practiced the lie on the drive up, and it still sounded clunky and untrue. Using Willa's pseudonym feels like cotton on my tongue.

"Oh, dear. I'm sorry to hear that. Is she doing all right?" Her voice is thick with an indulgent country twang.

I hurry up the path to follow my lie with another lie. Willa's been dead nearly a month, but the Wynnes don't know that. My heart races as I give her a fake name: Sarah Drew. I think of the canary-yellow spines of the Nancy Drew mysteries that lined a small shelf in Willa's and my bedroom growing up and feel a secret connection to my sister through my new pseudonym. I wonder if the reference is obvious to Grace, that she'll know I'm playing detective, but she lets me in the house without pause. I wonder if I'd be as trusting if I had a baby kidnapped from my house.

She leads me into the kitchen, where she pulls two ceramic mugs from the cabinet and fills them with water. A rotten-egg stink pours from the sink. She places both mugs in the microwave.

"Sulfur," she explains, looking over her narrow maroon eyeglasses at me as she dunks a tea bag into a steaming mug. "From the well water. It's safe to drink but unpleasant to bathe in."

Instantly I picture Willa's wrists leaking in a bathtub filled with stinking rotten-egg water. I shake the image away as I follow Grace into the sitting room facing the lake.

"Is your husband—?"

I stop. Hundreds of photos are tacked to the shiplap walls from floor to ceiling. The effect is overwhelming. I step closer, my eyes darting across the wallpaper of faces. They're all shots of different people, mostly kids: all ages, all hair colors and complexions, all manner of moments captured and affixed to the wall.

Grace lowers herself into the rocking chair, and the medallion on her necklace clinks with the mug.

"They're all from local yard sales or flea markets." She takes a slow sip. "It's desperate, I know, but I'm hoping to catch a glimpse of Melody, or even her favorite toy, in one of them. My husband, Jack, he hates it, but he lets me have it. I think he knows it's something when we have nothing."

"Is he home? Your husband?" I ask, forcing myself to look away from the sea of kids' faces staring at me.

"No. He's at the clinic, but he usually comes home for lunch."

"So have you ever found anything in the photos?"

She fluffs her short-cropped gray hair as she scans the walls. "I've found hundreds of places where she isn't. That must count for something."

"How long have you been collecting them?"

"Not as long as you'd think. If I saw this room, I'd imagine it would take decades to find this many photos that families are willing to discard. But I've only been doing it for a few years. Since . . . oh, I shouldn't tell you this. Will you include it in the book?"

I shake my head vigorously, alert with the promise of a secret. Wait, though. Maybe a real reporter is less willing to take things off the record so quickly. I lean back in the lumpy couch and take a sip of tea.

"After I heard that Merrill Vaughn died, I worked up the courage to go to his estate sale. I was certain that being in his house would reveal something about Melody. I dressed like a tourist and kept sunglasses on the whole time—like a low-rent spy." She laughs.

I feel my cheeks turn pink, and I lift the mug to pretend the steam colored them. I recognize Merrill Vaughn's name from the online article—one of the top suspects in Melody's disappearance.

"Anyway, he lived in Pullman, in this giant Italianate farmhouse. A former B and B at the turn of the century. The last century," she clarifies. "It's a fifteen-minute drive from here. God, the things I imagined on that drive." She shakes her head to chase the memory away.

"The funny thing was, I felt like *I* was the criminal for attending his estate sale. Not he, for taking my daughter," she confides, her voice now brittle. "The only thing I purchased was a family album. Again, hoping to catch a glimpse of Melody, as if he'd be foolish enough to print it locally and paste it into an album. But this was the first set of photos I ever purchased, and I didn't think it through."

"Do you still have them?"

She shakes her head. "Bottom of the burn pit. I was sickened to see him living a normal life in the photos."

I nod, and we fall into silence, both looking out at the lake. The house is set close to the shore, close enough that I can see fast but clumsy dragonflies buzzing near lily pads. A squat willow tree skims its leafy branches across the water. A whisper of color catches my eye. I squint to see better, then regret it as the shape shows itself. A plastic baby swing. Canary yellow.

"Are the police still working the case?"

Grace casts a sidelong look at me. "How much has Christine told you?"

Damn, damn, damn.

"Only the basics. She wanted me to be unbiased when I talked to you. Form my own opinions. See if I have a different take than she does so the book can be comprehensive . . ."

"Detective Campbell is still working the case. He has been since Melody disappeared. He was a deputy in the sheriff's office back then. Now he's ranked as a detective lieutenant, and he oversees three sergeants in his bureau. Truth be told, I don't know if that consistency helps or hurts us anymore."

She ages as she speaks. She must be in her midsixties, but the lines on her face deepen every time she says Melody's name. I try to rewind time's effect on her face to see the woman she was before her daughter was taken, but I can't take the loss out of her eyes.

"So . . . the police aren't doing much. Have you ever taken the investigation into your own hands? Since the estate sale at Merrill Vaughn's?"

"I'm not a vigilante, I'm a mother," she says with a sigh. "Jack and I hired a private investigator years ago. We paid him thousands of dollars, but no real leads were ever generated. Merrill Vaughn, now dead, and Abel Bowen are the only two men who were ever suspects. Abel lives down the road, at the turnoff where the pavement meets the gravel. I've always kept an eye on him—how could I not? Detective Campbell could never prove either man's involvement, though."

I think of the online articles. The detective could never prove that Abel or Merrill was involved, but he couldn't prove that Grace and her husband weren't either.

"What does your gut tell you?"

Her mouth set in a grim line, Grace eases herself from the rocking chair. The chair slaps the floor and her knees creak, but I am silent as I lean forward. Grace gazes out the picture window at the lake. The still surface of the water ripples when fish jump.

"You're so different from Christine."

I startle. "How so?"

"The way you interview. It's complimentary, I suppose. She's much more formal than you. Notebook, recorder, the whole nine yards. Asking about evidence and facts only. Steering me back when I talk too much about my feelings. You seem more perceptive to the emotional side of this story. And God knows it's a tearjerker," she says with a cheerless smile.

"You've got to feel your feelings," I say with a shrug. I redden again and curse myself for sounding so flippant. It's something we say in spin class, but it's not something to say to a grieving mother. "I don't mean that to sound so empty," I backpedal. "I just believe in trusting your intuition."

"Of course, dear," Grace concedes, her voice tender. "Truth told, my gut has always told me that Merrill was responsible for Melody's disappearance. He came to visit us here at home early on. He came three times in that first month, claiming to be a psychic. I was so vulnerable, I believed him. He wanted to learn more about Melody, to help us find her, he said, and I believed him. I *believed* him," she chokes, still emotional after all this time. "When he died, Detective Campbell told me he found newspaper clippings about missing children in his house."

"Oh God," I breathe. My knee bounces with anxiety.

Grace nods sagely. "I know. But Jack and I are divided. He can't be convinced it wasn't Abel. He says it's black and white: Abel is a convicted felon. We didn't know it at the time. But he's a criminal who lives a mile down the road, on sixty-odd acres of wooded land. Jack still searches, though it's trespassing. Abel doesn't even try to stop him. That's why I think it wasn't him. He'd have more to cover up if he took her."

But not if she's been gone for more than twenty-five years.

12

Sawyer

"WE DIDN'T HAVE cicadas this year. That was appreciated," Grace says as the screen door opens and sets the air-conditioning unit in the window rattling.

An older man with graying hair and rimless eyeglasses walks in. His welcoming face turns stony.

"Who are you?"

I jump to my feet. "Sarah, sir. I'm here for Christine. She asked me to fill in for her. Temporarily." Is it my imagination, or does my voice hitch on the last word?

He looks to Grace, and I know he sees the shiny tear streaks down her cheeks.

"Honey, I told you not to speak to any more reporters." He turns to me. He's not much taller than I am, but I still feel intimidated. "We have a good relationship with Christine. If she can't finish what she started, we don't want to talk to another reporter."

"I'm not—"

"We're not going to start this all over again. We're not going to dredge up our family's pain every few months and years, every time there's an anniversary. This case will never be solved. The police made mistakes and dragged their feet. There will never be a trial or justice. We just want to move on."

"Christine wanted me to talk to you about what happened," I try again. It was a mistake to come here, to invade their home. I set my mug down on an end table and inch toward the door, expecting Jack to demand I leave.

"Nothing happened. Grace heard nothing. She saw nothing. The police found nothing. There's nothing we can tell you," he says.

Grace puts her hand to her mouth and bows her head. She pulls a small, intricate quilt over her knees. It's embroidered with tiny bluebirds, and I realize it must be the baby's quilt. It breaks my heart.

"Grace isn't to blame for Melody's disappearance," I say, thinking out loud.

Jack's eyes dart back to Grace. Her shoulders curve as she smooths the hand-stitching on the quilt in her lap. When he looks back at me, his eyes have softened.

"I don't blame her. No one does," he says. "Take a seat. What did you say your name was again?"

"It's—"

"I do," Grace says. "I blame myself."

Cautiously, I sit on the edge of the saffron-yellow chair cushion once again. I think about what Remy said at the funeral: it's an intrusion to peer at someone's grief. I wonder again if I should leave.

"Of course I feel guilty," she says. "You have no idea how many times I've said, 'If only . . .' I just wish I could bring my daughter home, even if it's bone by bone."

Jack's weathered face hardens again, and he strokes his salt-and-pepper beard. As the sunlight filters in, I see that his clothes are covered in pet hair. There are no pets in the small cottage; he must work at a veterinary clinic.

Grace says, "I used to see the shadow of her little body, just learning how to walk, when the sun went down in the evenings. I used to wake up to her phantom cries in the middle of the night. And I used to hear this sound. At first it was subtle but reliable, like a metronome. Then I realized what it was: the imagined sound of Melody's measured, sleeping breaths through the baby monitor. I left it in the house that afternoon instead of bringing it into the garden with me. It haunts me. I collapsed when I realized it wasn't really her; it was my guilt. Like the telltale heart."

"Grace," Jack warns, more aware than she is that I'm supposedly a reporter. A shark waiting to expose their story, or so he thinks.

"I used to dream about Melody," she continues, ignoring him. "I'd awake from my dreams with a grainy anxiety that something was wrong. Then I remember. I lost her. Lost her like someone forgets an umbrella or a shopping bag. But I don't anymore. It's like the mother in me has disappeared, just like she did. I don't see her or hear her anymore because I didn't see or hear when it was most important."

"You'll never stop being her mother," I say gently. I sense that Jack is preparing to shut me out for good. My presence is too disruptive to Grace.

"I'm going to leave you two together. I'm so sorry to uproot your day like this," I say. "Christine wanted me to check in with a few of your neighbors. Are there many who were living here when Melody disappeared?"

Jack stands, grateful I've excused myself. His bulky frame crowds me to the door. "Most of the neighbors are summer folks. Only Roberta is still around. I know Christine talked to her on a few occasions. She's right over there," he says, pointing to a cheerful cottage nestled under the overhang of towering trees. "She docks her pontoon in our boathouse. Of course, Abel still lives down the road. But he won't talk to you. He's never answered questions from a reporter."

I nod my good-byes and cast one last look at Grace sitting by the window. Silent tears have started to escape behind her bold glasses. As the screen door rattles shut, I hear Jack's gruff voice speaking loudly, purposefully, over the sound of Grace's quiet weeping.

"Detective Campbell, please."

I pause to listen, mindful that they can surely hear me crunch down the path and drive away just as clearly as I can hear them inside the thin cottage walls.

"What's the sudden investigative urgency around my daughter's abduction?" He pauses. "What I mean is that another reporter came today."

I pull out my phone and pretend to be engrossed in listening to a voice mail so I can justify lingering on their front porch.

". . . and she was alone with Grace. I don't know how long . . . Well, I know there's nothing you can do if she lets them in. But I wanted you to know there's yet another new reporter looking into the case."

With soft steps, I reach Willa's car and ease myself inside. The leather's boiling hot and covered in a fine dust from the dry gravel road working its way through the vents.

I don't doubt it's normal for the parents of a missing child to have close contact with the police officer on their case. But after nearly thirty years?

As the car crawls away from the lakeside cottages and into the woods, I wonder how far Jack would go to protect his wife, and if the Wynnes should be unspoken suspects.

Cry of the Cicadas: The True Story of Melody Wynne's Disappearance

Emergency Call Transcript

August 4, 1992
3:06 P.M.

EMERGENCY DISPATCHER: Nine-one-one operator. What's your emergency?

GRACE WYNNE: Please, she's gone. I need help. Please help.

DISPATCHER: Okay, ma'am, I am going to help you. What is your name?

GW: Grace. Grace Lynette Wynne. It's . . . I need the police.

DISPATCHER: Okay, Grace. Explain to me what's going on.

GW: My daughter's gone. Oh God. God, hurry, please. [*Inaudible*]

DISPATCHER: What's your address, please, ma'am?

GW: It's four six one eight Lakeview Lane. God, please send help.

DISPATCHER: I'm sending help now, ma'am. How old is your daughter?

GW: Um, she's eighteen months. She's . . . she's not old enough to count her age in years yet. She's my baby.

DISPATCHER: And how long has she been gone?

GW: I don't . . . I don't know. I was in the garden and went inside, and she was gone. There's no

note. Are you sending the sheriff or just an
officer?

DISPATCHER: I'm sending the nearest officer over
now. Don't hang up. Help is on the way.

GW: Oh God, tell him to hurry. There's only one
road out. [*Inaudible*]

[*Call disconnected.*]

13

Sawyer

THE CONCRETE WALLS absorb the sound. That seems to be the only positive about Leo's tiny office.

His officemate made a grumbly show about being displaced when Leo asked for privacy. His chair is empty, but I stay standing, bouncing on the balls of my feet as I look out the window at the rainy afternoon. There's a row of Troll dolls lined up on the marble windowsill, more than a dozen in all. Not Leo's collection, I'm sure.

"So I have more information about the project she was working on. It's a book. Not an article. An entire book," I emphasize. "A major undertaking. Something you'd want to see through. A huge accomplishment."

He sighs. "I get it, Sawyer. You think she was too much of a go-getter to kill herself." He's dressed almost identically to when I last saw him on campus: a plaid shirt with rolled cuffs, dark jeans, and scuffed brown shoes.

"But did you know?"

"Know what?"

"About the book. It's about a kidnapping in rural Michigan that happened twenty-six years ago. She was writing a true crime book, just like the ones she read all the time. She could have been the next Ann Rule."

"So?"

"So she was visiting the family of the missing baby. She was interviewing neighbors. Suspects. What if she uncovered something about the case? Something that led to her death?" I steeple my fingers together anxiously and look at the ceiling. "I went there. I met the missing girl's parents. I told them I'm working with Willa, that I was there on her behalf. If I can piece together what she knew, what she was working on . . ." I trail off when I look down from the cracked ceiling to Leo's incredulous face.

He stretches his skinny arms over his head and leans back in his chair. His brows knit together in a skeptical frown; his lips purse into pale lines.

"I'm in disbelief that you think you can solve not only Willa's supposed 'murder' but a cold case about a missing child in another state as well. Visiting the missing baby's parents, Sawyer? That is so reckless I can't even begin to comment on it."

My cheeks flame, and I stare out the window to cover it. He has the same blunt criticality that Willa had. Maybe they were more similar than I thought.

"It's not my place to say it, but Willa always thought you careened from one self-created dramatic disaster to another. I don't want to be in the middle of another Stannard girl's struggle, for truth or justice or boredom or whatever this is."

I let the silence stretch between us before I speak again.

"I believed you when you said Willa became mean to you," I say. "She judged those who were closest to her the harshest. She was brutal in her judgment of me, so I'm not surprised you've heard all the mean things about me. I've heard them about you too. She was good at seeing flaws. It meant she cared enough about you to want you to be better.

She knew how to wound you with words, and it sounds like you know how too." With a tug, I tighten my ponytail. "Should I leave?"

Leo rubs hard on his temple until his fingers turn white.

"Sawyer, I'm sorry. I—"

"I don't want to hear it. I've heard enough sorries to last a lifetime," I say, thinking of the note Willa left behind.

"You're not going to let this go, are you?"

"Willa hated that I'm not good at finishing what I start. I have to get closure, for her."

It was a point of contention between us: my flightiness, as Willa called it. She accused me of wanting what everyone else had, even if I didn't want it. She said it was the reason I dropped projects, friends, and money so freely. She resented me for failing to see things through to the end. Ironic that she was the one to give up on herself.

With a sigh, Leo leans forward and rummages through the desk drawer. He pulls out a pen and a piece of paper.

"What's the name of the missing girl again?"

I tell him what I know, and he scribbles on the back of what looks like a student's homework assignment.

"If you're going to look into this case, do it right. Try to find Willa's notes, and do more research before you do another impromptu interview. Don't be careless. If anyone is going to believe you're working with Willa, you have to be as on top of your shit as she would have been."

I nod vigorously, my ponytail bouncing.

"And I'd avoid the yoga pants if I were you," he says, eyeing my daily uniform.

I laugh, and my mouth falls into an easy smile. I look away suddenly, embarrassed. Laughter feels like flirting. A moment of levity feels like disrespect. I turn away and look out the paned window again. The rain has slowed to a fine drizzle, and the campus seems deserted except for a pair of robins tussling near a marble birdbath. I think of the embroidered bluebirds on Melody Wynne's quilt, and I know I can't get distracted on this. I have to see this through to the end, wherever it may lead me.

"I can call the local police department," Leo offers, "but if it's a small town, they might close ranks. They like to protect their own, sometimes even the guilty. I'll present it as research for a case study for one of my classes. I'll see what I can find out for you."

"Thanks, Leo. I need to find out more about the biggest suspects in the case: the so-called psychic and the convicted felon. And the parents. I need to know more about them too."

"For the record, I'm totally against this," he says, his voice taking on a judgmental, professorial edge. "You're completely unqualified to go sniffing around a former felon or grieving parents in an attempt to solve a cold case that may have nothing to do with Willa's death." He takes a deep breath, as if he's readying himself for an oration in front of his students, but he lets it out heavily, and his chest deflates. "Which, for the record again, I believe was a suicide," he adds.

"The official record notes your concern," I say sarcastically. "At least tell me you agree that it's odd Willa died while investigating and writing about an unsolved crime. For the record."

Leo rakes a bony hand through his hair and smiles. It reminds me of what Willa once said in an uncharacteristic moment of enthusiasm—that there were two things that made her fall for him: his book collection and that he smiled. In her field, everyone was too self-involved, too cool to smile.

"I think you're nuts for thinking you can inject yourself into a case that police haven't been able to solve for decades," he says, tapping a pen on the marred wooden desk.

I shrug. "How hard did they really try?"

Cry of the Cicadas: The True Story of Melody Wynne's Disappearance

Part 1: The Investigation

It was reported in September 2002, ten years after Melody's disappearance, that the Trowbridge County Sheriff's Office interviewed more than sixty people involved in the case, investigated four potential suspects, logged 180 items of evidence, and built a case file approximately seven thousand pages long.

At the sheriff's office in Mapleton, it was a quiet summer afternoon when the call came in that a little girl was missing from her home. In 1992, the understaffed sheriff's office employed three detectives in the investigative services unit, serving the thirty-two townships in Trowbridge County.

An hour before the call came in, Sergeants Eric Lewis and Marty Paulson had left the station to investigate a report of a drug offense in a rural trailer park. Sheriff Wiesel was out of the office presenting his monthly crime retrospective to the town board. Deputy Corbin Campbell took the call that afternoon.

Well before eight that morning, Campbell arrived at his neat office at the station, where not a paper clip was out of place and a maple tree waved out the window in an early-morning breeze. With fewer years on the force than his counterparts, Campbell didn't have experience in missing persons cases. Then again, neither did Lewis, Paulson, or even Sheriff Wiesel.

Reserve officers had erected roadblocks around the county by five o'clock in the evening the day Melody was abducted. By then, she had been reported missing for nearly two hours and could have been more than one hundred miles outside Trowbridge County.

Campbell was, and still is, assigned to the central townships, which include Lake Chicora in Cheshire. Though a rookie at the time of Melody's disappearance, Campbell was the first officer at the scene of the crime, and he has remained, uninterrupted, on the open case since then, including a brief period when state investigators took the lead during a spate of heightened publicity.

Campbell faced criticism from the citizens of Trowbridge County for the cost of the investigative measures he ordered in the days, months, and years following Melody's disappearance. Money and resources are scarce, and many members of the local population are unemployed or underemployed—and quick to point a finger at the rising cost of the Wynne case when tax hikes have been proposed since the abduction, regardless of the actual effect of the case on taxes.

The week Melody disappeared, Campbell ordered dive teams to drag the lake to search for any trace of the eighteen-month-old girl. Bloodhound searches occurred in the two miles of wooded land surrounding the Wynne house and Lake Chicora. Work at factories, dairy farms, and even the JCPenney in downtown Mapleton halted as workers took time off to join the volunteer search.

Logjams and trotlines were searched. Persons of interest were given lie detector tests, and round-the-clock surveillance was performed. Years later, modern DNA testing revealed no hits.

Thousands of dollars in investigative costs and police overtime led to no viable clues or discernible progress in the case. Now, more than twenty-five years after Melody disappeared, Campbell is no closer to figuring out where she went than he was the first evening he arrived at the Wynne cottage on Lake Chicora.

CHAPTER

14

Sawyer

THE NEXT DAY is Thursday, and I'm scheduled to teach a spin class. The jumps and sprints and resistance and jogs feel cathartic. We promise a soulful experience through a steamy room and curated music, and today I feel it. I might be high on endorphins, not exercise, but I welcome the forty-five minutes of release.

After, exhausted and nearly sick, I drive Willa's car to my mother's house in Hillside. It's small—Willa and I had no choice but to share a room growing up—and set along a road with dozens of monument businesses, funeral homes, and cemeteries. Bleak, but it provided for us, and the village capitalizes on it. They sell tickets to an annual cemetery tour to visit the graves of Chicagoland legends. Working at the florist that outfits the funerals, my mother is immune to the macabre. Her specialty is sympathy wreaths. Yet once I saw her rip a makeshift cross out of the soft grass along the roadside. She said she didn't like the notion of marking the exact spot where life left a body. She preferred to commemorate it with tasteful and overpriced white flowers instead.

I park on the crumbled asphalt driveway, pleased to see that Oz's truck is not there. It means my mother is marooned at the tiny house. Carless and unfriendly with neighbors, she doesn't leave the house unless it's for work.

Inside, I settle on the lumpy plaid couch, the same we've had since I was a kid, and Claudia lowers the volume on the TV. Always on, it's an indication of the time of day when the shades are never open: from the coffee-fueled cheer of the morning shows to the unencumbered shrieks of daytime TV to the somber dictation of world events in the evening.

"So the lady cop called yesterday. She got the results of the . . . whaddya call it . . . the toxic report?"

"The toxicology report?" I ask, alert.

"That's it. Well, Willa's blood-alcohol level was high above the legal limit. She gave some numbers, but they didn't mean anything to me. I'm no expert. Anyway, it was so high, and with the note, and no evidence of a break-in, they're ruling it a suicide and closing it."

"They're closing her case? This fast? What did she say about the DNA?"

Claudia shrugs. "She didn't mention it."

"Did you *ask*, Momma?" My voice is incredulous.

"Look, Sawyer, I'm happy it's closed. I haven't been able to sleep for a month, not since I found out that Willa died. I'm going to have a hard time getting her insurance money, but I just want it solved," she says. Her face, full of calculated resignation, reminds me of the women who gave limp, pitying hugs at Willa's funeral while they clutched handfuls of prayer cards as if they intended to trade souvenirs later.

"But it's not solved at all! How can you care so little about your daughter's death?"

"I can see how you feel like that, and I'm sorry. But the police are comfortable closing the case, so I trust them."

"Trust?" I scoff. "It's complete blind trust. It's as if you're hiding your feelings so you don't upset the police, who are the ones who are supposed to be investigating it. If you, her mother, don't push them—if you cow down just so you please the police—they will never find the truth. They're not going to investigate possible foul play if you, of all people, don't even care."

"I'm sorry, Sawyer. But it's what's best."

"Sorries are cheap," I spit. *I'm sorry* is her favorite phrase; she accepts blame and guilt so easily. Her favorite activity is being pitied. It infuriates me to see the way she compromises herself if it means people will like her. I exhale loudly and fight the urge to retreat to my old room.

I think of the way my mother dealt with the grief of losing our father during those early years when it was just the three of us and she hadn't yet turned to a revolving door of needy men. She'd retire to her room with a wineglass and paint elementary watercolors of beaches. During those years, she spoke of God and how he was salvation, but painting was the only thing that seemed to bring her solace. Never church, though we still went every Sunday. The memory of our father—gone when I was just a baby, never to be spoken about—outshone all the living options, not that any of the men who came later were worth her time.

But I wanted to speak about Willa. I didn't want her name to become unmentionable like our father's.

"She's not going to go away, you know. Even in death, she still has a voice," I say. "Did you know she was working on a book?"

"A book?"

"Yeah. She was working with a publisher on a true crime book. She was investigating this cold case. Interviewing and writing about it."

"Well, whatever she was working on won't be published. It couldn't, right? She didn't finish it."

"Someone might pick it up." I shrug. Someone like me? "She's a dethroned news queen who was making her way back into investigative journalism when she died while looking into this case. If anything, it's probably *more* publishable."

"That would be a dishonor to Willa."

"Why do you care? You'd probably be the one to receive royalties from it. Besides, I think it's a bigger dishonor to allow the police to close her case than to publish her book posthumously."

"Sawyer, why are you talking like this? You know I don't like to fight. You've always been my good baby girl." Momma sits with rolled shoulders and her hands clasped in her lap. Her eyes are heated yet apologetic below her absent brows.

"I'm not—" I shake my head and stand up. The couch groans under the shift in weight. "I'm not trying to fight with you," I say as I walk into the kitchen. I fill a plastic cup with tap water and take greedy gulps.

"But if you won't do it, then I'll get the police to reopen the case," I call from the other side of the wall. It's still easier to talk to Claudia when she can't look directly at me; she's too erratic and overemotional to face head on.

I turn the corner and lean against the wallpapered wall. Outside, I can hear the familiar sound of graveside bagpipes wafting over from St. Cyril Cemetery across the street. I move to the window and push the paned glass down the warped frame to drown out the sound.

"I can't shake the feeling that there's foul play involved in Willa's death," I say. "Now we find out she was writing about a missing persons case. What if it's related? If she found something that led to her death somehow?"

Claudia scoffs. "First you accuse Oz, saying he killed her for the insurance money. Now you think it's an old kidnapper who vowed revenge on a reporter."

She sounds like Willa when her papery voice turns harsh. It's so rare it startles me. I straighten.

"Do you have any idea how crazy you sound?" she asks.

Part of me wants to concede, to agree she's right and apologize, to get her to say *good girl* in a way that might be patronizing to me as an adult but just gives me relief.

Instead, I set my jaw and steel myself for her disappointment. Convinced I'm onto something—my gut is rarely wrong—I know I have to see this through.

"It may be crazy, but at least I'll know I tried."

15

Willa

Three years before

THE SNOW SAWYER tracked into Claudia's house was nothing more than a smattering of puddles ringed with dirt when Willa arrived. The worn cotton rug in the entryway slid under Willa's pointy-toed stiletto boots as she stumbled gracelessly into the house.

She steadied herself with a manicured hand against the wall and leaned over to remove her boots until she thought better of it. It had always been a "no shoes" home, but Willa was feeling belligerent about everything today, and defying the long-standing house rule felt satisfying.

She tottered into the living room. The evening news blared from the television, casting the darkened room in a pale glow. Brooke Conroy offered a somber, knowing nod as a field correspondent concluded a story, then brightened as she shifted to the weatherman. She looked comfortable in Willa's seat at the news desk, though it had only been a few days since her panic attack.

"Jesus Christ, Mom. Couldn't you have on any other channel right now?" Willa spit.

Claudia looked up in alarm and fumbled with the remote. She was settled deep in her recliner, legs propped on the footrest, bare, unpainted toes sticking into the chilly air that rushed in when Willa arrived.

"I always watch your station," Claudia protested. "The more viewers, the better paycheck, right?"

"Not when I'm not on the air. And I'm never going to be again," Willa said, stomping to the television set. She punched the power button and wobbled in front of it.

"Have you been drinking?"

"It's my boots," Willa said, lifting a toe into the air and giggling.

Sawyer padded into the room in stockinged feet. She flashed Willa the wide smile of the sorority girl she'd never gotten the chance to be.

"You made it," she cheered.

"I don't know why I'm here," Willa said. She stepped carefully across the room to hide the way the vodka had seeped into her long limbs. Framed photos hung in mismatched frames on the wall. She stooped to examine them, as if seeing them for the first time.

"It's my birthday," Sawyer said dumbly. Willa could hear the hurt instantly tinge her voice.

"Is it?" Willa asked absently as she ran a finger along the pink-cheeked face of Sawyer as a chubby kindergarten graduate. Beside her photo, Willa's own face, with her angular chin and narrowed eyes, offered a cautious, academic smile.

She hadn't meant to work so hard all her life. At first, it came easy. The straight As tumbled in almost by accident. Book-smart Willa performed well on tests and breezed through papers, earning herself a reputation in elementary school. Maybe it was the relief in her teachers' faces that spurred her on; she was happy to prove she understood. Her teachers championed her. Willa had promise, they said. She didn't want them to be wrong, so she delivered the grades, sculpted essays that guaranteed her scholarship money and college apprenticeships with envied writers, and scooped her classmates' stories in journalism school and wrote them better. She became merciless, and she loved it. She overcame a stutter that threatened to defeat her. She hadn't meant to become the anchor on the evening news on the best television station in Chicago, but by then she'd grown addicted to proving herself.

What no one had told her was that she had to *keep* achieving.

And Willa was bone-tired.

"Of course it is," Claudia snapped, bringing her back to the moment. She smiled indulgently at Sawyer. "Baby, maybe you should bring in the cake."

"I don't understand why we're celebrating," Willa said, overenunciating her words, her voice too loud in the small living room.

"Willa."

"Momma, please," Sawyer said. She turned to Willa, her face melting with empathy. "I understand. It's rude of us to celebrate when you're having such a bad week. Do you want to talk about it?"

Willa closed her eyes slowly, willing the room to disappear. When she opened them again, Sawyer and Claudia tilted into place, both wearing matching frowns of concern.

"If one more person asks me if I want to talk about it, I'm going to kill myself."

Sawyer held up her hands in surrender. "Fine, fine. Forget about it for the night. Have some cake!" Her voice oozed with fake cheer.

Willa rolled her eyes. "This is some party," she said, gesturing around the room. Some might describe it as "humble," but Willa was embarrassed by the house now that she was an adult. Now that she knew better.

"You should be out with your friends. Or a boyfriend. Not us," Willa continued.

Suddenly she had the sensation she was hovering over the room, an objective observer. Claudia gnawed on a nail while fixing Willa with an anxious gaze. She was always offended, always hurt, by something. Lately, it was usually Willa who wore the blame for upsetting her thin-skinned mother. In contrast to Claudia's lumpy form still settled in the faded recliner, Willa was all angles. From her jutting elbows and structured shoulder pads to her sharp eyebrows and asymmetrical haircut, everything about her was pointed and harsh. And then there was playful, affectionate Sawyer. She had a halo of blond hair and emanated warmth. *She deserves more than this, than us*, Willa thought.

"I don't have a boyfriend," Sawyer said, her eyes downcast.

"Maybe you need to move to Chicago," Willa suggested. "There are thousands of guys you could date in the city. You're holding yourself back by staying in the suburbs."

"There's nothing wrong with Sawyer living here. The city is dangerous. I don't want her there," Claudia said.

Willa scoffed. "But it's fine if I live there, right?"

"That's not what I said."

"Momma, Willa, please," Sawyer said. She tucked a strand of hair behind her ear, and Willa caught sight of tears glistening in her eyes.

"I don't understand why you won't grow up and move to the city. You'll meet a guy there. If you lived there now, I guarantee you'd be at a bar with some pretty girlfriends drinking expensive drinks. You'd have a blast. Instead, you've shuttered yourself in with her." Willa jutted a thumb at Claudia. "Shut yourself out, bowed out of the whole thing. Gave up before you even tried. God, how old are you? Twenty-five? You're a baby."

Willa knew she'd taken it too far, but she didn't dare apologize. Sawyer needed to separate herself from Claudia, from this life, this house. Willa didn't even know why she was pushing so hard for Sawyer to live in Chicago anyway.

The glittering lights of Chicago used to have so much depth, promise, life. But lately, she'd felt like she was looking at a picture when she looked out the window of her River North condo. It had only been a few days since her panic attack, so she knew she couldn't blame the feeling on that. She'd felt numb long before the panic attack ruined her career.

A hiccup rose in her chest.

"You'd better call Leo to bring you home," Claudia said, half rising from the recliner.

"Innocent Leo has to fix broken Willa," she said as she lurched across the room and into the hallway. Her shoulder brushed against a bouquet of blue cornflowers wallpapered on the wall. "Did you know," she called as she entered the kitchen, "that Leo has only lied once in his whole life? That he admits, anyway. He cheated on his first eye exam because he really, really wanted to get glasses."

"That's pretty cute," Sawyer said quietly. She'd followed Willa into the kitchen. "He's a nice guy."

She stepped around Willa to retrieve an aluminum baking pan sitting on the stovetop. She opened a drawer near the sink and rummaged to find a knife to spread frosting on the birthday cake. Chocolate on chocolate, Sawyer's favorite.

Willa leaned against the refrigerator after a quick peek into the freezer to see if a bottle of vodka might serendipitously show up there, ready to save her from this night. No such luck. She watched Sawyer scoop thick gobs of frosting onto the cooled cake.

"You know, I read an interesting article the other day," Willa said thoughtfully. "It was about how fatherless daughters are more likely to have eating disorders. And when they're longing for that relationship, they could develop what's called 'father hunger.' Have you ever heard of it? It's this deep insecurity that women try to fill with bad coping habits, like trying to control their food intake. It's fascinating. It sounds just like you."

Sawyer's arm stiffened, and she stopped spreading the chocolate frosting. She stood above the cake with her head bowed and shoulders hunched and tense. Willa waited patiently for her to comment, because she genuinely thought the topic would resonate with Sawyer. Details weren't her strong suit at the moment, but she didn't miss the first huge teardrop plopping onto the frosted part of the cake, creating a dark little lake on the smooth surface. Another and then another fell. They reminded Willa of the time fat raindrops hissed on the hot pavement and the sweaty arms of all the salsa dancers at the Taste of Chicago a few years ago.

But Willa didn't move. She didn't step forward to comfort Sawyer, and she didn't offer an apology either. If anything, she was sorry she hadn't bluntly addressed Sawyer's eating disorder years ago.

She thought that if she kept moving forward, achieving, the others around her would be motivated to be better too. But Sawyer was floundering, in Willa's opinion, and Claudia was a lost cause.

It was then that Willa knew she couldn't be with them, like this, anymore. She had to be loyal to herself.

16

Sawyer

I FIND MELODY'S NAME in a thread about midwestern cold cases on an online forum for amateur sleuths. Looking at the responses, I see that Melody's case isn't as obscure as I thought; there's a subthread in which two or three users regularly toss around theories and dissect evidence, while others pop in to offer recriminations of the parents, the police, or both.

> LAXFOX: eh, this will never be solved. she was too
> young. can't trace her footsteps. literally
> PROMENTICA01: can we all agree she's dead tho
> LAXFOX: yea i think we're past that promentica01
> SHOOTMI: The area is rural. There are old farms,
> undeveloped land, and water by way of lakes,
> creeks, ponds, and wells. Her body could be
> almost anywhere in Trowbridge County.

I take a sip of green tea as I scan the thread. I consider creating a username and commenting. *I'm not an investigator, but I'm determined to tell her story*, I'll write, and it'll ignite the thread once again. But I read their posts and soak in everything I should have known before visiting the Wynnes.

> LAXFOX: problem is there's no smoking gun . . .
>   grass too dry in august . . . no footprints or
>   tire marks or n e thing
> SHOOTMI: Those are the obvious clues. In a case
>   like this, the smallest thing might be impor-
>   tant. We need to find linkages.
> PROMENTICA01: nah the cops do
> LAXFOX: n e one else think it's weird that the
>   parents stayed together ???
> PROMENTICA01: oooh good point laxfox
> LAXFOX: every1 knows that most marriages end in
>   divorce when a kid dies. :/

I shouldn't be surprised by the comments. Most people are armchair detectives when given the opportunity; there's a universal interest in catching the bad guy, and no one wants to think that criminals can outsmart not only law enforcement but them too, as they sit in a darkened room in front of a glowing laptop.

I click on ShootMI's profile. There's no identifying information. Maybe it's a hunter in Michigan. It could be someone who knows the case well, someone who lives near Lake Chicora. For a brief moment, I wonder if it's Willa. She wouldn't compromise her grammar on a discussion board either, and maybe the username alludes to suicide.

I sigh and click back to the thread. I'm on page three of thirty-nine. I take another sip of tea and settle in.

*   *   *

When Leo calls, I'm three hours into a Google rabbit hole of searching for more information about the case. The

forum thread holds more information than most news articles from the time, and certainly more information than
I've been able to find in Willa's apartment. I drove here from
Claudia's house and scoured what's left of her belongings for
her notes about the case. I searched for stacks of handwritten notes or tapes of on-the-record interviews with illicit
off-the-record details. I came up with nothing but a folder
of digitized phone books with impossibly tiny font. I turned
to a search engine to tell me what everyone else already
knew.

"I may have done more harm than good," says Leo when
I pick up.

"Tell me."

"Well, I called the local police station. Detective Corbin
Campbell has been on the case since day one, and unsurprisingly, he is protective of it and the Wynnes. He's never
worked a missing persons case before or after this one. And
now he's on high alert. First Willa goes poking around, then
you, now me." He pauses. "Did you tell the Wynnes your
name was Sarah?"

I swivel in Willa's desk chair and kick my feet onto her
bare bed. I drop them back to the floor when a wave of guilt
prickles my stomach. "Yeah. I heard Jack, the father, call the
police when I left their house. Willa went by the name
Christine Fleury, her pseudonym from *TruthShout*."

Leo harrumphs.

"What?"

"Christine, like Christine Chubbuck. That newscaster
who killed herself on air in the seventies. It's grim, but it's
probably her own version of gallows humor."

"Oh God," I moan. I push away from the desk and
stretch my legs as I walk down the low-ceilinged hallway
into the living room. "So what did the detective say?"

"Very little. He only confirmed what's easily accessible
to the public. That there were two persons of interest in the

case from the beginning, and that police took measures to investigate both men but never found anything conclusive."

"Merrill Vaughn and Abel Bowen," I say as I take a seat on the couch.

"Right. And Vaughn is now deceased. It sounds like Detective Campbell picked him up for questioning somewhat regularly. He had injected himself into the case early on."

I think of Grace Wynne sitting in her chair overlooking the lake, Melody's bluebird quilt in her lap.

"He posed as a psychic to get information from the mother."

"That's sick," Leo says. "So he was never ruled out, but now he's dead. I'm more worried about the other person of interest, Abel Bowen."

"The Wynnes told me he's a criminal," I confirm. "Did the detective give you any details?"

"Bowen is a convicted felon, Sawyer. He served time for a second-degree murder charge and a felony count of malicious destruction of property."

"Murder? He's a convicted murderer living down the road from where the baby went missing?" I feel the goose bumps rise on my arms. How could the Wynnes have continued to live in that cottage less than a mile from Bowen all these years?

"He was convicted at age seventeen but tried as an adult," Leo reports. "It's really freaky to think about, but he threw a rock off an overpass that killed a passing driver. Just, poof! A rock falls from the sky and you're dead. It takes a messed-up person to do something like that."

The chills continue to roll up my arms.

"Look, Sawyer," he continues, "I said this before, but I really think you're in over your head. I don't want you looking into this case. It's not safe to drive up there alone and antagonize criminals. Please. I know more about crime than most care to ever know, and I know this is a bad idea."

"I won't do anything stupid," I say, shrugging him off.

"I'm serious."

"So am I."

"Your stubbornness reminds me of Willa," he says. "If you're not going to let this go, I want you to meet with one of my colleagues, another professor at the university. Her name is Dr. Nomi Ito. She's a forensic psychologist. I'll set up a meeting for you, but don't take that as me condoning what you're doing."

My eyes settle on the wall of professionally mounted awards standing at attention with laser-precision spacing between them. "I'm not giving up on this," I say, my voice too loud in the empty apartment. My mind whispers, *Even though Willa did*, and shame makes me tear my gaze away from her accolades, evidence of the accomplished life that wasn't enough for her.

His exhale rattles in the earpiece. "What happened to the goofy, bubbly little sister?"

My heart warms. I can't believe I let myself smile flirtatiously at him the other day. He is, and will always be, my big sister's boyfriend. A protector.

We chat a bit more before saying good-bye. When the beeps signal the end of our call, the apartment seems to shrink and darken. There's no doubt it's a depressing space.

So many people don't want me to continue this project on Willa's behalf. Leo fears for me; my mother thinks I'm betraying her. Even Willa left no notes and no easy way to pick up her trail. She wrote dozens, maybe hundreds, of articles as a journalist, but nothing long-form. I wonder again why she chose this case to begin her career as an author when she was preparing to end it so soon. What is it about this case?

A word I've never associated with Willa flits through my mind: *personal.*

Is this story personal to her in some way? Is it more than a cold case she found through a search engine?

* * *

It takes less than ten minutes to walk down Kinzie Street to the Green Line station, but alone, at night, it feels much longer. My mother's cautionary tales dance through my head as I pass shadowy alleys. She didn't show her love by offering affectionate touches or raking her hand through my hair; she wove tapestries of fear and danger to prove she was the only person I could trust. Now her words thunder in my mind, flutter in my chest.

The clanging metal stairs announce my arrival on the platform. The Pink Line trains board here too. Twin antennas atop the Willis Tower twinkle as I wait in line to purchase a single ride ticket.

"All yours." Tangy breath behind wine-stained teeth hits me as a woman totters away from the ticket-vending machine, bumping my shoulder. Instinctively, I clamp my purse to my body. My mother warned about this.

Ticket in hand, I feel my nervousness exposed under the buzzing fluorescent lights. Cleansing my face of the worry from the walk from Willa's apartment, I adopt a nonchalant expression as I wait for the El to bring me back to Oak Park.

I'd never admit it to anyone, but a tiny, secret part of me finds satisfaction in spending time in Willa's apartment alone. In the years since we shared a bedroom, Willa's homes have always been polished and tidy. But this apartment is more grit than glamour. I get to see it for what it truly is, and it's worse than my apartment. I've never been superior to Willa at anything—she was smarter, thinner, richer, and she even had more long-term boyfriends than me in spite of the easy way she tossed out scalding remarks. I've felt inadequate as long as I can remember. Forever the desperate little sister hovering in Willa's shadow. Maybe that's why I felt a tiny thrill when I spotted a centipede on Willa's immaculate couch earlier in the night. I know my apartment wouldn't be envied by most—trains rumble in the distance and the paper-thin walls invite you into the neighbors' arguments—but it doesn't have bugs.

A breeze lifts my hair off my neck as I scan the other people waiting on the platform. A boy, college age, tosses a rakish smile in my direction. My gut fills with a desperate, girlish longing. I think of the extra place mat and empty hangers waiting to hold a man's jacket in my apartment. I break eye contact.

The woman from earlier stands near the bumpy tiling bordering the track. The force of an expected train could sweep her onto the track, she's so close to the edge. Seeing her eyes trained on her phone screen, I watch for an oncoming train.

Then a thought hits me. It's so morbid, a shudder shakes my limbs. I wonder if Willa considered this platform, these rattling tracks, when she thought about how she'd end her life.

I close my eyes and push my hand against the chain-link fence behind me to steady myself. I loop my fingers between the grimy rungs as I look up again. I can't watch the woman with the wine-stained teeth anymore.

Farther down the platform, near a white metal garbage can, stands a hulking form. Snub nose, brutish chin, a shock of dark hair.

Oz.

What is he doing here? He has a truck—a rust bucket named Becca, a detail that makes me pity my mother for the jealousy she must feel toward the nickname.

The college boy tosses his hair with a flick of his neck as I approach, but I pass him, stopping in front of Oz. I feel my heart bang against my chest. Under the platform lights, his skin is ashen, the lines on his face pronounced. He smells of cigarette smoke and, faintly, of a dinner heavy in garlic and onions.

"Are you following me?"

"No," he barks.

"What about Becca?" I feel the eyes of the others on the platform watching me now. Wondering if I'm confronting this man about another woman.

Oz shrugs.

"I'm going to tell my mother that you're here. That you followed me from Willa's apartment."

A telltale rumble of the wooden planks warns of an approaching train. I step closer to Oz as he spits over his shoulder.

"She's the one who asked me to watch you," he says, his words nearly swallowed by the sound of the train shuddering to a stop.

The refrains of an announcement—"Transfer to Metra trains at Clinton"—tumble out of the train car as the doors open and passengers surge onto the platform. I step onto the train in their wake.

"Leave me alone," I say, my voice quivery but loud over the whoosh of closing doors.

I feel my cheeks blaze red as I stumble toward a seat. Oz remains on the platform, his shuttered face trained dully ahead with indifference and stoicism.

As the train hurtles away from the city, I feel the pressure in my chest give way to a churning in my stomach. It doesn't make sense.

Why would my mother ask Oz to follow me if she believes Willa killed herself? Does she know more than she's letting on?

17

Willa

Three months before

OVER TWENTY-ONE HOURS of recorded conversations and nearly 150 pages of notes.

She didn't know where to start.

The problem was that the story didn't begin when Melody went missing, even though that was what the book was about. Her disappearance was a symptom of a sickness that had begun decades before.

Willa leafed through the notes on her desk, and her eyes flicked across the words. Abel's words. There was no doubt he'd been reluctant to let her in when she'd knocked on his door, not because he didn't want his story told, but because he didn't want to implicate the girl.

And that was really where this story started, where all stories start: with two people meeting.

Like so many stories of damaged kids hungry for respect and love, this one didn't have a happy beginning or end.

Willa had a good eye for lies after all the years of writing about controversy. Truth was uncommon among those involved in something worth investigating. But Abel's story rang true.

He was sixteen years old when he met her. There was no question he was insecure, even if he didn't say it in so many words. He was overweight at the time. His mother, Dorrie, a religious fanatic, refused to let her sons leave the dinner table until every bit of food was gone, but she'd never adjusted the portions to cook less, even after the death of Abel's father and, later, his only brother.

Years of living with Dorrie's obsessions gave Abel his own hang-ups. His sense of reality was so distorted and his feelings of worthlessness so strong that by the time the girl showed any interest in him, he couldn't see that it wasn't love. He still couldn't.

The part he couldn't tell Willa, the part he didn't know, was that the girl was damaged too. Abused by her uncle as long as she could remember, she was numb. Needy. Troubled. She was worse for him than he would have been on his own.

But as he talked, even Willa could see the anger and impulsivity and frantic efforts to avoid abandonment in his words. He might have lost the weight and the girl, but he hadn't changed that much from that disconnected teenager in 1973.

So many of the notes were about how much he loved her and how he'd do anything for her. But Willa wasn't writing a love story. She set down her notebook and stared at the frame on her desk. She was just a little girl in the picture, young enough not to know how everything in the world goes to shit. She was maybe four or five in the photo. The year, she calculated, would have been before Melody Wynne was even born. Yet here she was, writing a story about a missing baby, though it wasn't really about her at all.

Willa tapped her ragged nails on the desk as she thought. She'd hurt more people if she told the true story after all these years. But . . . that was what she had vowed to do by telling Melody's story, and wasn't it better for everyone to know the truth, even those who thought their story was closed?

She'd have to include it in the book, because it was the cancer that had started the whole mess.

Once the reader understood Abel's childhood, they'd understand what led to that day, she reasoned. His desperation following Dorrie's death, his destructive behavior, that suicidal undercurrent. He wasn't self-aware enough to voice these things himself, but Willa could piece together the patterns in his words enough to visualize the teenager that stepped onto the overpass that day.

Two words stuck out at Willa as she scanned her notes: *my disciple.*

It was how Abel referred to the girl when he got to the part about what happened on the overpass. In his warped mind, Dorrie's flawed teachings of the Bible had led him to believe the girl was doing his bidding that day. When she picked up the rock, tested its weight, and readied herself to heave it off the railing at the next passing car, Abel believed she did it for him. And if she'd do that for him, as his disciple, he'd die for her. In his mind, he was Jesus. Laying down his life for the sins of others.

God, she'd be happy when this story was over.

She smiled ironically to herself. *That's a joke*, she thought. *I'll be dead by the time this story comes out.*

18

Sawyer

THE VIRGIN MARY smiles benevolently on me from the university's chapel as I wait for Dr. Nomi Ito's class to end. A sign tells me that afternoon Mass doesn't begin for another hour, but candles are already lit, and their flames gleam against the polished wood floor.

Though Willa's funeral wasn't overly religious, peering into the chapel reminds me of the day we put her in the ground. I feel exhausted thinking of the crumbly smiles of the mourners and their furtive glances at the police escort in the cemetery.

I tear my gaze away as a group of students in nurse's scrubs breeze past me on their way to their next class. The hallway is suddenly full, raucous. It's jarring after observing the reverent quiet of the chapel. Swarms of students buzz down the corridor. The soda machine rumbles to life, and the unyielding wooden benches become backpack holders and shoe-tying stools. I'm staring down the hall at a group of girls full of loud laughs and easy smiles, thinking I used to be like that, when I sense someone at my side and startle.

Dr. Ito barely clears my shoulder. "Sawyer, I presume."

"Yes," I say, thrusting my hand in her direction. "Do you want to go to your office to chat, or maybe a coffee shop?"

She looks at my eager hand and raises her eyebrows. She's carrying two cups of coffee and a thick white binder that seems impossibly large for her small frame. The scent of old cigarette smoke clings to her.

"Take one," she instructs, holding out a cup. "It's not very good, but it's free in the faculty lounge." She hefts the binder onto her hip and nods toward the chapel. "Till Mass begins, this is the most private place we'll find. And even then . . ."

Dr. Ito throws her shoulder into the wooden door and pushes her way through. Reluctantly, I follow. I don't count myself as religious, but it feels wrong to talk about death and murder in a chapel.

Bowlegged but quick-paced, she weaves between the pews. Her orthopedic shoes squeak as she crosses the length of the chapel, and the sound of her binder hitting the pew as she settles in the back is a thunderclap in the quiet space. She brushes her thin chestnut hair over her shoulder and turns to face me.

"I'm not sure how much Leo told you about me, but it's probably all wrong," she says bluntly. "Not that Leo told you incorrectly, or that you misunderstood. It's just that no one really understands what a forensic psychologist does." She takes a sip of coffee and wrinkles her nose. Her face is flat, round, and her skin is pale and light.

"I'm not sure how you can help me," I admit. "I don't really know what I'm doing."

Dr. Ito smiles and reveals a bunny tooth. "Do any of us really know?"

I return her smile but shift uncomfortably in the pew. "Well, I'm not sure how much Leo told *you* about *me*, but it's probably right. He probably told you I'm in over my head. That I should forget this case and forget following my sister's final footsteps." I sigh. "My sister was Willa Stannard, the newscaster? She and Leo dated."

"I met with her. Bright woman."

"You did?"

"Yes, about the case you're here to discuss today. She interviewed me. I was her 'expert,'" she says, tossing up air quotes and an ironic smile. She shakes her head, and stale cigarette smoke invades the air. "So I know a thing or two about the case. Probably even more than you. No offense."

"None taken. Like I said, I am trying to pick up the pieces. I'm not a writer or an investigator. I teach a cycling class, for heaven's sake." I glance up at the Virgin Mary near the altar again. "But Leo said I should talk to you, so I here I am. I need to figure out what Willa knew about this case. It was the last thing she worked on—the last thing she showed interest in or cared about—before she died. I don't know why, but I know it's important that she was writing about this crime, this family, this town. It has something to do with her death. If I can figure out what it was, then maybe her death will mean something."

"Trying to find meaning in suicide is as useless as finding meaning in life," she says as she takes a sip of lukewarm coffee. "Perhaps you can solve this crime, but it may not resolve the chaos. That's what she was trying to do, isn't it? Bring order to confusion?"

That's all Willa ever tried to do: tie a perfect bow around an elusive answer and file it away. It's why I can't comprehend why she'd leave me with a mess of unresolved questions.

"She was a relentless journalist, in the best way," I say. "She found answers to questions others didn't even know to ask."

"I admire that. This world needs people who will ask the hard questions. In my job, I figure out how to ask those hard questions, and how to evaluate the answers." I nod, and Dr. Ito continues. "So where I sit is at the intersection of criminal justice, psychology, and law. I teach here, yes, but my job is really a consultant. A media consultant, a jury consultant, a police consultant. I help law enforcement with interrogation strategies. I perform mental health evaluations." She ticks the roles on her nicotine-stained fingers. "Everyone wants to know the reasons someone kills. I'm never out of work."

Dr. Ito sets her coffee down on the wide white binder beside her. It reminds me of the three-hole-punched packet of glossy pages I sifted through at the funeral home, one page after another depicting a sturdy, shining casket, each one promising comfort and security to the person who now needed it least. There were questions I'd never thought I'd ask: Bronze or birch? Copper or cherry?

I take a sip of my coffee to combat the chill that prickles my arm at the thought of Willa in a casket. The coffee is sour and bready. It tastes punishing, so I drink more as I turn away from the watchful eyes of the saints.

"In this case, though, we know that Melody Wynne was abducted, but we don't know that she's not alive somewhere," I say, keeping my voice low, barely above a whisper. "Are the reasons for kidnapping the same as murder?"

"No. But kidnappings by strangers are rare, just the same as with a murder case. I believe the victim knew the offender."

I cast a wry smile in her direction. "She was eighteen months old, Doctor."

She flaps a hand in the air to wave away the technicality. "I use the term loosely. It could be anyone on the periphery of the family. Think mailman, garbageman, hairdresser, grocery store clerk—the list goes on. Once you have to look outside the family, the crime is much more complex. Knowing what I do about this family's history, I'd be surprised if drugs or gangs or organized crime is involved. So what does that leave?"

"If you ask the internet, a self-proclaimed psychic and a former felon are the top suspects in her disappearance," I say, thinking of the online discussion boards that tossed out accusations amid misinformation and rampant rumors.

"Ah," Dr. Ito chirps. "Let's unpack that. As with anything, a crime boils down to the concept of gain. What can the killer, or kidnapper, gain from committing this crime? It could be a straightforward gain—monetary. Or it could be a means to quench feelings of jealousy, fulfill a sexual urge, alleviate a stressful situation, or quiet a psychosis. Between the psychic and the felon, do any of those motives strike a chord with you?"

"I can't say. I haven't met either man personally. But something tells me you posed this question to Willa too."

"I did."

"What did she say?"

"She asked for statistics about the rarity of the role of psychosis in crime. She allowed that delusional compulsions may have been a factor if the felon abducted the toddler."

"What does that mean? What are delusional compulsions?"

"The best way I can describe it is by using this phrase: *The devil made me do it.* It's when someone tells you to kill and you believe it. It's a diagnosis reserved for those who suffer from psychotic episodes, who can't distinguish right from wrong, reality from imagination."

"And she thought that described Abel, that his psychosis could be the reason he kidnapped and possibly killed Melody?"

"She cited auditory hallucinations as proof of the theory."

I lean back and suppress a whistle. Willa knew so much more than I can hope to uncover. How could she have known about Abel's hallucinations without direct access to him?

"What about Merrill, the psychic? Did she discount him as a suspect?"

"She wanted to know more about why someone would inject themselves into an investigation, as I believe he did in the weeks following the abduction. It's simple, really. Sometimes a perpetrator likes to control the investigation by staying close to it."

I nod and bite my lip. I take another sip of the bitter coffee and wince as I swallow. I paint an image of Merrill Vaughn in my mind, cobbling together what I can remember from his photograph in online articles—thin blond hair, a mocking smile, amused eyes behind oversized glasses—and sketch in the rest, adding a bulbous nose, jowly chin, and hands too small for his body. If he hadn't selfishly muddied the investigation with psychic claims so early on, would the police have found Melody? And if he knew something and didn't tell anyone, wouldn't the guilt have killed him one day?

"Willa must have found someone close to the investigation to speak to, to get as much information as she had."

"She'd been working on it for at least, oh, a year or two, I'd say," Dr. Ito says. "She interviewed dozens of people. She spoke to the felon at length. In fact . . ." Her eyes dart around the chapel. "In fact, I wondered if I missed something when we talked. I wondered if her book ignited her death. If the real perpetrator wasn't getting credit, so he got involved. If he was so narcissistic that he had to stop publication if he wasn't recognized for his crimes. If he was so proud, you know?" Dr. Ito talks with her hands as if she's trying to hold his pride, to squeeze it into a tiny ball. "It sounds counterintuitive, I know. For a criminal to want to get credit for a crime." She drops her flexed fingers into her lap. "You think I'm a conspiracy theorist now."

"You think someone could have killed her to stop her from telling the story," I say, talking fast and leaning in. "That it wasn't suicide after all. That she wasn't depressed."

Dr. Ito leans away from me. "I don't know what I think," she says, backpedaling. "It's a crazy theory, and it's usually the simplest explanation that's the truth. That someone in the family or close to them kidnapped the baby. And, if the police believe it to be true, that Willa committed suicide." Her voice has changed; it's no longer strident with possibilities but limp with sympathy.

She downs the rest of her coffee and wipes her hands on her brown pants vigorously, as if to warm them. Within a few minutes, she excuses herself, and the only sound is that of her thick-soled Velcro orthopedics squeaking out of the chapel.

I sit on the pew while my back starts to ache, after the priest intones the readings and the rites and the candles snuff themselves out. I turn over Dr. Ito's words until I know what to do. I let her voice rattle in my brain—"it's usually the simplest explanation"—until I can't quiet my combating mind shouting, *But what if it's the most complex?*

* * *

"I wanted to talk to you about the Melody Wynne case—"

"We're sorry. You have reached a number that is no longer in service."

"Writing a book—"

"Your call has been forwarded to an automated voice messaging system."

"A few questions about Melody Wynne, if you don't mind—"

"The number you have dialed is not a working number."

* * *

Night falls, and I realize I've never had more disconnected calls in my life. I roll backward on the balance ball I'm using as a desk chair and stretch my arms overhead. The small town is impenetrable. These same people have probably lived through nearly thirty years of being pumped for a quote for some sensational, explosive story, maybe even most recently by my own sister. But I'm different from those reporters, because I don't care so much about what happened to Melody as about what happened to Willa as she investigated Melody's case.

I need to talk to people. People who were there, people who remember.

19

Sawyer

I HAVE TO ADMIT, it feels good to press my foot down on the accelerator, hard, as the city falls away and the road-work gives way to the open highway.

At first I worried the time alone would give me time to think, time to regret. But it feels freeing to be away from the girls at the studio. They sport seasonally appropriate spray tans, look good in yellow and oversize florals, and drive larger-than-life Wi-Fi–equipped SUVs. Willa called them "big-footprint women." I aspired to be them. But the fizzy enthusiasm I love about them seems grating when I can only think about how to search out answers in Willa's death.

I've thought about reaching out to Emily, my coworker from my short-lived time working in sales. A few days ago, a story Emily told me about her dead brother popped into my head. Over drinks, she talked mostly about how she felt after he died. One week, I asked her to tell me something about him when he was alive. She took a long, thoughtful sip of beer and told me about the soap. How he used to carve funny messages into a bar of soap for her to find when she went to shower later. After I knew about the soap, I felt Emily's loss too.

Even though she's weathered the grief of a sibling's death, I know I can't get together with her. We wouldn't help each other heal; we'd wallow. And it'd be too easy to succumb to self-pity and the carbs Emily loves to order on the side.

I've only made the drive once, but I feel a sense of familiarity as I pass the weathered campground signs and the field of sunflowers, the last of the season, all standing at attention in the same direction. This time I follow the road when it bends instead of bumping off onto the gravel road leading down to the lake. I pass a wide-open country cemetery and a one-room town hall. A dull-red tractor sits in a farm field across from town hall, and soon the pavement gives way to the same pockmarked gravel that leads to the lakeside cottages. GPS doesn't do me much good out here, but this road should take me to the north side of Lake Chicora.

Beeches and maples, ashes and elms overtake the road and offer a reprieve from the midday sun. The road curves uphill, and the overwhelming scent of sap and freshly cut logs pushes through the car's vents. My tires crunch over crushed stone, and I pass a logging truck. A few delimbed trees stand like amputees in the clearing, and harvested timber is stacked near the roadside.

I pass more trailers than houses. Ahead, there's a sign: *Lake Chicora Outpost Store. Beer and Liquor. Bait and Tackle.*

Tacked to the white vinyl siding are rusted metal signs for beer, cigarettes, and hunting gear. I pull the car to a stop and kick up a cloud of dust. A group of bare-chested boys and shoeless girls sitting in front of a sign for Wild Turkey whiskey don't flinch as the dust settles on them. I squint into the sun as I step out of the car and run my hand discreetly along the door to lock it without a conspicuous click.

I toss my hair over my shoulder and smile as I approach the teenagers.

"Hi there, do you have a moment for a few questions?" I ask. "I'm a reporter." I paste a sunny smile on my face. I feel the back of my neck turn red as I'm met with unflinching faces.

"A reporter? Ain't nothing worth talking about happen here." One of the girls says this. She looks like she has a habit of sucking on strands of her hair; the ones within reach of her mouth are ropy and crusted.

"It happened a long time ago, actually." As I say it, I realize these kids are too young to know much about the case. I'm off to a messy start.

"What did?" asks a boy with a buzz cut, scabs around his mouth, and the glazed eyes of a meth head.

"A kidnapping," I say, edging toward the screen door of the shop. It feels wrong to say Melody's name to these smirking teenagers.

"Oh, the baby. 'Cross the lake," the girl says with a flick of her neck.

"Yeah," I say, pausing. "Could you tell me what you know?"

"What's in it for us?" One of the boys cuts me with a leering smile.

"Uh," I stutter, eyes darting around. Would Willa have offered a six-pack or some cigarettes to get a local source to talk?

A gold pickup truck pulls in. A man with a graying beard lumbers out and hefts a propane tank from the truck bed. He eyes the teenagers and me as he drops the empty tank into the dirt with a thud.

"No trouble, ya hear?" he says. I'm not sure if it's directed at the kids or me, but one of the girls rolls her eyes as she digs her naked toes into the dirt. He enters the outpost store with a rattle of the screen door, and I turn back to them.

"You must be a writer, 'cause you ain't got a TV camera with you. Someone find the baby?" The girl tugs on her cutoff shorts, which reveal sunburnt thighs scattered with purple veins that resemble constellations.

"I'm writing a book. Can I ask what you think happened to the baby?"

"She's dead." It's the boy with the scabby mouth and unfocused eyes.

"Why do you say that?"

"Been missing before we was born. Ain't no way she's alive."

"Yeah." The girl nods. "They just gotta find her."

"And where do you think she is?" I say, darting my eyes to the door of the store again. The man in the gold truck is probably a better source than these kids.

"Open your eyes." One of the girls gestures broadly and smacks the shoulder of the boy with a crooked nose and a permanent sneer. An angry zit on his bare shoulder erupts and sends a trickle of blood down his chest, but he doesn't flinch. "This place is nothing but woods. She's buried somewhere in this shit town."

"And who do you think took her?"

They exchange glances, and for the first time I wonder if they can offer any useful information. The girls whisper to each other while eyeing me. One of the boys tries to skip a rock over the gravel, and it hits my ankle. A bell attached to the door rattles, and the bearded man walks back to his car, but not before shaking his head at me when I catch his eye. Intrusive questions while he drops off propane tanks and picks up night crawlers are probably nothing new; he may even be one of the people I called who hung up on me so abruptly.

"Bad Bowen, bad Bowen, don't get him goin'." The girl punctuates her chant with a self-conscious giggle. She digs her toes deeper into the dirt and avoids looking at the boys.

I scan their faces to see if they corroborate. "Abel," I say.

"He's fucked up," says the boy with the blood leaking from his popped pimple.

I feel my hackles rise, and I inch forward. "Can you tell me more about Abel Bowen?"

"You here alone?" Scabs asks, his eyes waking up to take on a hungry gleam.

"Yeah, where're you from?" one of the girls asks.

With a step back and a nervous swallow, I say, "Chicago."

She whistles and sticks a strand of wheat-colored hair in her mouth. "Big-city girl."

"Writer from Chicago's got to have a budget for information, right?" says Scabs. "I'll tell you what I know. Won't cost you anything. Any money, anyway."

He leers at me again, and I realize that even though I'm twice his age, he's trying to belittle me. He licks his crusty lips, and I take a stumbling step backward. I tug on the car door handle and stumble again when it's locked. I fumble with the keys and drop them in the dirt. My neck burns again as they cackle at my back.

I punch the gas pedal, and the car swings in a noisy arc as it crunches on the gravel and scrabbles for traction. With a glance in the rearview mirror, I see one of the girls staring after me, but she's the only one. The other girl turns her attention to pick at the zits on the boy's overexposed shoulders, while the skinny boy with the scabby mouth pulls a lighter out of his pocket, flicking the flame on and off.

With the back of my jittery hand, I swipe at my forehead to mop up sweat. Behind me, a horn sounds, and with a swerving screech, a dark-colored Jeep passes me, cutting too close in front of the car and sending a cloud of dust into the windshield. Instinctually I cough at the dust despite the closed windows. I hit the brakes and take a wild turn at a sign for a boat ramp. Tires crunch over last fall's leaves and into a grassy clearing. There's a break in the tree line, and beyond I see the choppy gray water of the lake roiling and receding from the shore.

A middle-aged man kneels by the hitch of his trailer and glances up as I get out of the car. Hands on knees, I take a few gasping breaths. How did Willa do this?

"Are you lost?" the man calls in a loud, ringing voice.

Straightening my back, I force a weak smile. "No. I'm just having a hard day," I offer.

A muddy mutt of a dog comes tearing around the trailer, and the man catches it with a few quick leaping steps. He grips its nylon collar and smiles ruefully. "Well, I don't want to make it worse by getting you smelling like the lake. Are you on your way to work?"

I run my palms along my suit pants to smooth them down. "I'm a reporter," I say, the lie getting easier each time. "I'm working on a story about a kidnapping that happened here in 1992."

The man's face falls. He strokes the matted fur on the dog's neck and casts his gaze through the clearing as if he can see the Wynnes' tiny cottage across the lake.

"This town will never get over Melody Wynne," he says into the breeze. I can't tell if his voice is wistful or accusatory.

"Did you live here when she went missing?"

He shakes his head, and the dog, playing a game, shakes his in response. "I don't live here now. I'm from Macatawa, up north. But we get the same TV stations there, hear the same stories. They trot out Melody's story at least once or twice a year, even now."

I lift my hair off my sticky neck and flap my hand as a fan. "Well, you must have an opinion, then, as to what happened to her. Any thoughts you can share? Off record," I add, my only bargaining chip.

The man shrugs and stands. Commanding the dog to stay, be good, stay, he picks up a wrench from the crabgrass clearing and turns his attention back to tightening the trailer hitch.

"My old fishing buddy had some thoughts, that's for sure. You've got a lot of hours to kill in an ice shelter waiting for a northern pike to bite. What I know, I know from him." The wrench clicks rhythmically. "Well, what I *think*, I should say. I don't *know* nothing, and neither does he."

"And what does he think?"

"Eh," he grunts as he secures the hitch and checks it with a firm tug. "He grew up in Pullman, next town over. He was a couple years behind Edwin Vaughn in school. Still lives up in Pullman at the family house even now."

Edwin Vaughn. The man Willa emailed for an interview. Phony psychic Merrill Vaughn's son.

"Did he know him well?" I ask, swatting a mosquito from my hot face.

"Nah, I wouldn't say that. There's a levee not far from town where we'd drink beer and listen to the Steve Miller Band. Edwin was there from time to time. Invited my buddy over to his house a few times, I suppose. It seems funny to call it a house when you can call that a house," he says, jerking a thumb across the street at a tract house lacking landscaping, curtains, and personality. I recall that Grace said Merrill lived in a giant mansion outside of town.

"No one knows about this, even though their family's history was dragged through the press years back. Edwin's dad set up this photography studio in the house when Edwin was still in school, around the time my buddy went over there. Like I said, that house is huge. Not everyone can add a studio willy-nilly. But his dad did, set up the whole thing real professional-like, said he was going to open a business. Never did, far as I know, but my buddy always thought it was creepy. His dad was like that, always doing things on a lark, but for some reason the photography studio stood out. With everything that happened, your mind can't help but go to the dark side of that. Kids' photos, you know?" He shakes his head, as if he's trying to keep from exploring the sinister thoughts of a man with a private photography studio and an unsettling interest in kids.

"How far from here is the house?"

"Couple miles down CR-82, I reckon. You can't miss it." He adjusts the bill of his red baseball cap and studies me against the sun. "Be careful, all right?"

"Of course," I say, feeling guilty. I used to consider myself unfailingly honest. I wonder if a life of assumed identities and false claims helped Willa believe she could lie about the important things too.

*　*　*

It's a fifteen-minute drive from the gravel road to the rural estate. The farmhouse is enormous, in proportion with what has to be nearly twenty acres of rolling land. Surprisingly, the drive isn't private or gated, so I creep down the road toward the old house. Online searching told me it's a historic landmark now: built in the 1890s and the first bed-and-breakfast in the county, just as Grace hinted.

The drive winds through gentle alfalfa fields and a patch of mature Golden Delicious apple trees. It's a sharp contrast to the constricted, damp feeling at the lake. I wonder why anyone would jeopardize all this by inserting himself into a missing persons investigation.

I park the car and follow wooden planks that carve a path to the house. A ceiling fan twirls lazily on the porch, and the entryway windows are stained glass, the colors rich and bright in the setting sun. The house is so beautiful that I'm not thinking of danger when I knock on the door.

The door lurches open, shouting its solid weight, the kind that existed before building materials cheapened. A man's face peers out. He's about twenty years older than me, but he's carrying enough weight for two men, and his face and neck sag.

"Edwin?" I say, flashing a smile. I took Leo's advice and ditched my yoga pants and sneakers for the trip, but judging from the instantly suspicious look in Edwin Vaughn's eyes, I wonder if it was a mistake. If I'd dressed more casually, I might have had an extra minute or two before he guessed at my purpose.

"I'm not interested," he says, easing the door shut.

"Wait, wait! We exchanged emails," I say. "You know me."

"We did? Who are you?"

"I'm trying to tell an unbiased story about your father's involvement in the Melody Wynne case," I say, avoiding giving a name. "I'm not trying to implicate him. I'm just trying to get the full story. Can we talk?"

"My father was nothing more than a red herring," he spits. "He got dragged into that case, and it distracted investigators. His visits to the family were an isolated piece of inconclusive evidence."

"That's fair," I say, angling myself in the narrowing opening as he moves to shut the door fully. "Your father's lack of involvement: that's what we can talk about. I'm not trying to pin anything on him. I just want to talk."

"Just talk?" Edwin says sarcastically. "Christine, is it? You're writing a book. You're trying to profit off a family's grief. You should be ashamed."

The door thunders closed.

20

Willa

Six months before

"THE SCREEN DOOR rattled when it closed. I remember saying that to Merrill Vaughn."

"What was going through your mind when you answered the door for him that first time?" Willa asked, pen poised above her leather notebook.

"Hope. At that time, every person at the door or on the telephone represented hope to find Melody. Every time it wasn't the police, that is. I thought they would only contact me with bad news, but everyone else represented possibility."

"How did he introduce himself?"

"He claimed he had experience working with police. That his visions, as he called them, had helped find people before. He said he wanted to help . . ." Grace's voice broke.

"So you invited him in," Willa prodded. "What was your first impression?"

"Looks-wise, he wasn't anything impressive. Nothing about his appearance was slick, so it didn't cross my mind that he was conning me. He was, oh, medium height, slightly stocky. He had thinning hair. It was a touch of blond, I think. I remember his eyes, though. Or rather the way he looked at me. He'd pause a long, long time before responding or saying anything. It made me feel like he was just, you know, sizing me up. He looked at me like he was slightly amused. His had these wide glasses that magnified his drooping eyes."

"Did you believe he was psychic?"

Grace sighed and shifted in her sun-faded armchair by the window. She looked at the morbid wallpaper, the photos of children other than her own, instead of out the window. A dusting of late-winter snow covered the frozen lake. Willa knew from her frequent trips to Lake Chicora that when it snowed, it could be days before a plow truck cleared the way for residents. The first snowfall used to be a time for celebration. The "lifers" who spent the winters there used to slide a decked-out Christmas tree onto the frozen lake, but it stopped after Melody disappeared. It was cruel, they thought, to be festive when the Wynnes were grieving so hard. They'd lost a sense of community when Melody went missing, and it had never been regained.

"I know now how desperate it was to invite him into my home. To believe him. But I did."

"When the police later questioned Merrill, he knew information about Melody and intimate details about your house, such as the way the screen door banged twice before it latched, or what times of day the air-conditioning window unit turned on. How much of that is information he extracted from you on his visits? That he observed or that you willingly told him?"

Willa knew she was leading the interview subject. It was as unprofessional in journalism as it was in law enforcement, but she couldn't help it. She knew the legal implications of going undercover—she'd sat on a panel about it at a conference in Miami five years ago—but she couldn't help but feel as if she was raising a host of thorny ethical issues as she sat here with Grace. She wasn't after sensationalism, and she wasn't shamefully abusing her skills as a journalist, but she felt an incredible dishonesty that nearly compromised her work.

"Too much, I'm sure," Grace said, almost breezily. "I knew even at the time that it was wrong to talk to Merrill. It was shameful of him to take advantage of a grieving mother like that. I know that. But instead I felt guilty, like I was the one who invited him into our lives instead of the other way around. I knew it was wrong to talk to him . . . because I didn't tell Jack. But he found out."

"What happened then?"

"He called Campbell immediately."

"Tell me about your relationship with Detective Campbell," Willa said, shifting topics. She'd found she could get her interview subjects to give up more information if she denied them the ability to follow their story through its usual narrative arc.

"When I think of Campbell, I think of the way his face changed when I told him what happened on that first day. He was somewhat new to the police force and so eager. To this day, I think of the eagerness in his face when he arrived that afternoon. I could see that he thought he'd save the day. But I can't divorce that image from the way the urgency left his face when he glanced at the lake."

Grace was funny, Willa thought, in that she tended to describe how people looked and how she felt, above all else. She was a former artist, after all. She'd quit her job at the arts council in town, giving up the chance to organize summer camps and commission artists to bring sculptures to the downtown river walk, when Melody disappeared. But she held on to that artistic perceptiveness, painting a scene in her mind as she talked.

"I appreciated the way Campbell wrote down everything I said. It gave my words weight. He asked me what I thought happened. I didn't realize until later, when Jack told me, that he wanted to know my *version* of events. As if it was only my opinion and not the truth." Shyly, she tucked her chin to her chest and looked away, as if the memory alone made her feel insecure.

"Jack later castigated Detective Campbell publicly. The effect was more that the public turned against you and Jack instead of focusing on police efforts," Willa said. Grace clearly felt valued when given attention, and it might make her open up more if Willa indulged her, so she took feverish notes to show she trusted Grace's words. "How did that make you feel?"

"Frustrated, of course. We only wanted to bring our daughter home," Grace said simply.

"Let's rewind. It's the night that Melody disappeared. August 4, 1992. Sun's going down. You and Jack are feeling desperate. Tell me something that sticks out in your mind from that evening."

Grace took a long sip of tea. Always the same floral mug, always the same Lipton tea. Willa had wanted to bring her a token gift early on in their conversation, something to show she paid attention and cared, but the imported teas in specialty flavors—blueberry ginseng, goji berry, honeyed pear—sat unused on the chipped Formica countertop.

"I'll never forget the endless cicada chorus from that day. They were louder than my thoughts. I'll never forget them because I had this thought a few weeks later, when it was harder to hold on to hope. I thought the cicadas would end up living longer than my baby."

21

Sawyer

IN THE DEAD stretch between Pullman and Cheshire, fizzy fireflies light up the open fields. It's beginning to get dark, and I haven't planned on making more stops this evening, but with Vaughn's refusal to talk, I consider knocking on the door of one of the Wynnes' neighbors.

I don't notice the lights flashing behind me until the car is right on my tail. Maybe I'm lulled by the intermittent bursts from the fireflies, but the headlights catch up to me out of nowhere in the trailing dusk. I grip the steering wheel tightly. There's nowhere to turn off, nowhere to lose them. I fumble for my cell phone with one hand. A single bar flickers on the screen: even my phone knows the area is unpopulated. Who could I call? Momma? Leo? The police?

The car swings around to pass me. Thank God. I'm just driving too slowly.

But then it swerves into my lane, narrowly missing a swipe to the front bumper. Taillights shout at me as the driver stamps on the brake. I swing the steering wheel wildly and swerve to the side of the road, bumping on the dusty shoulder and barreling over a wall of cattails and wildflowers. When the car stops bouncing, I realize my hands are covering my neck and my body is tensed, waiting for a collision. I lower my shaking hands and place them on the wheel. I try to steady my breathing, but then I see someone get out of the car. Approaching fast. I paw at the gearshift, but I'm too slow. Fear batters my heart against my rib cage. Someone is at the trunk and close enough that I can see it's a woman.

With the motor still running, I roll down the window just a crack.

"Are you hurt?" the woman calls.

"I don't know," I respond, testing my neck.

"Good gracious, I didn't mean to run you off the road." The woman's voice is buttery and soft. She's stopped by the trunk, hesitant to move any closer. "I just wanted to have a word."

I clamp a hand over my neck and pivot slowly. She's a plump woman with a wide, open face and heavily freckled skin. Her wispy, corn-silk hair flutters in the wind, and her crop pants don't conceal her swollen ankles.

"I'm Justine, Edwin's wife," she says. "Merrill Vaughn was my father-in-law."

My muscles go rigid.

"I followed you from the house," Justine continues. "I saw Edwin turn you away. But I want to help."

"Why?" I choke.

She takes a step closer and tilts her head to look inside the car.

"I can tell you what you need to know. Mind if I sit with you?"

I glance at the passenger seat littered with my purse, phone, a Kind bar, and printed directions. Rationally, I know I shouldn't let a stranger into the car, especially not one who ran me off the road. But she seems sincere, and I want to know what she has to say. I fumble with the controls until the locks pop open with a swoosh.

As she slides into the supple leather seat, she doesn't pause to admire how nice the car is, something I couldn't get past when I first started driving the relic from Willa's TV days. Then I remember the size of Vaughn's estate and know she must be used to nice things.

"I married Edwin in 1999, years after Merrill became a suspect. Everyone in town already knew everything there was to know about the Vaughns by then, and they all thought I was crazy to marry into the family," Justine says.

"So you must not have believed it, then," I say, unsnapping my belt and swiveling to look at her.

"I was a teenager when the baby went missing. We all thought Merrill was a creep for visiting the mom and telling her he was a psychic. There's no denying that. But once Edwin introduced me to him, I knew he couldn't have done it."

"Why do you say that? Excuse me—"

I lean through the seats to reach into the back. I grab a notebook, left over from my college days, and turn to a blank page. A reporter should take notes.

Justine looks at the poised pen and shakes her head. "Off the record."

Good. Less pressure. The pen drops from my hand.

"Merrill came from wealthy parents, but he didn't make much of himself. His father was a business magnate. He traded stocks, ran a construction company, and acquired property. Merrill inherited the family's house and wealth when his parents died, but he was never a successful or talented man himself. The business about being a psychic— that didn't start till later, when Edwin was out of the house. He never said or did anything that would suggest he was psychic that I saw, but he became incredibly spiritual later in life."

Justine's looking down at her feet, and I follow her gaze to see that she's slipped off her sandals and is tracing her unpainted toenails on the floor mat.

"But it's not so much that I know Merrill didn't do it. It's that I know that Abel did."

Something about her voice draws my attention from her feet to her pale eyes.

"Cheshire is a small town. I grew up not far from Abel, across the lake. Have you made a stop at the Lake Chicora Outpost yet? It's the campground store on the northern side of the lake. I grew up in the trailer park next to the Outpost. I didn't always live in a mansion," she says sheepishly.

I think of the cramped bedroom I shared with Willa and feel an affinity for Justine, respect for her modest background.

"So you knew Abel?"

"Not personally. He was older than me. But my brothers knew him, and his family was a bit of a legend on the lake."

"How so?"

"Well, his mother was from Bath, so the family was kind of famous in that way, to start."

"Bath?"

"It's a small town about an hour and a half, two hours east of here. Now, it's not much more than a tiny town. But Dorrie, Abel's mother, was just a little kid when the school disaster happened in the twenties. A disgruntled farmer set off a bomb at the local school, killing dozens of children. Dorrie survived with no injuries. But her siblings all died. A tragic thing to happen to a child, for sure. By the time Dorrie had the boys, she was extremely religious. That always seems to be the case, you know. You experience something awful, and you either give yourself over to God or you don't. There's no middle ground," Justine muses.

She pauses to contemplate that, and we sit in silence, looking out at the open field. Dusk has fallen, and the fireflies are in full bloom.

"So Abel and his brother grew up with Dorrie's tragic past hovering over them. It wasn't surprising that she kept them home from school for years. But I imagine she'd have been more, I don't know, motherly, protective, toward them. Are you a mother?" she asks, glancing at my stomach as if she expects to see evidence of a child.

"No." I shake my head. "Not yet," I add, superstitious, scared to leave it off.

"Well, Dorrie wasn't the maternal type. Any joy or love or compassion those boys ever had was sermonized and slapped out of them by their mother. She rarely let them leave their property, but you could hear her shouting at them if you were anywhere nearby. My brothers said it sounded like an animal was let loose till you realized what she was saying. She'd repeat the same word over and over again: *bad, bad, bad, bad, bad,*" Justine chants.

I shiver and pull my knees up to my chest. I feel as if we're girlfriends sharing gossip over drinks, not strangers in a borrowed car crashed in a field.

"Now, I don't know what went on in that house after their father died, but I heard that Dorrie used to make the boys crawl into the oven when they were bad. This was when they were real little, of course. But one day she forgot Abel was in there, and she turned on the oven. He got out before being burned alive, but his hands and arms were still burned real bad."

"That sounds like a rumor," I protest. "The inside of an oven is pretty small, and he could have been killed."

She shrugs her sunburnt shoulders. "You forget how old their farmhouse is. Ovens were bigger then, I think."

"Still," I say, unbelieving.

"Well, this I know for a fact happened: Dorrie once called a priest to the house to perform an exorcism on Abel. The priest was my mom's brother. Like I said, small town," she says when she catches my glance. "So my uncle got to the house. They lived in a creepy old farmhouse in the woods even then. Abel still lives there. My uncle gets there, and he sees Abel in the woods. He's torturing a baby fox. He said his eyes showed no conscience and no remorse. This was before his brother shot himself, before Dorrie died, and long before Melody Wynne disappeared. So there you have it."

Crickets chirp loudly outside the car. Another car hasn't passed us since we pulled off the road. I shift in my seat and idly rub my neck.

"Have what?"

Justine stares at me. Her eyes are so pale they're disarming. "Proof that Abel did it."

"It sounds like proof of animal cruelty, sure, but not of kidnapping. Well, hearsay more than proof . . ." I trail off.

"He *loved* to kill things."

"We don't know that Melody is dead—"

"Hurting animals is one of the signs of a serial killer."

"We definitely don't know that he killed others. Do we?"

God, I need to do my homework better.

"Listen. Abel killed animals as a kid. He was suspended when he brought bones to show-and-tell one day. Later, when he got out of jail, he took up hunting. He'd patrol the Lake Chicora woods with a hunting rifle all the time. He knows every inch of those woods. And the police found that bag of blood and hair in the woods right by his property. Put two and two together," she says urgently.

I feel the light-headedness of vertigo wash over me. I reach for the steering wheel so I can hold on to something solid.

A bag of blood.

And hair.

Cry of the Cicadas: The True Story of Melody Wynne's Disappearance

Part 2: The Evidence

Though no forensic evidence was ever found that resulted in a viable lead pointing to Melody's location or abductor, the county sheriff's office wrestled with several leads soon after the abduction.

When Deputy Corbin Campbell arrived at the Wynnes' house on August 4, he spotted a piece of fabric snagged on a low-hanging tree branch near the boathouse. The fabric, light pink and cotton, was determined to be a scrap from a child's nightgown. Grace Wynne denied that Melody owned anything matching the fabric, but it still left the uneasy notion that foul play had occurred near the lake. Years later, the nightgown fabric was tested for DNA, but it yielded nothing—including no skin cells or saliva to indicate that the nightgown had once belonged to Melody.

The location of the fabric scrap adjacent to the boathouse required that Lake Chicora be searched for Melody's remains. A two-man team from Lansing arrived on August 6. They worked in relentless sun and temperatures hovering in the midnineties; it was a summer when the heat settled on your shoulders like a heavy wool blanket.

After two twelve-hour days spent searching the lake, the dive team recovered piles of debris but no body. They found plenty of everyday objects with no consequence to the case, such as fishing rods, lawn chairs, and coolers—the detritus of summer tourists.

Most interestingly, though, was the .300-caliber Savage Model 99 rifle found in the lake. The Savage 99, popular for hunting game and costing less than a hundred dollars in the early sixties, featured a rotary magazine promising six quick shots. It was not something you'd expect to find discarded in a body of water forty feet from shore. Though impossible to link to Melody Wynne while she remained missing, the rifle was often referred to as "the murder weapon" by locals.

Six days after the disappearance, volunteer search parties continued to canvass the woods surrounding the lake, covering the ground that the bloodhounds had tracked days before. Marcy Edwards, a fifty-three-year-old schoolteacher, discovered the most alarming items recovered in the case to date.

Less than a quarter mile north of the Wynnes' home, just across the silty creek, Marcy stumbled into a shallow hole that measured eighteen inches wide, twenty-five inches long, and twelve inches deep. The hole had neat edges, indicating the use of a shovel; it would be a difficult task to dig a hole that size in the unyielding dryness Cheshire faced that summer.

Alongside the predug hole, Marcy found a black garbage bag. Marcy could tell from the bag's bulk that there was something inside. She used a whistle to call for help before she touched the bag. When a visiting member of the state forensic team arrived on the scene, he sliced open the bag to reveal a bloody mass of what appeared to be hair and intestines.

"It was a sight I can never unsee," recalls Marcy Edwards, now retired from teaching and in her eighties. "I was nearly hiding behind a tree when the officer opened the bag, the same way a small child hides behind a blanket at the scary part in a television show. I'll never forget it. Before my brain had time to register what I was seeing, the stench hit me. It was unbearable. Even with what we know now, at that moment, I truly thought it was the baby in that bag."

But of course, it wasn't Melody Wynne in the bag. Lab tests revealed it was the remains of a deer.

After the discovery of the rifle and the bloody bag in the woods, the Wynnes voluntarily removed themselves from the public eye. They demurred when asked to appear at press conferences at the local and state level.

In a statement released one week after Melody's disappearance, Jack Wynne said, "We will no longer be accessible to the public for comment about our daughter's abduction. It seems obvious that the media is more interested in capturing our reactions to gruesome updates than helping us find our daughter."

The refusal to comment on the case left a bad impression in the court of public opinion. The Wynnes' avoidance of reporters, coupled with early evidence of the fabric found near their home, led to much speculation by locals that Jack and Grace were involved in their daughter's disappearance.

"There is no other physical evidence in this case that could lead to a breakthrough or an arrest," Campbell said in a plea to the public. "All evidence has made its way into the public domain. We need your help to solve this case."

Campbell was faced with the choice to keep the story local to southwestern Michigan or go national with it. Though national attention doesn't necessarily deliver viable leads, the decision to keep details about Melody's abduction local cost the investigators. They didn't receive tips about slow-driving cars, cars with darkened windows, suspicious men, and men who weren't suspicious enough.

The community was at once captivated and frustrated by heavy local news coverage, but the media attention didn't return any new leads.

22

Sawyer

Picturing a bag of blood and hair turns my stomach, but I can't help it. Why didn't the Wynnes mention it? Why are they still looking for Melody?

Justine continues to talk, but her voice becomes muffled as I fall deeper into imagining the moment some poor person found the bag in the woods. Her freckled hand on my arm brings me back to the present.

"Someone's here," she says, her voice lowering.

I spin in the driver's seat, and I'm blinded by another car's lights. The high beams are on, and the car idles behind us. By instinct, I reach for the key to turn the engine back on, but Justine grips my wrist when I make the movement.

The night's become fully dark, and even the fireflies have started to fade away. The field is illuminated by the car's brights, and I see that we're parked in knee-high wild grass. It's silent but for the hum of the car behind us.

Someone gets out of the vehicle, and this time I can tell it's a man from the stocky frame and broad shoulders. His stride is slow but purposeful. He raps hard on the trunk, and Justine and I both jump. My throat constricts as I realize my window's still open a crack, though if he's here to hurt us, it probably makes no difference.

"Police," he announces. "Roll down your window."

Again I reach to turn the key to activate the power windows, eager to please and too scared to think.

But Justine tightens her grip on my wrist. "What are you thinking?" she whispers harshly. "You'll give him a fright if you start the car."

Right. I've barely ever driven, and I've never been pulled over. I turn to shout through the crack in the window, and I'm met by the flare of his flashlight turning on, so intense I see little white shapes dance in my eyes for a moment while they adjust. I clamp my hand over my eyes, and he takes a fast step away from the vehicle. I realize my mistake and drop my hands to my lap.

"Sorry, Officer. What seems to be the problem?"

"You tell me. You have an accident?"

He lowers the flashlight, and I can see his face. He's in his midfifties with a square face, bushy gray eyebrows, and enviable posture.

"No, sir. It was a misunderstanding," I say, glancing at Justine. Her wispy hair glows like a white halo in the headlight beams. "We were just talking."

"Heck of a place to talk." He tilts his head to look into the vehicle. "Edwin know you're out here talking, Justine?"

She doesn't respond. The officer tuts and shakes his head. He gives the roof of the car another startling rap, as loud as a gunshot in the silent field.

"Go on and get a move on. And next time you wanna talk, go to the diner in town. Not a field at night."

He strolls back to his vehicle at a languid pace.

"God, that scared me half to death," I breathe.

Justine gathers her purse in her arms and rests a hand on the door handle. "Not a word about what we talked about, you hear? It was off the record."

I raise my hand. "Scout's honor."

She snorts. "Right. Word'll get out now that Campbell saw us here. But if Edwin reaches out to you, you're not to tell him what I said. Got it?"

"Got it," I say. "Wait. Campbell? As in Detective Campbell?"

"The one and only. I should've known he'd pull up here. He must know you're sniffing around about the missing baby. Small town, remember? Your Illinois plates give you away." Justine grips the door frame and heaves herself out of the car. "Good luck with your story."

Blazing high beams turn to disappearing taillights as Detective Campbell and Justine pull out of the field and head west back into town. I turn the car on and ease backward out of the field, from what's probably a bucolic view in the daytime. But right now it's a void of darkness. No streetlights. No houses. No cars.

I ease back onto the road, and within minutes, it curves where the dirt road intersects it. I take the turn slowly, thinking of how the car filled with dust when I bounced over the rutted gravel last time.

The woods begin almost immediately, thick and full and canopied over the road. I can see only ten, fifteen feet in front of me as I drive. The road is mostly straight. I slow to a crawl and try to squint through the brush. It's too dense to see through, but still, it's hard to believe Abel's old farmhouse is nestled back there, completely invisible from the road. The crickets are loud, and the damp air creeping through the window carries the scent of cedar wood.

I don't hit the brake when a single stop sign is illuminated on the lonely road. It's riddled with bullet holes, as if someone used it for shooting practice years ago. I estimate I'm a half mile away from the lakeside houses now.

It's foolish to come here this late, I know. It's past eight o'clock, and twilight has set in. The Wynnes' neighbor might not even be awake. But I keep driving, now impatient to talk to another person about what Justine told me.

Willa hated the way I'm too spontaneous and never aware of the time. She was so conventional, always sticking to rigid plans and schedules and expecting everyone else to too. She'd never pull up for an unscheduled interview.

I don't want to admit it, but I'm excited. Terrified, yes, and full of self-doubt, but I feel energized. Even Willa wasn't able to get an interview with the Vaughns, and yet I did. And I may know something she didn't know. I feel an explicable closeness with her as I trace her footsteps. But I still need to know why she chose this case, of all the possibilities. There must be hundreds of children who disappear from their families in Chicago. Why did she choose to drive out here, into these unforgiving woods, to this void of a lake?

I roll to a stop in front of the little cottage that the Wynnes pointed out. It's smaller than the Wynnes' cottage and the others down the road. It stands out with its home-made attempt at a wraparound porch. Only one bedroom, if I had to guess.

The crunch of the tires as they come to a stop on the gravel announces my arrival. A woman on the porch becomes visible. She doesn't stand but calls out a greeting, as if she's been expecting me.

23

Willa

Six months before

S HE WAS ON the porch when Willa arrived. The winter thaw hadn't yet lifted, and Roberta wore a warm red plaid jacket atop a white turtleneck. She was in her rocking chair, emanating a calm as if she'd be content sitting there staring into the woods for hours.

She ushered Willa inside matter-of-factly. They'd spoken over the phone first—Roberta didn't have an email address, or an internet connection, for that matter—and Willa could tell then that the old woman was no-nonsense. In her late sixties, but not frail. She was compact: short and wide.

The first thing Willa noticed inside the tiny cottage was that one wall was lined with bookcases. They were flimsy particle-board creations, but they were filled with real books. Willa took solace in this. When everything was digital and journalism had gone to shit, real books were salvation. Complex concepts had to be boiled down to witty thought fragments ready to disappear in an instant. Books felt permanent, and it helped Willa settle in on the plaid couch.

Roberta offered her coffee, black, as she admired the books, and Willa smiled. This was the type of person she tended to get along with, not insincere people like Remy and Noah. Roberta planted herself beside Willa on the couch, opposite a boxy old television. When she sat, her self-hemmed jeans revealed thick woolen socks.

"Trowbridge Township has five thousand people in fifty square miles. But I know you're here to talk about only five of them," Roberta said.

Willa turned on the recording feature on her phone and set it beside her on a low end table. Most expected her to conduct her interview linearly, but she rarely did that. "Let's start with what you remember about Merrill Vaughn and Abel Bowen."

"Merrill I didn't know personally. But it was no secret he was under surveillance by the police, and it didn't take long for word to spread that his lie detector test was inconclusive."

She'd been right: Roberta was no-nonsense. "And Abel?"

"Well, now, Abel I did know. Once you live somewhere long as I've lived on this lake, you know the locals," she said as she lifted the mug to her lips. "I'll give you the abridged version: Abel was a loner. His father died, then his brother died, and finally his mother died. He was a lonely, troubled boy, but he wasn't a kidnapper."

"He was a convicted murderer at seventeen," Willa pointed out. "And Roberta, you know I'm here for more than an abridged version."

"I'll get there, I'll get there," Roberta said as she reached for a crocheted afghan beside the couch. She draped it over her lap. "Every year it feels colder and colder to me. Spring seems to last longer than before."

Without asking, Willa turned the knob on a nearby space heater pointed at the couch.

"Thanks, dear. You know, before all of this, Lake Chicora used to be a bit of a tourist attraction. It's tucked away, but it's well kept, and there are plenty of crappie and muskies in the lake. But with all the negative publicity following Melody Wynne's disappearance, the lake's been all but forgotten. We can't seem to shake this air of tragedy—like Dutch Lake, not too far away. Two kids drowned there in the early 2000s, and that town hasn't recovered yet either."

Willa gave a solemn nod. "The lake lost its sense of community," she said, thinking about how the Christmas tree tradition had died after Melody was taken.

"The Bowens, though, they never really tried to be part of our community. Dorrie Bowen was intractable. She was a willful lady, even before her husband died. Put a little bit too much stock into what the church told her to believe, if you ask me. Their farmhouse is about a mile down the road, but when I was younger, I'd traverse the woods more often. I could hear Dorrie shrieking at the boys."

"What would she yell about?"

"Oh, everything. She sounded like a banshee, going on and on about their wickedness. She railed against poor Abel and Leroy. It took its toll on Leroy, obviously. And that's not to say Abel got out unscathed either." Roberta held her still-steaming mug to her mouth until her large, round glasses fogged up. "He is simply a troubled boy."

Willa thought of the catalog of stories Abel had told her in their interviews. For a year now, she'd lived with Abel's accounts of how they'd recited endless prayers, the way Dorrie had clutched him when she found Leroy dead in the basement, and all the woodland animals he took it out on.

"So are you suggesting 'boys will be boys'?" Willa asked, forever the instigator.

"No. What happened to that lady driver was a tragic accident, and Abel used poor judgment."

"You must believe the best in people."

"No, dear, I believe the worst. I was on the receiving end of tragic calls for years, and I know it's often the person you trust the most that causes you the greatest harm."

Willa fought a shiver at the blunt truth in her words. "For Abel, that's Dorrie. And for Melody, that's her parents. You believe it was the Wynnes who did this," Willa concluded. This was good content, Willa knew. No one had vocally pointed a finger at the Wynnes in her interviews yet, though it had been a common speculation for years. It had been rare to find anyone who'd blame the Wynnes for Melody's disappearance at first, but now that the little beauty pageant queen had gone missing in Colorado, it seemed to be in style.

"There were rumors, of course," Roberta acknowledged. "The most common was that they covered up an accident at their boathouse. They don't use it anymore, and I dock my boat there now. But then, it was an accident waiting to happen for a toddler."

"Police dragged the lake and never found a body," Willa debated.

"That's the troubling part. I never thought it was intentional, but you'd have to have a malicious soul to dispose of her little body after an accident."

"Why do you think it was the Wynnes, then?"

Roberta set her empty mug on the end table, nudging aside a tattered, warped stack of books that looked as if they'd taken a tumble into the lake. She thought for a moment.

"I worked as an emergency dispatcher for Trowbridge Township at the office in Mapleton at the time of the disappearance. I was the one to take Grace Wynne's call."

Willa sat up straight. This she hadn't known. She'd read the transcript, of course. Tracked it down with a

Freedom of Information Act request and filed it away for her book. But she had been told the dispatcher's identity was private. Even her lawyer couldn't help her get a recording while the case was still open.

"Grace never mentioned Melody by name, and she used the word *gone* instead of *missing* or *taken*. It's not something one would pick up on in the moment. But I couldn't get the call out of my head. It was always a niggling feeling until I realized why it bothered me so much. Grace wasn't lying; Melody *was* gone."

Willa thought back to the transcript, but she couldn't remember it verbatim. It would be the first thing she reviewed after the interview.

"Was this emergency call the main thing that made you uneasy, made you suspect Grace Wynne in Melody's abduction?" Willa was careful to keep her voice impartial. She could have listed off all the reasons the rest of the town criticized the parents, but she wanted to hear Roberta's thoughts.

"No. Later that evening, before the dive team arrived, Jack took the boat out. I understood it at the time: he was a desperate father searching for his daughter. I had just gotten off my shift at dispatch and was as frantic about Melody as the rest of us. But when she wasn't found and I thought about Jack searching the shores alone, it made me uncomfortable."

Willa scoured the crime catalog in her mind. There had been a time after the "bushy-haired stranger" theory lost its popularity and suspicion turned to the parents but before DNA evidence became critical to a conviction. Had Melody gone missing during that window, Jack might be in a cell right now. As the police officer on scene was a rookie, it wasn't surprising that Jack had gotten the chance to fire up his motorboat—loaded with a body or even a speck of blood, for all the police knew—while Grace stayed home, waiting for news.

"If you were truly uncomfortable, why did you stay? You're the Wynnes' closest neighbor," Willa pointed out.

"Like I said: I never believed it was intentional."

"And if it happened like your theory allows, it was bad judgment on behalf of the Wynnes. Someone is missing, maybe dead. But they didn't mean to harm anyone. But doesn't that still make them murderers, just like Abel tossing the rock off the overpass?"

"I'm no lawyer, but I suppose it boils down to the semantics of manslaughter versus murder," Roberta mused.

"But isn't guilt, guilt?"

24

Sawyer

ROBERTA HANDS ME a steaming mug of coffee despite the late hour as she settles on the couch next to me. Between her nearly antique television and her wide glasses that haven't been in style since last century, I feel as if I've stepped back in time. I take a polite sip, and it's a bitter black.

"How long have you worked with Christine, Sarah?"

My heart leaps in my chest. Willa once revealed that I blink rapidly when I lie, so I open my eyes wide and innocent. "Oh, off and on for years now."

Roberta gives a brisk nod. "It takes a certain sense of entitlement to claim to know someone else's story well enough to write a book about it."

I set the mug down on a battered end table beside the couch and take a deep breath. I should have known that the Wynnes' neighbor would be wary of an invasive reporter and less loose-lipped than Justine Vaughn.

"I can appreciate that. I'm coming in as an outsider, trying to tell your story," I allow.

"It's not my story to tell."

I can't help but think of Willa. She chased rumors and followed legends and probed deeply into the lives of everyone she talked to. Her whole life was about telling other people's stories. But even as her sister, I never knew her story or that she lived a secret, private life of depression.

"But you're a part of it," I argue. "Don't you think it's worth telling your perspective and sharing how you felt? If it would help save even one person, isn't it worth it?"

"That this interview could save someone is a lofty ambition."

God, she's no-nonsense. Book smart too. Her tiny one-room cottage is nearly overflowing with newspapers and books, and not the type of candy-colored beach reads scattered around my apartment either.

"I understand that true crime books purport to delve into a criminal's mind," she continues. "But is that why people read them? Isn't it really just a basic morbid curiosity? I suppose I got over that quickly when I worked in emergency dispatch."

"So you were on the receiving end of a lot of sad calls. You were the first person to hear about countless tragedies," I say. "Then you understand that if this book can help us understand why Melody Wynne went missing, then it's worth it so the dispatcher at the desk where you used to sit may have one less missing-child report to file."

Roberta rummages in the pockets of her plaid jacket and retrieves a tissue. She dabs at her nose discreetly and pats at her short-cropped gray hair. She looks like the type of woman who'd carry a compass in her pocket, not tear up at the mention of her former career. I may have gone too far.

"There's an insatiable desire to understand these monsters. But in the end, they're just regular people without guilt or remorse. That's what a psychopath is. We don't even know what causes it—upbringing or Mother Nature. Your book won't change that."

I run my sweaty palms across my dress slacks. A relic from my days in sales, they were buried in one of the laundry baskets permanently housing clothes in my room. Not for the first time, I wonder why Willa subjected herself to the bitterness and hurt of the Lake Chicora residents for this project.

Maybe she wanted to feel something when everything else felt like nothing.

"You're tougher than you look," Roberta observes. "I've been visited by countless reporters through the years. All the local ones would have given up by now."

She looks at me appraisingly as she takes a slow sip from her mug.

"You're not as impartial a journalist as Christine. She's all business. Just the facts and the details."

"I like to dive into the heart of the story," I hear myself saying, as if I've got a strategy or a background in journalism.

We're quiet for a moment. I can hear the deep, resonating sound of bullfrogs lining the lake. Night has fallen completely outside; it's full darkness out the window, which is covered with plastic wrap to keep out the early autumn draft. With a half acre between us, I can't see the Wynnes' modest cottage or even their old boathouse in the dark.

Roberta must follow my gaze, because after a moment she says, "This is a place where people leave their doors open. It sounds trite, but it is. Yet regardless of how safe we think it is, it's no place to raise a family."

"But it was safe before Melody, right?"

She shrugs. "Was it? There's two hundred acres of natural water right outside my door, forty feet at its deepest. The shoal areas are heavily weeded. It's a fine fishery if you want to catch bluegills and muskies. Better than Blueberry Lake or Mud Lake. The woods aren't maintained, any beachfront is man-made, undocumented tourists come in and out all summer, and the trailer park by the Outpost drove down the value for everyone else. I wouldn't say it's a safe place to raise a family, no."

There's no doubt in my mind she's right. The sound of a stick breaking in the dark is enough to make me lock myself in a room with the covers pulled over my head. It's scary out here, especially at night, and I wouldn't want to live here, isolated, let alone raise a baby here.

"Besides Melody Wynne, were there any other children living here before she went missing?"

"There was another family, many years ago. They were on the other side of the Wynnes. No one's lived there for a long time. I took it upon myself to trim the branches of the oak in that yard after it broke the window twice one windy spring. They moved out just a few days after Melody was kidnapped."

"How did they leave so soon? Had the house been on the market before the disappearance?"

"You can't imagine anyone choosing to live here after that happened. I understand that," Roberta concedes. "But no. They just up and left. I can't blame her, of course. She was a young mother, with two small daughters of her own."

"Two daughters? She must have been terrified."

"Everyone was shaken. But she packed up her little girls and never came back. Her name was Claudia."

Cry of the Cicadas: The True Story of Melody Wynne's Disappearance

Interview Transcript

Mapleton Sheriff's Office, Investigative Services
    Unit
Part 1 of Recorded Interview with Roberta Skinner
Date: 08/25/1992
Duration: 56 minutes
Conducted by Deputy Corbin Campbell

CORBIN CAMPBELL: Can you explain why you
    took down the missing-person posters from
    the campground store on the lake?
ROBERTA SKINNER: It's been three weeks, Officer.
    Anyone who visits the outpost store knows
    Melody is missing. I was picking up some
    night crawlers there when Jack stopped in for a
    gallon of milk. He stared at the poster so long
    he nearly forgot to pick up the damn milk.
CC: I see. You know it looks suspicious when you
    go around town taking down her missing
    poster, though, right?
RS: I know that baby's not coming home alive
    unless you stop worrying about the posters
    and focus on finding out who took her.
CC: Right. Well. Let's get on with it, then. I'm
    sure you've heard that we're looking into Abel
    Bowen, given his background. How would you
    describe your relationship with Abel?

RS: We're neighbors, I suppose. He lives about a mile down the road from me.

CC: And how long have you lived at your residence on Lake Chicora?

RS: Nearly thirty years.

CC: So you've lived near Abel since he was a young child. Tell me about him.

RS: What do you want to know?

CC: Well, have you had any interactions with him that stand out to you? I'm just trying to understand a little more about this guy.

RS: One instance stands out in my memory, but it wasn't an interaction. It was an observation.

CC: Go on, Roberta.

RS: Well, Abel went to jail, that's no secret. But when he returned, a young girl came to live with him for a few months. I heard from someone at the Outpost that she was claiming to be his dead brother's daughter. Whether that's true or not, I don't know. But I do know she stayed on with Abel for several months. I make a point not to meddle or pry, but it made me uncomfortable. She was a teenager. Too young to be living with a man nearing thirty, in any regard. But you know, I'd watch out my window or sit on my porch and see them. Every day, he'd walk up and down the dirt road dragging this dusty blanket while the girl sat on it, cross-legged and glassy-eyed. He'd drag her on that blanket from his house in the woods up to the lakeside cottages every day that summer. And then one day, she just disappeared. It wouldn't have been so noticeable that she was gone, I suppose, but he took to dragging the empty blanket behind him for the next few weeks, as if she was still sitting right there.

CC: Do you know anything more about the girl?

RS: No, but Claudia might.

CC: Why's that?

RS: I'm no gossip, Officer, but I believe that she and Abel are friendly, oddly enough. Late at night, when I return from the swing shift at dispatch and sit on my porch to unwind, I see him walk toward her house now and then. I can't explain it, why she'd let him in with two little girls in the house, but hers is the last stop on the road, so I know that's where he goes. Have you talked to her yet?

CC: The night that Melody was reported missing, I spoke with her.

RS: I take it she didn't see anything, then. What about her older daughter? She plays near the Wynnes' house and in the forest.

CC: She and the younger one were asleep when I visited. I peeked in on them. But Claudia denied a one-on-one interview with the older girl. And now it seems they've left town, at least until it's safe.

RS: Is it unsafe now?

CHAPTER

25

Sawyer

WHAT DID SHE look like? How old was she? How old were her kids? What did they look like? Was there a father in the picture?

I try to probe for more information, but it's useless. Roberta's memory is good, but it's not infallible. It's been almost thirty years since this woman and her daughters lived on Lakeview Lane, she says, and don't all kids start to look alike after a while?

She offers me her couch for the evening. I take her up on it, thinking I'll text Cami or Ainsley to take over my morning class instead of fessing up to Kelly that I won't be in. What I don't count on is the complete lack of cell service. My phone's inoperable out here.

The couch's padding is so thin that the wooden support beams are as pronounced as if I decided to sleep on a pallet. Roberta settles into her twin bed before long without a hint of awkwardness about the stranger on her couch. She places her giant glasses on her bedside table and begins snoring almost immediately.

I lie on the couch for a few hours, listening to the hum of Roberta's snores and the evening rhapsody of relentless bullfrogs.

Darkness penetrates the cottage. My eyes adjust just enough to see the shellacked scales of a mounted fish above the couch. A black gill, eternally flapping open, hangs right above my sight line. I'm staring into it when I hear a crunching sound.

Cocking my head, I strain to listen. It's a measured sound, and it's getting closer. It's rhythmic: four crunches and a pause, repeated. My muscles tense and I hold my breath.

Footsteps, I realize. Footsteps on the gravel road, approaching Roberta's cottage.

Crunch. Crunch. Crunch.

I glance at Roberta, but she hasn't stirred. Should I wake her?

The steps are cautious and halting. Waiting.

Then: nothing.

I exhale softly.

Click. Click. Click.

It's closer now, a sharp tapping against the brick pathway leading to the cottage. It sounds like ladies' heels snapping against a tile floor. Pointed and urgent, yet restrained. *Click. Click.*

I pull the blanket higher, tucking it below my nose so my hot breath balloons the fabric. It's Abel, I realize, lurking around the lakeside houses while the residents sleep. I picture him pushing his face against the window. I picture him looking at me now, and at Roberta each night. I picture his weathered face, thirty years younger, peering into Melody's crib beside her window.

Click. Click. Thud. Thud.

I swallow. He's on the wooden porch now. Will I hear the metallic rattle of his hand on the doorknob?

Without moving my head, I strain my eyes to see better in the dark room. Is there a weapon I could use? There's another set of dull thuds on the hollow porch, and I imagine cowering in Roberta's bathroom while she racks a shotgun.

The footsteps pace the porch.

As slowly as I can, I tilt my body off the couch, gently easing onto the damp-smelling carpet with my wrist, then my knee, then the rest of my body. I let the musty blanket cover my back. On hands and knees, I crawl to the window. I move slowly, testing the squeakiness of the cottage floor. I imagine Abel's wild hair silhouetted against the moonlight reflecting off the lake.

Instead, the outline of a rangy raccoon takes shape on the porch. It shuffles across the beams, dragging its tail and sniffing into corners for forgotten scraps of food. After a few minutes, it taps its claws back down the brick path and dissolves into the darkness.

I stand and wrap the blanket around my shoulders. I look again at Roberta. Her snoring has quieted, but she's still asleep. My cheeks turn pink with embarrassment at the thought of the brusque way Roberta would brush off my fears.

I lie back down, but my mind refuses to settle.

Memories and questions whip through my head. Did my mother ever say anything to suggest that we lived here, on the lake? Is that why Willa pursued this story?

My thoughts grind to a halt.

Willa. I can't remember her face. The harder I try to picture it, the fuzzier it becomes. Of course I know what Willa looked like. But if I had to draw her right now, could I? *Concentrate, Sawyer.* I build a skinny face and a pointy chin surrounded by a halo of white-blond hair. She had a standing appointment for a platinum root touch-up every month because the station already had a brunette, she told me once when she was still on the air. But what did her eyes look like? Was her nose sharp or blunt? Suddenly Willa seems more like a feeling than a memory I can reconstruct.

I'm grinding my teeth on my beaded necklace. I pull it out of my mouth and feel my legs start to twitch. I'm no good at staying still when my mind is racing. I push the blanket off me, quietly swinging my legs off the couch. With a glance at Roberta's stolid sleeping figure, I creep to the door and ease it open, stepping gingerly on the porch. The porch slopes to the left, and the planks don't match up well. As I pad across it into the dewy grass, I wonder if a neighbor helped Roberta construct it.

Behind the cottage is a labyrinth of overgrown trees and weeds. The moon doesn't filter through the brush, but the chirping crickets suggest that the woods are expansive.

I keep to the nighttime-wet grass to mask my footsteps instead of crunching on the gravel like the raccoon. The Wynnes' house is silent as I pass it, but still I'm scared Jack may see me outside and call the police. A dim light flickers from the decrepit boathouse in the distance.

Roberta is right. The oak is planted too close to the front window. I stop at the A-frame cottage next door to the Wynnes and shelter myself from view by walking to the far side of the house. A wide window overlooks the lake, but when I peer inside, all I see is my pale face reflected back at me.

What was I expecting, our family's photo to be tacked to the fridge?

Nothing is familiar here. How old would I have been when we left? *If we really did live here*, I remind myself.

I step away from the house, and my foot catches on something in the tall grass, sending me stumbling. The white wire frame of a croquet wicket clings to my shoe. I shake it off and see that it was in a soldier-straight line with three other wickets. It's the type of easy shot a child would indulge in. With a trembling hand, I push it back in line with the others.

A dozen feet out from the cottage sits a wooden well with a mildewed roof and a rust-colored pump. I train my phone's light down the well. Darkness. Morbidly I wonder if the police searched here for Melody all those years ago.

The lake's edge butts up against a retaining wall on the property. I inch toward the edge and see that the water is low and still. Easing myself onto the embankment, I swing my legs over until they're dangling a few inches above the waterline.

The lake is silent except for the hum of the frogs and the occasional splash suggesting catfish that have come out to claim their food in the dark. I have an unfettered view of the stars.

It's easier to think out here. My thoughts have finally slowed. *Start from the beginning,* I remind myself. What do I know for sure?

A baby went missing twenty-six years ago, and Willa decided to write about it now.

That's it, I realize.

Everything else is speculation.

She might have chosen to write about this missing girl because we used to live next door to her. She might have uncovered something that led to her death. Or, I realize, researching an abduction and visiting grieving parents might have accelerated her lingering depression. Might have led to more drinking, less caring. Did she feel shame at her depression when there was so much worse to feel bad about, or did it feel worse than death itself?

I scour the last six months. The last year. Two years. How long do I have to go back to see Willa's fall?

Leo's convinced she was depressed. Angry. I sort through my catalog of moments with my sister, all those years we shared a room and a walk to school and complaints about our mother. Willa didn't spit outrage. She wasn't bitter. She was self-contained. Blunt. Logical and loyal. A quiet force.

She was only thirty-three.

And yes, she was judgmental. Her personal convictions guided the way. She excelled in seeing flaws. She judged me, but no one escaped her judgment, not even Willa herself.

Out of habit, I glance at my phone. Away from Roberta's cottage, I have a weak signal. Instead of trying to text one of the girls at the studio, I dial my voice mail. Press seven to listen to my saved messages.

"Isn't it funny how people still begin their voice mails by droning on with a laundry list of information that the phone records automatically? I don't need to identify myself or tell you when I'm calling. I don't need to insist you call me back, because voice mails are so passé that, if I'm leaving you one, you better know it's important. But I'm a pragmatist, so here are the facts: this is Willa Stannard calling for Baby Sawyer. It's nine P.M. on Thursday. It's important. Call me back."

Every time I replay it, I'm scared I'll delete it by accident. I've played it dozens of times since she died. Thursday at nine P.M. was right before the coroner estimated her time of death. Now the voice mail is forty-two days old, my phone informs me.

The police know she called and that she left a voice mail. They must then think that the note she left that night was real, even though I insisted it was a forgery, a fake. They must think she called to apologize, and when I didn't answer, she wrote it in her last sentence before taking a razor blade to her wrists.

With a deep inhale, I breathe in the damp air, humid even after the sun's gone down. It's full of algae and decaying wood and fish, but it smells good. Not fresh, but real. Chicago stinks of exhaust and stress. Here the smell calms me and slows my racing heart.

Sitting beside the lake, I find it hard to believe anything bad could happen here, even with Roberta's warnings resonating in my mind. As the fright from the raccoon fades away, I begin to feel comforted by the remoteness. It seems so far from the danger I know how to quantify: Chicago's break-ins and drive-bys and drug deals. This isn't how I feel in my apartment, or even how I felt growing up at our house in Hillside.

Here, it feels like any danger is internal. Deeply isolated, this place seems to nudge the part of my mind that harbors the darkest places of my imagination. The biggest threat to my safety is my conjuring mind.

But Grace Wynne probably never thought her worst fears would materialize here.

Why would anyone come all the way down this quiet road to take a sleeping baby out of her room?

Cry of the Cicadas: The True Story of Melody Wynne's Disappearance

Part 3: The Suspects

Police immediately raised the question central to finding Melody: Who would have had access, opportunity, and motive to abduct the eighteen-month-old?

Most popular is the intruder theory, followed by "the parents did it" theory. Each side points to crimes that received sensational coverage in the media to support their opinion: those who believe that an intruder abducted Melody cite the disappearance of Elizabeth Smart, who was taken from her home and held captive by a stranger in 2002; and those who point a finger at the Wynnes refer to Casey Anthony, the young mother accused of the death of her two-year-old daughter in 2008.

Early on, two local men were separately investigated for any involvement in or knowledge of Melody's disappearance.

The first person to garner attention as a potential suspect was Abel Bowen, a thirty-five-year-old man from Cheshire. Bowen lives in a two-story wooden farmhouse in the woods near Lake Chicora, situated just off the only gravel road leading to the lake. With a home in close proximity to the Wynnes and a criminal background, Bowen was an obvious suspect.

In 1973, when he was sixteen years old, Bowen was convicted of second-degree murder and malicious destruction of property after he threw a rock off an overpass and killed a passing driver. Bowen was sentenced to twenty-five years in prison but got out in twelve years on good behavior.

A known felon, Bowen received immediate attention from the police. Bowen refused to participate in a lie detector test, citing that such tests are inconclusive and often inadmissible. With no evidence or witnesses to tie Bowen to Melody's disappearance, police did not have any recourse.

In the weeks after the first public announcement about Melody, another potential suspect came to light. Forty-six-year-old Merrill Vaughn from Pullman, Michigan, injected himself into the case when he paid repeated visits to the Wynnes.

Vaughn was not a successful or talented man. His father, Lacey Vaughn, had run a large construction company, acquired property, and traded stocks, building a large fortune. Upon his father's death, Vaughn inherited his father's wealth and chose not to work a traditional job. Instead he claimed to be a psychic and made supplemental income by offering his services to tourists.

Days after Melody's disappearance, Vaughn arrived at the Wynnes' house, offering his psychic services to help find Melody. He claimed she was alive, that he had dreams of her. Two men from Chicago took her, he said, and he smelled ammonia when he channeled her. He suggested that Grace perform rituals at the lake, in the boathouse, at midnight. She complied. He asked for one of Melody's onesies. She complied.

After repeated attempts to learn more about Melody, Grace Wynne reported Vaughn to the police. Though an unusual man, he had no criminal background. Again, there was no evidence pointing to Vaughn's involvement except his unsettling, intrusive behavior.

While Bowen and Vaughn continued to be considered the primary persons of interest, police had nothing to tie either of them to the case besides uneasy feelings. If Campbell made the decision to arrest Bowen or Vaughn, he had to be prepared to go to trial within six months, adhering to Michigan's right to a speedy trial. He simply had no evidence to warrant an arrest.

Campbell would be remiss if he didn't investigate Grace and Jack Wynne as well. Campbell met with both parents the evening of the disappearance. Jack, normally a gregarious man, in his midthirties, had an alibi for the time of the disappearance: he was working with another staff member at the veterinary clinic he owned and operated out of Mapleton.

Grace, however, received more scrutiny as the caregiver at the time of the disappearance. Grace worked part-time for the Mapleton Arts Council, where she routinely booked artists to come to town and organized workshops and summer camps for children.

For her part, Grace Wynne's story held no inconsistencies. Yet still rumors would fly that she was involved in her daughter's disappearance and, many speculated, death. Some believed she had hidden Melody's body to cover up a boating accident. Other theories were more sinister: that she'd done it for insurance money to revive Jack's struggling veterinary practice.

But she didn't so much as flush when caught off guard, though her eyes narrowed each time she was asked a question she found offensive. She was fully cooperative and, Campbell believes, fully transparent and honest. The Wynnes have no history of abuse or mental illness in their family.

Outside of Abel Bowen, Merrill Vaughn, and the Wynnes, attention also focused on transients. Lake Chicora was not a popular tourist destination, but there were still out-of-towners who visited summer cottages on the weekends and visitors who used the boating access for fishing and water sports.

Part-time residents who lived on Lakeview Lane, typically wealthy Chicagoans eager for an escape, denied having been at their cottages on the Tuesday of the disappearance.

While a fishing license is required in Michigan, no conservation officers reported checking identification on Lake Chicora that week. Tracking visitors is impossible; the Trowbridge County sheriff relied on individuals to come forward if they were at the lake that day.

"It was a quiet day on the lake," said Lake Chicora resident Aimee Buttrell. "No motorboats, no Jet Skis. Hell, it was brutal—nearly one hundred degrees with the sun beating down on you. Even the fish were hiding. It had been like that for a few weeks. Thank God we don't rely on tourist money for anything. We wouldn't have had it that summer. It was too damn hot."

The investigation continued. With no other viable leads, Sheriff Wiesel, in his last order before retirement, announced that everyone in Cheshire was being asked to submit an alibi to rule out involvement in the abduction.

Refusal to comply was rampant. A meager fifty-four people of the estimated 1,800 men and women living in Cheshire submitted an alibi to the police. The debacle revealed no leads but succeeded only in violating the privacy of the citizens and turning the police, and by proxy the Wynnes, into public enemies.

26

Willa

One week before

I F WILLA HAD thought she would feel relief when she hit send, she was wrong.

Relief was never something she felt when she submitted an article. She'd published hundreds of articles since graduating j-school, and she only ever felt the sickening lurch of perfectionism fold over her. It could have been better, she knew; it always could have been better.

Yes, she liked the closure. She preferred to have projects finished, deadlines settled and met promptly. But the finality never brought her release from self-criticism.

This time was different. This time her publisher would call. She'd be more confused than angry, trying to figure out if a fact-checker by profession had gotten the details wrong.

Willa wouldn't answer the phone, of course. She let it ring endlessly now. Mostly it was the landlord calling about the rent, or Frenchie calling about a missed deadline. For a little while, it had been men calling: "I'm outside; open the door." The quickies helped with her anxiety until the numbness took care of that and she didn't need them anymore. So she'd let it ring and ring and ring.

She tapped her index finger on the computer mouse, thinking. She shoved aside the slow, deliberate stuttering exercises that crawled through her mind late at night. Her stutter's burden had lifted long ago—now she overenunciated with sharp, defined consonants, because taking a task to the extreme was how she operated—and she concentrated on the screen.

Maybe she should find a way to make sure the story got out, even if the publisher stopped production.

She didn't have much time, but for once, it didn't need to be perfect.

CHAPTER

27

Sawyer

WHEN MY CLASS begins at nine thirty and I'm not in the studio to lead it, I brace myself for a call from Kelly. Michigan becomes Indiana. Three lanes become one. Traffic comes to a grinding halt somewhere west of Portage.

I woke on Roberta's couch with tears in my eyes this morning. I didn't know it was possible to cry in your sleep, but since Willa's death, tears leak from my eyes in an uncontrollable way. It's not so much that I'm crying; I don't even know it's happening, like the way your eyes water when you look at the sun.

Between the morning sun's glare, the jackhammers, and the sleepless night, I feel a headache begin to thunder between my eyes. The familiar tinkle of an incoming call finally arrives, and I swipe without looking.

"'Lo?" I say as I suck on my teeth to relieve them of the furry brine coating my mouth.

"Good morning. I'm calling to speak with Sawyer Stannard."

"This is she," I squeak as I roll up the window to drown out the construction noise. With a flick of my wrist, I glance at the screen. Not a local area code.

"Sawyer, this is Gemma Matthews. I'm with Red Folio Literary Agency. Do you have a few minutes to talk?"

"Of course." I nod into the phone and punch up the volume with my thumb.

"Great, thanks for taking a moment to speak with me. First, I'd like to start by saying how sorry I am to hear about Willa's death. I understand she was your sister." She pauses. "Willa was a great talent, and I was looking forward to working with her. I thought I'd finally found my golden-child true crime author."

I smile into the phone as traffic inches forward. Gemma has said the first authentic thing about Willa that I've heard since her passing: that she was a good writer, and that Gemma would have benefited from Willa's life, not her death.

"I'm just now returning from maternity leave, so I apologize for not responding to your email sooner," she says.

The email. I sent it before I ever even made my first trip to Michigan. It seems so long ago now, though it's only been a couple weeks. I forgot about it.

"Willa submitted her final manuscript to me shortly before she died," she continues. "I am interested in publishing it posthumously, but that's not why I'm calling right now. What I would like to know is if she left behind any draft content, any notes, or any alternate writings that you may be able to send to me."

"Why would you need notes if she already sent you the final copy?"

"Our fact-checking department cannot validate the conclusion she submitted. We will, unfortunately, have to reject the manuscript and cancel publication if we can't confirm the ending she provided. I can't publish a story that may be contaminated."

"But Willa *was* a fact-checker. That's what she did at *TruthShout*. She wouldn't have sent inaccurate materials."

"I understand that. I'm as baffled as you. I'm not saying it's not true. Rather, I need evidence or notes to corroborate its validity."

I think of the times I've searched Willa's apartment for anything even suggesting that she was working on a book and come up empty-handed. What did she do with all her interview notes? Her recordings? Her drafts?

"There's nothing. I've been through her papers and digital files. She must have deleted everything before . . ." I trail off, remembering the way the boxes in Willa's closet were labeled and sorted with finality. As if she intentionally prepared for her death. I shake off the thought. Willa didn't kill herself. "In fact, I really need to read her manuscript myself. Can you send me a copy?"

Gemma is silent for a beat. "I'd have to check with our lawyers first. We may need Willa's next of kin or executor to sign an agreement. You understand, I'm sure."

If it's up to Momma, I'll never see that manuscript.

With a promise to keep looking for Willa's notes, I end the call with the agent.

Knowing that Willa submitted a final manuscript to her agent throws my mind into a tailspin. I knew she'd submitted a proposal, and Jack and Grace and Roberta all confirmed she'd been by their cottages for interviews. If she submitted her work, she wasn't just investigating: she had a conclusion. And if the publishing agency couldn't find validity to it, it meant she'd uncovered a new ending. Maybe a previously unreported clue.

I pound my fists on the steering wheel.

Something new. Something that would allow her to submit a conclusion other than *this case is still open*. Something that may have killed her.

* * *

Because she insists on closing the blinds during the day, and since she doesn't have a car to park between the privacy evergreens lining her asphalt driveway, it's almost impossible to know when my mother is home.

I drive straight to Hillside after Gemma's call. The wind has picked up, bringing with it the promise of afternoon rain. As I pass St. Cyril Cemetery, I see a half-dozen balloons dancing in the breeze, anchored to gravestones. I hate them. The way they pop like gunfire when they hit the trees in the cemetery, and the way others deflate into sad, drooping bubbles, infuriates me. Growing up, it was the only thing that made me angry, that I found offensive, that Willa did not.

Willa is still dancing in my mind, more haunting than the graveside balloons, when I knock sharply and turn the knob. The TV is blaring, as usual, and my mother is sitting in the darkened room watching an overly excited game show contestant humiliate herself for an appliance. I'm greeted by the musty floral scent my mother carries with her constantly. She smells like a dried-rose sachet that an old lady would leave in the drawer with her delicates. I once told the girls at the studio that my mother was a florist, and they asked if she could hook them up with bee pollen for their mango-banana fitness smoothies.

Her limp, wavy hair needs a cut, and her skin around her nose is bloodshot, as if she's been crying. Her swollen calves rest heavily on the extended footrest of the recliner.

"Oh," she says, fumbling with the remote as I come in. "I didn't know you were coming by, baby. I would have cleaned up some. I'm sorry it's such a mess in here."

It isn't, really. Plastic cups are scattered on the folding tray table near her chair, but none of them look like they're rimmed with the telltale red stain of the wine she liked so much when we were growing up. A blanket is crumpled on the couch. I shove it over to take a seat.

"You don't look so good, Sawyer," she observes, wringing her hands.

"I didn't sleep."

I came in ready to confront her about living at the lake, but the permanent worry in her eyes slows me down. She tends to find herself attracted to needy people, and needy people are attracted to her. There is something about my mother's tendency to worry and coddle and give unwanted advice that I find very comforting. Willa hated it; she said our mother felt bored and worthless if she didn't have a crisis to solve or a person to help, and she wouldn't volunteer her problems for our mother's compulsions. But I kind of like it.

She brings a hand to her mouth, hiding the deep grooves in her chin. She rubs her face nervously and watches me.

I pretend to look around the room thoughtfully. I try to force a light note into my voice. "How old was I when we moved into this house?"

Her hand stops rubbing. "Just a baby."

"Where did we live before moving here?"

"Not far," Claudia says.

Her response hardens my gaze. "Did we used to live on a lake in Michigan? Lake Chicora?"

"Where? Where would you get an idea like that?"

"Is it true?"

"No." She lifts an empty cup to her lips and tries to take a sip. She sets it back down and rubs her lips. It's something she does when she's nervous. She rubs till they're cherry red and lets them crack and split and bleed. "You're acting crazy," she adds.

"I'm not." I roll a bead on my necklace between my fingers. "I think Willa remembered it. She was going up to the lake to talk to people for the book she was working on. I think she chose that case because the baby who went missing was our neighbor."

Claudia hoists herself up from the chair on wobbly legs and lurches around the corner into the kitchen. I lean on the armrest of the couch to follow her with my eyes. She raises a can of diet soda to soothe her inflamed lips. When she turns, her arms hang heavily at her sides and her face sags.

"You need to drop this. Willa is dead, but you're still alive. I don't want you to do anything illegal or get arrested. I've lost a child. I will not lose another."

I feel my tense shoulders deflate. I know she's right. She keeps talking, and it's a familiar refrain: I need to find a husband. Start a family. Stop being so independent. Look where it got Willa.

As she talks, I think again of my old coworker Emily. When her brother died, she said, she never had to compete to be the favorite child again, but she had to be more perfect to prove to her parents that they didn't fail. But I refused to compete with Willa when she was alive. If I never finished a project or achieved a goal, my average work could never be compared to Willa's ambitious accomplishments. I wonder now if that will change once Willa's shadow recedes.

Claudia's voice dulls to a hum as I shift on the couch and my fingers run across the blanket. Silky stitches catch a jagged, bitten nail, and I look down. Sewn into the old blanket is a tiny bluebird.

It's the same arctic-blue thread and delicate stitches from the quilt at Grace Wynne's house.

CHAPTER

28

Sawyer

WILLA KEPT A book of lists.
Inspirational people. Inspirational quotes. Movies that made her think. Movies that made her laugh. Lists to add to her book of lists.

One of the lists was things she could control. Her thoughts, her honesty, her investments, her smiles: these were all things that made the list.

I made a list too. Mine included the amount of food I ate and how often I exercised. I kept it secret because counting calories and exercising until exhaustion overtakes you is shameful when you're in a public role in the fitness industry. Everyone wants to believe you're the healthiest, so you sip matcha tea and pressed juice and talk about plant-based meats and high-intensity interval training instead of admitting that you skip meals and, on bad days, lock yourself in the bathroom with water running to mask the sound of you purging the frozen yogurt you couldn't resist.

It flew in the face of everything I built myself to be. It sucked my energy and passion and creativity. All I thought about was sugar and calories and fat and protein. It controlled me.

As I climb the stairs to my apartment, I'm trying to place the last time I ate a good meal. I can't let myself become so scattered that I forget to eat, I remind myself.

"Drink some water, eat an egg, take a shower," I say to myself as I round the corner, thinking out loud. The list centers me. Keeps me from thinking about that tiny bluebird on the quilt, proof that my mother is lying.

I freeze.

There's someone waiting at my door.

My vision starts to blacken, and I wobble, stumbling into the wall. My knees crumple, and I drop to the ground. Everything goes black, but I can still hear. Someone is talking. A man.

I pass out.

* * *

I'm on my back. I try to raise my head, but it's too heavy. Voices hover over me. I open my eyes, blinking slowly.

Alma Ruiz stands over me, balancing her baby on her hip and talking rapidly into her cell phone. The baby is wailing. I try to sit up. She barks at me in Spanish. I don't know what she says, but I drop back to the ground.

Then I see him. Leo hovers nearby, rubbing his fingers over a skinny blue tie. His eyes are huge behind his glasses.

"Pregnant?"

It's Alma. I try to shake my head, but it hurts too much.

"Husband says girls faint when they're pregnant all the time. EMT," she says. Her neck is crooked to the side to hold her phone between her ear and her shoulder.

"I fainted?"

Leo approaches. His slender shoulders are hunched, birdlike, as he leans in.

"Let's get some food in you." His voice is quiet, but his eyes are resigned in a way that breaks my heart.

He thinks he just transferred to another Stannard, I think groggily. *He thinks he has to take care of me now.*

I want to shake his hand off my back to prove I can handle myself, but I feel weak, so I let him guide me to my door. Alma drifts back into her apartment without breaking stride in her string of Spanish to her husband on the phone. The baby wails, and she ignores him.

"When was the last time you ate?"

Leo ushers me inside, and I collapse on the couch with a groan.

"Did Willa tell you about my eating disorder? That was in college." I rearrange a pillow under my head and blink at him in the sunny room. "That's not why I fainted, anyway. It was you, at my door."

"The sight of me made you faint? I must be better-looking than I thought," he jokes. He perches on the edge of my assembly-required modernist desk, in the same spot the uniform sat when he came to tell me Willa had died.

With a yank, I untuck my blouse. Yoga pants may be unprofessional, but they're much better for surprise sleepovers at the cottage of an interview subject.

"It was the way you were standing at my door. When I turned the corner, I couldn't help but think of the police waiting for me to tell me Willa was dead."

"Oh, shit."

His face goes slick and pale behind his eyeglasses. Aware of the guilt he's feeling, I offer a weak smile.

"You couldn't have known. I'm sorry." There it is again. Claudia's apologetic nature is drilled into me to the core. "You're right, though. I could use some breakfast."

He brightens and unzips the messenger bag resting on his hip. Producing a small brown bag of bagels, he grins. "Not exactly a health food, but you look like you could use one."

I wiggle my fingers, and he tosses the bagel bag onto my chest. Untangling his messenger bag from his shoulders, he drops it on the ground and retreats into the kitchen, under the arched doorways and past the pressboard shelves. Before I moved in, I thought the building's vintage charm and the short walk to the Green Line El were enough to make me happy, but the lack of closets and ceiling fans made themselves known frighteningly fast.

Before all this, the galley kitchen hummed with life. Eating disorders were something to be battled, brawled with, conquered. I quit the soul-sucking sales job and started to job hop in search of something I could do with a burst of energy, not a commitment to the long haul. Job postings with the word *flexible* were my favorite; I rejected anything with routine and rules and rigidity. When I signed on with the cycling studio, I took up cooking as a hobby and vowed to stamp out my eating disorder. After that, the sink filled with a mess of pots and pans as I fought—until I forgot it was a fight. But now I feel myself backsliding, eating less, to control the pain and uncertainty. Taking on Willa's battle has sapped me of energy to care about my own.

Leo sees the empty cabinets as he hunts for a clean water glass. I want to tell him he doesn't have to save me with food to make up for not saving Willa from alcohol and depression.

"Are you running the marathon?" he calls.

A flyer is tacked to my fridge, next to the training schedule I created.

"It's in two weeks. I'm not ready," I say, biting into the gloriously cream-cheesy bagel.

He peeks around the corner. "Keep carb loading and you'll be fine."

I shake my head. "I don't have time to train."

"Aren't you only part-time at the studio?"

I never pegged Willa as a sharer, but she seems to have told Leo a lot about me. It was probably in the context of all the flaws in my life, and all the ways they made her even more motivated to achieve. Then I think that while she might have accomplished more than me, she stopped at thirty-three, and though I'm already twenty-eight, her achievements are now finite.

"I'm investigating a kidnapping and becoming a crime writer, remember?"

"Right." His tone is sarcastic, but he returns to his spot on the edge of the desk. "About that. I wanted to tell you what I found out from a staff writer at the local newspaper, the *Trowbridge Gazette*."

"You called the newspaper?"

He shrugs. "Basic detective work. There are four people on the staff. An editor, a staff writer, a sportswriter, and an advertising rep. They're too small to care about protecting their story or closing ranks on me. Most of their pieces are either obituaries or about high school baseball pitchers with good games. This case is a perennial piece for them. They write about it whenever there's an anniversary. Every year new tips flow in, new perspectives, but no advancement."

"So what do they know?" I ask through a mouthful of bagel.

"I asked about the parents, mostly. I know you went to see them, and I wanted to know if they're dangerous."

"Oh, Leo," I interrupt, swallowing. "They look like there's nothing more in life they'd like than to be grandparents by now. They're not dangerous."

"They're suspects in their daughter's case, even if you got the warm fuzzies from them," he says slowly.

I roll my eyes. I know Roberta pointed a finger at them too, but I think there's a better chance that Abel Bowen harmed Melody than that her parents did.

"The staff writer actually knew Grace Wynne personally. He said she used to work for the arts council, and she commissioned artists to bring sculptures to the river walk in town. She gave a good sound bite to the newspaper when she did publicity for the council."

"She sounds like a monster."

"And Jack," he continues, ignoring me, "used to own a veterinary practice before Melody went missing, but he had to sell it to one of his employees when he ran out of money after spending so much on private investigators."

"Being that this is a small-town reporter, I'm sure he had some gossip to share too," I prod, anticipating.

"There are rumors about them, no doubt. When you were there, did you see a boathouse?"

I picture the wooden structure with its aluminum roof and uneven planks crowded with lily pads and seaweed— the last place you'd want a freshly minted walker to toddle over to while you were distracted in the garden. I wince at the thought but nod.

"Well, he thinks the boathouse is the key to the whole thing. He says there was a scrap of fabric found nearby. Baby pink in color. He thinks the whole case could have been closed on that one piece of fabric. Says he remembered writing about it not too long ago when the police ran it for DNA. Tests came up negative, but the general consensus is that the parents covered it up and lied about the baby not missing any clothes. The *Gazette* believes the case lives and dies on that piece of fabric."

"I need to know what Willa thought about all this. I'm trying, Lord knows I am. But I'm no detective. My mind gets too scattered for me to put all this together. She would have known if that fabric was something or nothing."

"Have you been able to find her notes?"

I massage my now-pounding temples. I still feel weak from fainting. "I searched her computer and her email as best I could, but I didn't find anything worthwhile. I think she must have deleted the files. She didn't leave behind hard copies. But I know there must be reams of notes. Did I tell you she finished it?"

He furrows his brow, so I continue.

"She did. Her agent called me just this morning, asking for Willa's notes so she could verify the conclusion. Willa submitted a final draft. I think she uncovered something, Leo. She found an ending in all this uncertainty. Do you think the agent will give me a copy if I request it? It could be as easy as that, I guess. I can't believe I didn't think to ask."

"Maybe. But you're not Willa's executor, so they might not release it to you. It might go to your mom. Posthumous publication needs approval, I'm sure. You might get into contracts and monetary agreements and release of rights to get a copy." He thinks for a moment, tugging on his tie. "I could try to find a forensic tech to help locate the files on her laptop. Deleted doesn't mean gone in the tech world."

"How soon can you do that?"

"What's the urgency?"

"Willa's dead."

He nods slowly. "Yeah, exactly."

"I need to go back this evening. I need to talk to the Wynnes," I say, thinking of the revelation that we may have been their neighbors. I wonder if Leo knows this, if the newspaper writer told him. Property records can validate my suspicion. I decide not to tell him until I know for sure. I'm exhausted but wired, and I need to confirm at least one thing in this mystery. "I have to cover Ainsley's class this afternoon since she took my morning ride. Then I have to go back."

"Sawyer, Willa's dead," he repeats. "You don't need to kill yourself following in her footsteps." He cringes at his choice of words. "Sorry."

"The least I can do is try to find out what Willa knew. She found an ending, Leo. I can't describe it, but it feels like the clock is ticking. I don't have much time."

Before the ending finds me too, I finish in my head.

29

Sawyer

ON THE DRIVE back to Cheshire, I think about the irony of how the locals believe a fabric scrap that tested negative for DNA proves a case for foul play on behalf of the Wynnes, while I couldn't get the Chicago PD to take the unknown DNA found in Willa's apartment seriously in the investigation into her death.

Battling for a voice with the police is not only draining, it's heartbreaking. As I near the turnoff for the gravel road leading to the lake, I realize how much I have in common with the Wynnes. Aren't we both just fighting for recognition, for someone to acknowledge what we know to be true, deep in our guts? Jack and Grace have been fighting for nearly three decades to prove what they know to be a fact: that someone took their daughter. That they didn't do it. Now I'm trying to prove that a smart, motivated woman didn't take her life willingly. I hope I'm not still battling in thirty years.

Overnight, it became autumn. The warmest part of the summer is decidedly over; the air has lost its humidity and replaced it with wind. As I approach the lake, it doesn't smell as muggy and stagnant as it did earlier in the week.

The car bumps over the grooves and divots into the grassy clearing in front of the Wynnes' cottage. Two cars are parked side by side, and I realize that it's Saturday. Talking to Jack and Grace together seems like a risk. Grace, she doesn't seem objective enough to see through me. She's stuck in her memories. But Jack, he's more cynical.

He's pushing a lawn mower over the mix of clover and crabgrass that passes for a lakeside yard when I pull up. He eases the lever on the handle, and the mower shudders to a stop. He wipes his hands on his jeans as he approaches. His sweatshirt is tight over his round belly.

"My wife has been hoping you'd come back."

"I'm not here to talk about the evidence and the suspicions. Christine did all that. I'm just here to understand a little more about life in the aftermath of all this," I say, gesturing widely.

He rakes his thick fingers through his salt-and-pepper beard, considering. With a resigned nod, he leads me to the cottage, past a garden of dead and dying plants, beaten by the sun and wind and neglect and gnawed by the deer. A wet mustiness hangs over the abandoned plants. Grace stopped working in the garden after Melody went missing, I realize. She couldn't bear to go out here anymore, and doesn't that show her innocence?

But I warn myself against catching a judgment and getting attached. If I consider the case against the Wynnes closed, I've failed Willa.

Before the door closes, I dart my gaze to the house next door. Does it have a garden? If we'd lived there, wouldn't my mother have left behind a floral legacy?

The screen swings shut with two rackety bangs, and I think of Merrill Vaughn visiting this vulnerable family. Am I any better?

Grace is wearing her red eyeglasses and scouring a stack of dog-eared photos in various sizes. She looks up when I enter, and the deep furrows in her brow are replaced by cautious warmth.

She insists on making tea and ushers me to the same seat as before, facing the picture window with the view of whitecaps dotting the choppy lake and the baby swing waving in the willow tree.

"Tell me, dear. How's Christine doing?"

I hesitate. Naively, I hoped they'd forget to ask about Willa. "She's recovering," I say. I take too large a sip of tea to avoid saying more, then cough when it scalds my tongue.

"I told Jack that I want to hear about what happened after Melody went missing, but not necessarily about the suspects or the evidence," I continue.

"You want to hear about the heartbreak, then," Grace says simply.

I glance between them, already nervous that Grace's blunt anguish will cause Jack to ask me to leave before I can steer the conversation toward the neighbor family. To my surprise, he nods.

"It was heartbreaking, the way the disappointments mounted after Melody's disappearance," he agrees. "The inability to pin the case on anyone, the constant reminder of Abel Bowen living down the road, the false leads from other psychics through the years . . ." He ticks off on his fingers. "Paramount to all of that, the knowledge that Melody would be older, less recognizable, every year, if she did live."

"Our community ostracized us," Grace adds. "I used to be so involved in community events and the arts. It really hurt when they turned against us."

"But they supported you at first, right? What happened to change their perception?"

"I call it the JonBenét effect. When the Ramsey case went public a few years after Melody was kidnapped, the town didn't believe us anymore."

I nod thoughtfully and sip the Lipton tea. I always thought the parents brought harm to their beauty queen daughter too. I'm just as bad as everyone who suddenly blamed the Wynnes.

"By the late nineties, we didn't have any allies. I lost my support system just days after Melody disappeared. My friend, our next-door neighbor, moved away without notice. It was almost too much for me to lose at the same time. I don't think I even realized she was truly gone until a few weeks later."

Here it is. My opening. The neighbor. I open my mouth to interject, to find out if it could have been my family, but Jack interrupts first.

"We were attacked when we couldn't pull ourselves together to make a coherent appeal for our daughter, and we were criticized for our callousness when we could. We were powerless. We thought about contacting John Walsh from *America's Most Wanted* to request publicity for the case but decided against it, which was something the public was highly critical about, in retrospect. We didn't want our daughter's abduction to be sensationalized. You know, AMBER alerts weren't created until a few years later. Could they have saved Melody? We'll never know," he says. "Every few years the police release an age-progression photo, which they run in that forsaken newspaper on the anniversary in August. It's a sober reminder about what could have been."

I look toward the smiling faces of countless children plastered to the walls of their house. They are grieving for a toddler, yes, but also for all the potential her life held.

"She could be alive somewhere. She could return. It's not unheard of. Elizabeth Smart, Jaycee Dugard—they were reunited with their families," Grace says. The desperation in her voice makes me lose eye contact. I stare into my mug of tea.

"She could have Stockholm syndrome, or she could have been sold. She was a beautiful baby," Grace adds, voicing the kind of dark speculations that give way to sleepless nights.

"It'd be better if she was dead." Jack crosses his arms over his belly and leans back into the couch. He has flecks of mowed grass dotting his sweatshirt, replacing the pet hair from the last time I visited. "I don't wish a life of imprisonment or shattered innocence on my baby," he says resolutely.

Grace bows her head and rubs her thumb across the glossy photo in her hand as if she's caressing the cheek of her baby, lulling her to sleep.

"We have to live with the fact that we'll never know," Jack declares. "The unanswered questions are an unquenchable grief."

Is this what Willa dealt with every day as a reporter? Did she stare sorrow and heartache in the face and then synthesize it into a palatable story, sticking to her word count and leaving out the emotions?

"So the question remains: Who took her?" I ask, steering them away from their pain but into equally dangerous territory.

"The real problem isn't who took her, it's when they took her," Jack says. "If the day comes when I can accept that Melody was kidnapped, it will still haunt me that it happened before we could rely on technology to find her. Now there's facial recognition. With artificial intelligence, no one's just a face in the crowd anymore. Amusement parks use it. Law enforcement uses it. They're thinking about installing it on all the street corners in Chicago. Who cares about privacy if it could find someone's baby? Even genealogy sites are helping to solve cases and reunite families."

"But Melody was so young when she was kidnapped. Would that technology have even helped?"

"It could have. And isn't that enough?"

"We've always known that exposure could lead to finding our baby. But at a certain point the police started to call it 'Melody's recovery.' They thought she was dead. He thought she was dead," Grace says, nodding at Jack. "But I know she's out there."

"That's why Grace took that girl in so easily." There's animosity in Jack's voice.

I realize I'm biting my nails. I drag the jagged edge of one across my pants like a saw, filing away at the serrated piece left behind, trying to smooth it out. Once, my mother paid me ten dollars to stop biting my nails. Scared we wouldn't love her if she disciplined us, she instead bribed Willa and me with small bills when she wanted us to change our behavior. I clamp my hand between my thighs.

"What girl?" My voice is muffled as I lift the mug to my lips. The tea is lukewarm now, but measured sips keep my fidgeting at bay.

"Lochlyn Farmer," Jack supplies. "She came forward years ago, claiming to be our daughter, after seeing a segment on TV with an age-progression photo that resembled herself. We took her in. It was stupid, but all we had to go on was that photo. It's not like Melody could talk or have memories we could validate. We were conned."

"We had to start all over again with no daughter," Grace says. "She was lost. She was part of our family, and we loved and accepted her."

"She was a con," Jack repeats, his voice stiff and angry. "She wasn't our daughter."

I make a mental note to find Lochlyn Farmer. Maybe she picked up on something while she lived with the Wynnes that could open up the case. Willa would have sought her out, I'm sure.

"That was just one more of the disappointments that continued long after Melody was gone. The false hope of someone claiming to be our daughter," Jack says, adding another tick to his growing list. "Not to mention the unanswered questions that Merrill Vaughn's death left."

We're all quiet for a moment. I don't want to say anything about Vaughn that might set Grace off. I know she considered him the main suspect. I contemplate their comments. They seem candid, not self-serving. Would they have protested more loudly, to counteract their guilt, if they had something to do with Melody's disappearance?

How do you know when someone's telling the truth?

And if I get to the end, and Melody's still missing and Willa's still dead, does it even matter?

Cry of the Cicadas: The True Story of Melody Wynne's Disappearance

Field Notes

Mapleton Sheriff's Office, Investigative Services Unit
Field Notes
Date: 08/04/1992
Time: 10:38 P.M.
Compiled by Deputy Corbin Campbell

I arrived at 4618 Lakeview Lane at 3:24 P.M., eighteen minutes after the call came in from dispatch. Upon arriving at the house, I met with Grace Wynne, who was flushed and sweating. She was able to speak coherently and showed me around the house. I did not observe any rips or tears in the screen door, and the handle and lock appeared to be in good working order. I observed several open windows around the house, all with undamaged screens. I saw that Grace's knees were streaked with dirt, and a rubber kneeling pad and hand shovel were visible in the garden, possibly corroborating her story that she was working in the garden prior to discovering Melody missing.

Melody's room appeared to be undisturbed. Grace recalls that Melody was wearing only a diaper during her nap due to the heat. She did not see any missing clothes. She did note that Melody's favorite toy, a doll with a rubber face, soft body, and rabbit ears, was missing. She called the doll "Jammie Pie."

After speaking with Grace, I knocked on the neighbors' doors to see if they saw or heard anything. At the house next door, a young woman in her early thirties answered. She was wearing a checkered blouse and jean shorts. I established that she had two little girls in the house with her, both sleeping in a shared bedroom. I asked her what she saw that afternoon leading up to the kidnapping, and she said she saw nothing, as she had spent the afternoon indoors with her daughters. I found that unusual, since the house was sweltering hot and she did not appear to have a working air-conditioning unit. The windows were open at the time of our meeting, so I inquired what she may have heard. Again she denied any knowledge of suspicious activities leading up to the crime.

I asked to speak with her older daughter, age seven, to find out if she witnessed anything. The neighbor denied me the option to speak with her. I did not find out anything of value that could lead to the recovery of Melody Wynne in my visit to the neighbor's house.

CHAPTER

30

Sawyer

WHAT I LOST when Willa slit her wrists was a chance to revive our relationship, but what Jack and Grace lost when Melody disappeared was the future.

And so, when the car bounces down the gravel road, deeply grooved from a heavy overnight rainfall that brought today's wind, I think about how their grief is so much bigger, so much more deserved than mine.

Willa and I shared a room and a mother, but that was about it. Responsible and ambitious, Willa should have been a dream child, but she was combative, fiery. The more she talked back, the more obedient I became. She was whip smart, smarter than our mother. Her behavior was a harpoon in our mother's loyalty-loving chest, and it cemented me as my mother's pet. I had a gnawing desire to be the daughter Willa refused to be. It bothered her. One time she told me, "We're sisters. We don't need to be binary."

If she lived, we might have met in the middle. We might have been friends.

It's different for Jack and Grace. They didn't have a chance to compromise their hopes with reality. They lost every scraped knee, every lie, every bad grade and bad choice in men. They lost every chance to make up with Melody, because they never got a chance to see her live.

Loss crowds my mind as I bump down the road. Then a thought breaks through: I forgot to ask Jack and Grace about their neighbor. "Damn," I say aloud, pounding a fist on the steering wheel.

I hit the brake to ease the car off the gravel onto the pavement, where the dense trees give way to unmanned cornfields, weedy yellow flowers, and cattails.

My head swivels to check for oncoming traffic even though the cutoff is isolated, and a flash of movement catches my eye. I keep my foot on the brake and peer closer.

There. In the reedy cattails. A man.

His limbs are folded in on themselves as he crouches in a ditch. If not for the wind whipping the cattails, I might not have seen him. His hair is wild, unbrushed. He's wearing a stained shirt over his bony shoulders. His eyes are wide and unblinking. He looks as if he's being hunted, not lying in wait.

I'm only a few feet away from him, but he doesn't stand, and he doesn't lift a hand in a wave. We lock eyes. I try to calculate his age from his weathered face. *It's him*, I realize. Abel Bowen.

A shiver sends goose bumps up my arms. I tear my eyes away and stamp on the gas pedal, hard, and lurch onto the pavement fast enough to send a dusty cloud in the air.

I take back every doubt I had about Jack and Grace and even Merrill Vaughn. If that's Abel Bowen, he certainly looks the part of a bushy-haired former felon that you wouldn't want living near your children. Forget the danger of making a judgment in a case like this; it's more dangerous not to scrutinize Abel Bowen for his part in Melody's kidnapping. At first, I couldn't believe he could outsmart the authorities, until it hit me: the thing he's smartest about is the woods, and the dense tree cover he roamed since childhood is the getaway vehicle of this case.

I race down the road, past the occasional ranch and a barn and a steepled church and a burned-out convenience store. There are no stoplights or even stop signs. I take hairpin turns without slowing and don't meet any vehicles when a sign warns me to yield.

What's he doing, hiding in the cattails and weeds, watching cars pass by?

I'm the only car, I realize. Only a handful of people live down the one-way dirt road. He was waiting for a glimpse of me.

I pass signs for a wool farm and Camp Kiskitowa. Another lake and another church until finally a stoplight announces that I've made it into town. The downtown area is charming, all brick-faced buildings with striped awnings and chipped white paint on turn-of-the-century window frames. Locust Street is lined with shops that, improbably, have stayed in business in this sleepy town. There's a newsstand and a barber, a pharmacy and a Curves. City hall is nestled between an antique shop and a Pizza Hut. Parking is abundant, and I pull into a spot behind a light post with an American flag attached.

The doors to city hall are flanked by two pots of colorful chrysanthemums. Nothing special, my mother would have said, but they add charm to the concrete-and-glass facade that screams endurance, the same way bank architecture used to resemble an impenetrable fortress to symbolize wealth and worth.

A woman with a rouge-streaked face the color of a bruised peach looks up from her computer screen as I enter. She offers a friendly smile as she folds her hands and plops her heavy breasts atop them on the desk.

"How can I help you today?"

"Hi," I say. "I'm looking for information on address records."

"That would be the register of deeds. Records, land contracts, mortgages, liens, and lease agreements," she lists in an adenoidal voice.

"Perfect. Who should I speak to?"

"That would be me, honey," she says with a laugh. "I'm the one-woman shop for all city records and voter registration. What's the address, dear?"

"Four six two zero Lakeview Lane, in Cheshire." I feel my cheeks flame as the woman pecks at the keyboard with shiny metallic nails. I think of the old A-frame house on the lake and wonder if this woman will tell me my mother lied to me.

"That property is currently unoccupied." She turns from the screen and sizes me up, no doubt taking in my cherubic face and buttery blond hair that make me look younger than twenty-eight. "You interested in moving in there, hon?"

My cheeks burn brighter, and suddenly I wish I had her peach blusher to hide the guilt coursing through my body.

"Does it say who owned the property last?" I ask, guessing that it's been unoccupied since news of the kidnapping surfaced.

"That would be a Mr. Morris J. Stannard. Owned the property from 1978 to 1993."

Stannard.

The room tilts for a moment. I wonder if I'm going to faint again. I lean forward to rest my hands on her desk. I'm steadying myself, but the clerk must think I look conspiratorial. She looks around the empty lobby and tucks a fist under her chin.

"Morris was a drunk. Abusive. He let his poor niece Claudia live in that house in exchange for her silence. A lot of us suspected he was up to no good, but there wasn't much we could do to help back in those days," she says, lowering her voice to a gossipy stage whisper. "Three other girls from the community pointed the finger at him but didn't file charges. Back then it was just a he-said-she-said. Now they've got those DNA kits, at least."

I blink at her, uncomprehending. Claudia. My mother.

I raise a hand to my mouth while I rearrange my face into what I hope is an unreadable mask. It's what Willa would have done. Filed it away and continued on, only to pick it apart and analyze it later, alone.

"That's unfortunate," I choke in my best professional voice. "Say, can you do a sort of reverse address lookup as well? If I give you someone's name, could you tell me where she lives?"

"The name?" Her fingers arch like a cat's claws over the keyboard. She's disappointed I don't engage in her gossip, but she's not ready to turn me away yet.

"Lochlyn Farmer."

Her fingers jump but don't hit the keys for a moment while she traces the name through her brain. She begins to type and tosses a furtive glance my way, now even more curious to know who I am and why I'm asking about someone as undoubtedly infamous as the fake Melody Wynne, recovered.

Lochlyn may have intimate knowledge of the crime, since she immersed herself in the lie that she was the missing girl. I need to talk to her, if only to get another opinion about the Wynnes and to see if she knew anything about Abel Bowen. The image of him crouching in the cattails at the roadside flashes through my mind, and I shake my head to dissolve the way his eyes bore into mine.

"Lochlyn doesn't have a registered address on file. But I can tell you that she works at the Saddle Creek Inn in Grand Junction."

"Thank you, that's helpful." I avoid the woman's curious gaze and paw through my purse for my wallet. I pull out a twenty and place it on her desk gingerly. "For your help."

She looks at the bill disapprovingly.

Shit. I just made myself look even more suspicious.

"Have a good night," I call as I turn on my heel and throw my weight to open the heavy door.

There's still enough light to get to Saddle Creek Inn tonight. Maybe I'll get lucky and Lochlyn will be working. I rummage through my bag for the keys and press the button to release the locks. My fingers are reaching for the door handle when I stop. I back up slowly and crane my neck to look at the bumper more closely.

The license plates have been stolen.

31

Sawyer

I S IT A threat? A warning? Or just a punky teenager amused by the novelty of stealing Illinois plates?

Though the car was locked, it feels violated when I ease into the warm leather seat. I lock myself in and scan the street. Tampering with someone's plates is probably a crime, but I'm not sure I want to announce my presence and my real name to the police just yet.

The phone catches a signal in this downtown strip, so I thumb to the navigation map and type *Saddle Creek Inn*. It's a good forty-minute drive west, past the lake and the brush hiding Abel Bowen.

As I swing the car in reverse and bump over the brick-paved road leading out of town, I wonder if Willa interviewed Abel before she died. He's key to the case, so I have no doubt she tried, at the very least. Could she have written the book without his perspective? Maybe. Merrill Vaughn was just as critical a suspect as Abel, and she didn't get to interview him before sending her manuscript off for publication. It's unsettling to imagine Willa tromping through the woods to Abel's old farmhouse for an interview. If she found out something that tied him incontrovertibly to Melody's kidnapping, could he have found a way to kill her in her apartment?

I stay focused on thoughts of Abel and Willa to avoid the thing I most want to turn over in my mind: my mother's past and her lies.

Recasting her as a victim is easy. Her dependency and her self-esteem and her nerves. Check, check, check. Her erratic reactions. Check. I think of the way her eyes beg for love above her ruddy cheeks. I think of how her limp hair and sloppy weight problems are embarrassing, but I feel protective of her when I see others judging her. I think of her musty floral smell and I want to slide under her heavy arm on the couch like I used to do as a kid. She demanded uncontested love and constant reassurance, and I've always been happy to give them to her.

My feelings battle between sorrow for the abuse she's endured and fury that I had to find out like this. I guess that's what grief is, though: mourning and rage, all packaged up with passion.

* * *

Like most spots in this area, the Saddle Creek Inn, I realize quickly, is not a destination for girls' trips or overnight visits to the wine trails. I park in an unmarked, unlined clearing beside an old caboose railcar. A faded barn-red sign announces it's a relic from the nineteenth century, when the town was little more than a spot where two now-defunct railway lines met.

Six tiny cabins are scattered about the grounds, with a main building near the caboose. A wood-burned sign announces that the building is the inn's reception. I swat away a mosquito as my sneakers crunch on the weedy gravel leading to the building. They don't spray poison out here like they do at home.

To call it a lobby is a stretch. A handmade sign announces, *Ask us about blueberries!* next to the wooden desk, which bears an old metal bell and a rack of guides about local hiking trails and kayak outfitters. There's a breakfast nook to the right and an enclosed porch to the left, which overlooks a wooded expanse and a creek running through the property.

A lantern-jawed man with a toothpick hanging out of his mouth sits on the porch. He turns his head when I enter but doesn't stand up.

"Help you?" He has the kind of face you'd call a mug.

I take a tentative step toward him onto the all-weather carpeting lining the porch. Barbs of wicker have started to poke out from the worn chairs, which humbly bear flattened floral seat cushions.

"Do you have any cabins available for the night?"

He shifts the toothpick with his tongue as he evaluates me. I glance around, hoping a motherly innkeeper, someone like Roberta, will bustle in.

"Just the one night?"

I nod.

"Most stay for the week."

I bite my lip and press my palm against my thigh to keep it from fluttering the way it does when I get nervous.

"Just the one night, sir."

"Sir," he scoffs, and the toothpick falls from his lips. He leaves it resting in the folds of his shirt.

I take a step back. I hinge at the waist and rest my elbows on the reception desk as I peer around the lobby.

"Where's your overnight bag?" His gravelly voice is a mix of lazy and biting. I realize that men who have lived out here their whole lives might find a young single woman traveling alone threatening to the status quo. I'm not in liberal Chicago.

"It's in the car," I reply. *And it's none of your goddamn business*, I finish in my head. I ring the forest-green bell twice, and my heart quickens.

A young girl emerges at the sound of the bell. Her wide, pregnant stomach is at odds with her elfin face.

"You need a room?"

I nod tightly. "Just one night."

She tucks a strand of shoulder-length hair from her overgrown bob behind her ear. Her fingernails are short and unpainted. She looks younger than I expected, but I'm sure it's her.

"Are you . . . Lochlyn Farmer?" I ask as she pushes a wooden key chain with the number six on it across the desk.

Her dark eyebrows rise in surprise, then fall in instant weariness.

"Can I talk to you? About your time living with Grace and Jack Wynne?" I lower my voice, but it's useless; the man is only a few feet away, and he doesn't bother to pretend he's not listening.

Her eyes travel to him, and they regard each other silently for a moment before she sighs and drops her shoulders in resignation. She leads me into the adjacent room that functions as a breakfast nook. A rolling cart houses single-serve boxes of cereal and a few empty plastic juice pitchers. I guess in the morning Lochlyn is responsible for setting out a plate of microwaved bagels for the cabin guests.

She's not wearing maternity clothes. Her jeans have rhinestones on the back pocket, and her T-shirt isn't long enough to hide the stretchy fabric she sewed above the waist. She lowers her bedazzled bottom into one of the mismatched, scarred wooden chairs. I take a seat across from her.

"I suppose you want to know why I did it." Her voice is tight, and I see now that she's perspiring and her hands look swollen.

"If you'll tell me, yes. But I mostly want to know what you learned while you were there."

"What I learned?"

I rub my hands across the table, smoothing the plastic floral tablecloth. "What you thought of Grace and Jack," I say. "What you heard while you were their daughter."

Lochlyn leans back in her chair and rests her hands across her belly. "I lived with them for three weeks. I probably could have stayed longer if their cop friend hadn't insisted they take a paternity test to prove I was theirs."

"Detective Campbell?"

She puckers her pug nose and nods, sending her fine hair slipping out from behind her ear. "I didn't have to do much of anything to convince them I was Melody. If not for that paternity test, I'd probably still be there today." She glances down at her stomach. "Well, maybe not."

"What did you have to do?"

"Nothing. Look like what they thought she might have grown up to be, I guess. She was so young when she left home that she didn't have any memories of them. There was nothing they could test me on."

She didn't exactly leave home, I think. *She wasn't a sullen teenager.*

"Besides your DNA," I finish.

She shrugs. "I didn't think of that, obviously. I was desperate. I had just been arrested—again—in Muskegon. I saw the story on TV, and I just . . . showed up. I'd seen them, and their house, and the lake, for so many years, I felt like I knew them. I'd heard Melody's story on TV three, four times a year, for as long as I could remember. It was stupid, but I thought that if I could just *be* her, it would solve both our problems. I thought I was doing good."

"And they took you in, just like that." I tug on a loose strand of hair, thinking. "Where did you tell them you'd been all that time?"

Lochlyn sighs. "I told them two men brought me to Chicago, just like the psychic said on the news years ago. It was exactly what they expected, so they didn't even question it." She looks down and twists the tablecloth between her bloated fingers. "Well, the cop did. He questioned everything. But by then, the whole thing just kind of blew up in my face anyway."

"So what was it like living there for those three weeks?"

"They let me sleep in her room. It still had a crib and changing table and everything. Little tiny dresses hanging in the closet. Stuffed animals in a bin. They took that all out and got me a bed. I still feel kind of bad about that, but they had made it into a shrine for her. It wasn't good for them, you know?" she says, her voice going high. "It's like there's an expiration date on when it's okay to keep a dead kid's room the same, and they blew past it. I almost feel bad telling you this, but Grace's car still had a baby seat strapped in the back. More than twenty years later. How messed up is that?"

I think of Willa's apartment and the ticking clock of unpaid rent and a broken lease agreement. I'll have to clean it out fast, before October is up. There's no time to build a shrine when you rent.

"So you think Melody—the real Melody—is dead?" I ask, catching on her words.

Lochlyn rubs her belly and seems to deflate deeper into the hard chair. "By now? Yeah, I do think she's dead. For what it's worth, I don't think Grace and Jack did it."

"Why do you say that?"

"Isn't it obvious?" she says, her eyes going wide in her delicate face. "Just the way they were willing to take me in. It means they weren't covering anything up."

I tap my fingers on the tabletop. "I could argue just the opposite. That they embraced you so quickly because it proved they were never at fault in the first place. It repaired their reputation in the public's eye."

"Then why make me take a paternity test?" she challenges. "Why not forget it and let me live there till I turned eighteen?"

I consider it. It still helps their reputation and the rumors about their involvement if Lochlyn turned out to be a fraud, I decide.

"So let's say she is dead," I say as I lean forward on my elbows, getting a little too close to Lochlyn. "What do you think happened to her?"

"God, there were so many crackpot theories about what happened to Melody. I grew up not far from here. I heard them all. The creepy criminal down the street, that psychic fraud, the parents, of course . . . even the melonheads."

"Melonheads?"

"The Michigan Monsters," she smiles ruefully. "Story goes, this group of inbreds gave birth to a bunch of kids who had these enormous heads. Like, giant. So they were shipped off to this insane asylum for sick experiments. Then, one night, they escape." She floats her hand, palm side out, in front of her face, as if she's performing a magic trick. "They scatter into the woods. You can occasionally see them roaming the woods still, mostly on rainy nights. It happened not that far from here. I've never seen them, but we used to get drunk and drive out by the woods in Holland to catch a glimpse."

"Sounds reliable."

"Look," Lochlyn says pointedly, resting an elbow on the table. Our faces are inches apart, like we're best friends sharing secrets. Sisters. I lean back when that familiar pang of loss thrums in my chest.

"You've got to understand this area. I can tell you're not from here." She's eyeing my leather shoulder bag. "Grand Junction, Cheshire, Mapleton . . . we're all poor. We're near nothing. Nothing to do, nothing to see. This is backwoods country."

"I get that," I say.

"I don't think you do. The news comes in, and they want to write about a missing baby. They don't understand what it's like here, so they focus on all the wrong things."

Like how it's not normal to hide in the cattails watching passing cars?

"You know Bowen?" she asks, and I nod. "Okay, so he hunts game. Hunters are a dime a dozen in Michigan, but the news made a big deal out of it. How he hunts for food. Then they took it a step further and said maybe he's the next Hannibal Lecter. But everyone here hunts. Russ hunts and eats it." She hooks a finger at the man still watching us from the porch. "It would be irresponsible not to."

"So you think Abel Bowen is just your run-of-the-mill hunter, not a suspect."

"Hell no! I think that bastard took her and kept her in the basement of his creepy old farmhouse."

"Like, she's still there?"

"Probably dead by now. Bowen is crazy. I used to know this girl, her name was Corinne. Her father built her a painting studio in the woods. She went out there a few times, but Bowen kept creeping around while she was painting. She stopped going, and eventually her dad sold their cottage and they moved to Dutch Lake." She leans forward and lets her belly dangle as she itches her foot, sliding it out of her rubber flip-flop. Her voice is muffled when she speaks. "Bowen is messed up. He literally lived in the walls of that house."

I wait for her to right herself. Her cheeks are flushed from the effort of the itch.

"That sounds like another urban legend, like the melonheads."

"It's not," she insists. "Everyone knows his mom used to lock him in the basement, and he hid in the walls. I heard that there was this hidden compartment built into the walls to hide liquor during the prohibition. The farmhouse is that

THE THREE DEATHS OF WILLA STANNARD 213

old. Anyway, he used to hide inside the walls as a kid. One day they'll find Melody Wynne in the basement of that creepy house too."

I twirl the key ring around my finger. Lochlyn's just like Justine, full of rumors but very little truth. I wonder how Willa extracted enough from these people to write a nonfiction book. Then again, the book's under scrutiny for its validity, so maybe she didn't get to the truth after all.

"It's getting late. I should check out my room." I push back from the table.

"They're not just rooms, they're cabins. Better than a motel," she offers.

"Thanks for your time tonight. I didn't think I'd be lucky enough to find you here."

She barks a laugh and nearly topples the table as she presses her weight on it to stand. "First time someone's been lucky to see me."

"I just . . ." I pause, thinking of the right words. Even though she's a liar, she looks like she can handle the truth. Appreciate it, even. "I just thought that you'd leave this area after what happened with the Wynnes."

Lochlyn slides her hands into her rhinestoned pockets. "Those who settle here never leave."

I cast a glance at the pock-faced man still watching us. He's redeposited the toothpick between his grooved lips. The setting sun shadows half his face, turning one side twilight purple; the side facing the window flames a golden orange.

If the furniture isn't bolted down, I'm going to slide it in front of my cabin door.

"Hey," Lochlyn calls.

I stop beside the blueberry sign and glance back at her.

"Don't forget. The walls of that house: that's where they'll find her."

32

Sawyer

Lochlyn's warning is still on my mind as I unlock the door to cabin six. I'm greeted by a full-size bed, a television leaning dangerously far forward, and a tile floor in need of a good mopping. It's not much, but it's better than Roberta's couch.

The comforter isn't one of those slick ones the low-cost chains use, and definitely not one of the fluffy white ones the boutique hotels let you luxuriate on. It's a faded quilt etched with ducks and foliage. I cringe as I perch on the corner, conscious of all the people who have come before me.

I thumb through my phone as I rummage through my overnight bag for a snack. Eight missed calls from my mother. I can almost hear the breathy panic that films her voice when I don't answer the first time. I'll call back when I get home.

The messages from Cami and Ainsley have slowed in the six weeks since Willa's death. Now that they're no longer frantic to check up on me and be near tragedy, our texts have become more businesslike and infrequent. I'm gutted when I realize that their lives, everyone's lives, carry on as they did before Willa died. I can't bring myself to respond to their texts with the ferocious speed required to stay on their social radar. Keeping up with the girls at the studio is a full-time job. I once visited Ainsley's parents' house and saw that they not only had a harp and an indoor tanning bed, but they left envelopes of money for her around the house, like a rich kid's treasure hunt. It cost time and money and dedication to grooming to be close with the studio girls, and all of those are in short supply at the moment.

There's a text from Leo, though. *Good news. Tech can check out Willa's PC. Pick up tomorrow?*

Thumbs-up emoji. *Chances he can find her manuscript?* I write. I toss a tahini-and-carrot-powdered kale chip in my mouth. *Eat so you don't go crazy,* I say to myself in a singsong voice. And I laugh, because food is the one thing that makes me most unhinged.

His reply is instant. *Deleted, hidden, encrypted, yes. Overwritten w/ extraction software or if she destroyed the magnet in the hard drive that stores data, no. Wouldn't put it past her.*

True. Willa knew how to keep a secret.

My thumb whips through icons on my phone after I read Leo's message. There's so little to do on a phone once you delete Instagram, but I can't face the unprompted reminders of Willa's life and death. I know I need to hit the green icon in the corner and report the license plates missing. I crunch on another chip while I look for something to delay me. Finally I punch the button and wait for the ring as the phone searches for a signal.

"Police, please."

* * *

Detective Corbin Campbell shows up nearly an hour later. I wonder what I pulled him away from. A petty theft? Drug possession? Land dispute?

He's stocky in his black uniform, and a silver watch weighs down his wrist. I remove the nightstand barricade from the door to let him in, but he hovers in the doorway. In this light, I can see him much better than I could the night he pulled up behind Justine and me. His short-cropped hair is brown, with a growing patch of gray at the temples, and he has what looks like a permanent frown line creasing the skin between his eyebrows. He smells like soap.

"Do you want to see the car?" I ask, shuffling my feet back into sneakers while trying to hold the door open with one hand.

"It's the black Audi with missing plates."

"Right, um, do you want to get a closer look?"

I glance past him to see there are two pickup trucks parked near Willa's car, both rusted in the forgotten way of a place where time slows and newness ceases to matter. The sedan looks glaringly out of place. Newness still mattered to Willa.

He doesn't so much shake his head as crook his neck to the side. "I've got enough to make a report," he says.

"Oh, okay. Do you, um, need more info from me, then?" I'm still holding the door open for him, but if he comes inside, we'll have to sit side by side on the bed. There are no chairs in the cabin, just a bed, a nightstand, a dresser, and a small bathroom with a stained and peeling tub.

He slides a spiral-top notebook from his pocket and flips it open at a languid pace. A moth bangs stupidly at the fixture beside the door, the light casting Campbell's face in shadow. His watch is too big, out of place for him and this town. I wonder if it bears an inscription behind the face. *With love on our 25th anniversary,* I imagine. Something from an eager housewife excited to spend his government salary on an ostentatious gesture.

"For my records, please confirm your name, miss. Is it Sarah?" He looks up without expression. "Or Sawyer?"

I swallow. This was a mistake. I wedge the toe of my shoe below the door and let it crush my toes while I think. Now I know he's trying to make me uneasy, standing in the door. It's a tactic to put me on edge.

"It's Sawyer," I croak. I'm positive Willa never let herself get found out so quickly when she went undercover.

"And Sawyer, do you have documentation to prove that the vehicle in question belongs to you?" A blank expression sweeps over his face, and he maintains eye contact while the silence between us grows.

"I'm borrowing it. From a friend," I say weakly, eager to fill the void with words.

"The vehicle that you're driving, and its missing plates, are both registered to a Ms. Willa Stannard of Chicago, Illinois. Ms. Stannard just recently passed away, is that right?"

I ruined everything by calling him, I realize. He'll tell Grace and Jack and maybe even Roberta. They'll shut me out, and I won't be able to find out what Willa knew.

"Look," I say, straightening. "Detective . . . I'm trying to retrace Willa's footsteps before she died. I want to learn about her last year with the hope that, maybe, I can solve the mystery of her death." I was never much good at lying.

Campbell eyes me with the gaze of a man who's accustomed to feigning simplicity while retaining everything. He catalogs and processes me.

"I heard it was ruled as death by suicide," he says finally, after letting the silence stretch unbearably long—an interrogation technique, no doubt.

"How do you know so much about my sister?"

He widens his stance. Another power move. I stretch my spine until I'm as tall as my five-five frame will allow, and I plant my feet wider too.

"An investigative reporter comes into my town to solve a crime where there's been no arrest. You think I wouldn't notice her?" he says. "I looked up Christine Fleury when she first started to meet with the Wynnes. Her articles appeared on a website called *TruthShout*. She checked out."

"Shouldn't you have been happy to bring more publicity to this case? Maybe she was approaching it in a new way. She could have had a new angle, a way to finally get someone talking. Maybe she could have helped you solve the case . . ." Even I can hear the wistfulness that envelops my voice.

"I've been working this case since I was a deputy. Twenty-six years. It's our most frustrating unsolved crime. And you think your sister nosing around could have been the agent of change. The hero," he says mockingly.

"She was an investigative reporter. She won awards for her work."

"No, not when she was writing as Christine Fleury. That's why I didn't pay her much mind, honestly. Most of her articles were feel-good stories about babies getting hearing aids and soldiers surprising their families at the holidays. She didn't seem like much of a threat."

"A threat," I repeat, latching on to the phrase. "So you would have felt threatened by her if you thought she could reveal something."

"I didn't say that." He pauses and levels me with a steady gaze. "But you, Sarah Drew, didn't have any articles on the internet and no affiliation with a newspaper or anything. Once you arrived, I started to dig deeper. Found out that Christine Fleury was a pseudonym for Willa Stannard, big-shot TV reporter in Chicago. And you're right. Willa Stannard did win awards for her investigative articles, but that was when she was an idealistic young cub. The bigger she got, the smaller the stories got. She regurgitated stories from the Associated Press on air until she couldn't even do that."

I want to defend her. I owe it to her. She was a good writer, no question about it. She just wasn't made to be on the air. Campbell's antagonizing me, trying to get me to leave town. He'll say anything to make me angry enough to leave.

"Who are you covering up for?" I spit. "Is it Bowen? Vaughn? Jack and Grace?"

"I have a duty to protect this community."

"But are you only protecting a few members?"

"Why are you and your sister back in Cheshire?" he counters. "Curiosity about the girl next door or something more?"

I exhale and take a step back. "How did you—"

"I told you. I've been working this case twenty-six years. I know the names of every resident living on Lakeview Lane in 1992. Willa and Sawyer Stannard. I poked my head into your room and saw you both napping the day Melody went missing, for God's sake." His jaw squeezes tightly below his narrowed eyes. "I don't know why you're here. I don't understand the allure of being near tragedy."

"I'm just trying to report some missing plates," I say, my voice innocent and my palms up. "And here you are, trying to run me out of town."

"I am asking you," he says, his voice measured to match his unhurried move to put the notebook back in his pocket, "to stop harassing the poor people of my town about a long-dead girl. I am asking you to leave."

I don't want to show it, but I feel my heart flare with excitement. Leveling my stare, I raise my chin in defiance.

"I'll give you a call if we find out who took the plates off your sister's vehicle."

He turns on his heel, and his boots crunch over the pebbles back to the squad car.

"Detective," I call, my voice honeyed in delight. "For the record, do you have evidence that shows conclusively that Melody Wynne is dead? You called her a 'long-dead girl,' not a missing toddler, after all. Are you planning to declare her legally dead?"

Campbell slams the cruiser door without a word.

When I close and latch the door, I slide the nightstand in front of it, but not before catching a glimpse of myself in the mirror. With my chin raised and my eyes glittering with a scoop, I remind myself of Willa. For the first time, I realize what she loved about her job.

CHAPTER

33

Sawyer

I T RAINS OVERNIGHT. Not much. But enough that I have
to dodge puddles. I decide to skip the breakfast of Kix
cereal and frozen bagels microwaved by Lochlyn. I spent the
night channeling Willa, trying to think about what to ask
Abel Bowen to break this case wide open. Whether I should
lead with the fact that my family lived there too, or conceal
it until the end.

With my overnight bag in hand, I cross the stretch to
the car. My eyes are like a magnet to the missing plate. Then
I see white gouges in the shiny black paint. Were those there
yesterday?

No. I would have noticed them. I looked right at the
bumper, at the trunk, outside city hall yesterday. The gashes
are new.

I quicken to a jog, the wet gravel sucking at my sneakers. A few yards away, I grind to a stop. The trunk is open.
Not a lot, but it's definitely ajar. I lift my overnight bag into
both my arms like a shield as I creep forward.

The trunk has been pried open.

I scan the lot and the cabins. The morning is quiet and still as it recovers from the storm.

Gingerly I drag my finger across the scarred paint. The grooves are shallow and frantic. I shift the weight from my bag and hook two fingers below the lip of the trunk, just below the scratches, and push up.

I jump back as if a jack-in-the-box is ready to spring at me. Craning my neck, I see that it's not empty. A black garbage bag sits in the center of the trunk.

My breath catches in my throat. My gaze darts around the inn again. Still no one in sight. No one to help.

No one to hurt?

My heart starts to thunder in my chest. I lower my duffel onto the gravel and peer closer. The bag is tied with a knot at the top. It's not the shiny plastic of a brand-new bag, but it looks sturdy. Whatever is inside must be fairly small.

It's heavier than I expect. There's a sound like sloshing water as I lift it out of the trunk. I set it on the ground. Suddenly I think of Justine's pale-blue eyes widening as she told me about the bag of blood and hair found in the woods after Melody went missing. I bite my lip and, with shaking hands, untie the knot. Once it's free, I jump back, scared of my own imaginings. The bag folds in on itself and deflates, spilling a rush of pungent water onto the ground and my shoes.

The bag is lumpy. There's something inside. With one hand I tug at the folds of the bag, trying to keep my distance.

Oh God. Hair.

Just like Justine said. I stifle a scream and back away, tripping into my duffel and stumbling. I bend at the waist and gasp for air as my breathing turns ragged.

It's not hair, I tell myself. *It was too short, not the right color. You only thought it was hair because of the story.* With a sob choking my throat, I inch forward. One quick movement and I grab the bottom of the bag and upturn it.

Something tumbles out.

Hair.

Legs.

A dripping tail.

A drowned long-hair cat. Its eyes are glassy and unfocused.

I allow myself to scream.

34

Sawyer

WITH A STRANGLED cry, I start to jog. My knees are wobbly, and I realize I left my bag by the car. By the dead cat.

I circle back to get it, making a wide arc around the deflated garbage bag and the wet cat corpse. I grab my duffel but think about leaving the trunk open—I don't want to touch it—but in a lucid moment realize the interior light will drain the battery if I leave it open. And I don't know how long it'll be until I can get my bearings and go near this car again. I leave the deflated bag on the wet gravel and hope that Russ, the gaunt-faced avid hunter, will know what to do with a dead animal.

Fumbling with the wooden key chain, I drop it twice before I fit it in the lock and swing open the door to cabin six. The soles of my sneakers protest loudly on the tile floor, and I kick them off frantically. I peel off my socks and toss them across the room and rub my palms on my pants, trying to get the moisture off them. The water from the bag soaked my shoes. I don't know if I can put them on again.

Everything—my pain and my fury and my doubt and anxiety—it all comes tumbling out with the gut-wrenching scream. I let myself sink to the floor, back against the door, and scream until my throat is raw. The same way I was terrified that these freestanding cabins would mean no one would hear me if someone tried to hurt me in the night, I am grateful that the distance means I can let my shrieks fade to moans without interruption.

I feel gutted. I take a shaky breath and tuck my clammy toes beneath me. I stay on the floor because it feels solid, but I reach for my bag and pull out a notebook.

I scribble notes.

Bag of blood and hair. Bag of dead cat and water.
Who knows?

Jack, Grace, Roberta, Justine, Det. Campbell. I think for a moment, pen poised above the page with a shaky hand. *Lochlyn. Abel? Woman from city hall?*

I want to cross off the Wynnes, or at the very least Grace. But I remember that Jack works at a veterinary clinic. Does that make him less likely to harm an animal, or does it give him access to dispensable stray cats?

I keep the Wynnes on the list. I try to steady my mind and my breath.

Are the missing license plates related to the dead cat? All night a thought flitted through my brain, too light to catch; then it hit me: Detective Campbell knew the car belonged to Willa even though he couldn't run her plates when he arrived. Did he steal them and use it as an excuse to harass me into leaving town?

"Willa knew," I whisper to myself. "Willa knew. Think like Willa."

I consider. My mind wanders to a time a few years ago, before Willa's panic attack, when she was still a blond with a sexy, throaty voice on the evening news. She was new to broadcast TV. She told me how the studio released footage with different cuts: ten-second clips to hook and entice, and thirty-second clips for brand recognition. Not for the channel, but for Willa. I think of how proud my mother and I were when we saw the thirty-second clips and knew KZTV cared more about promoting Willa than the story itself. And I think of the way Willa despised those short clips, not for vanity, but because she thought it was offensive to boil something down to headline length to capture viewers. "For the person this has happened to, this is the most important moment of his life. Everything has led up to it. It's disrespectful to treat it as anything else," she once said.

Think bigger, I tell myself. This is about more than the cat and the people who know I'm here. This is bigger than Willa's death. Go *before*.

Before Willa died, she sent a final manuscript to her publisher.

Before she died, she came here for a year, talking and digging and nosing around.

Before she ever became involved in writing this story, we lived right next door to the girl who was kidnapped.

I hunch over the notebook and tap the pen on the cool tiles, thinking.

It didn't start with Willa's death, but it didn't really start with Melody's kidnapping either.

Even though we talk about what happened after the kidnapping, everyone I've seen has mentioned the *before*. Before, it was an idyllic lake, right? Wrong. Before, there was still a convicted felon living in a farmhouse in the woods. I think of Leo's face when he told me how Bowen threw a rock off an overpass and killed a passing driver.

A phrase pops into my mind: *It takes an uncommon mind to commit an uncommon crime.*

I smile despite myself. Maybe I'm channeling Willa so much I'm starting to absorb her writing skills. An image flickers in my mind. It's Willa, lying on her back in bed in our shared room. The way she could raise one thin eyebrow, eyes still shut, and convey her contempt silently, was unrivaled. She would arch that famous eyebrow if she could see me now.

I need to talk to Bowen today, but not to ask him about Melody Wynne. I need to know about his *before*: all the things that formed his world before a baby was born down the road.

But someone's trying to scare you, a voice in my head warns. The missing plates and the dead cat are threats. I should go home and forget this. Let Gemma dig for the facts so she can publish the story. Let the Wynnes grieve in peace. Let Willa be dead of suicide, and let Melody stay missing.

I roll my lips between my teeth as I think. "She knew," I repeat. *But what?*

What's complex is not likely, I remind myself. Isn't that what Dr. Ito said?

Then what's obvious?

There are a few versions of what could have happened, I decide.

The Wynnes did it, and Detective Campbell is covering for them. Willa found out and lost her faith and killed herself. Or Abel did it and followed her back to Chicago to kill her when she found proof of his involvement.

I frown. Maybe Merrill Vaughn did it, and his son came after Willa. Maybe the cat was a warning from Justine. It seems unlikely, so I cross it out.

I think about Officer Curry from the Chicago PD and the dog hairs and the semen. Are they inconsequential, like Leo suggested? And what about my original theory, that Willa died in a struggle when Oz came to steal something? Is insurance money involved? Does her death have anything to do with Melody Wynne at all?

I shake my head, overwhelmed. I've slid right back into the present, or the almost present. Something in my gut tells me the key to this case lies in the past, and somehow Willa got tangled up in it.

To get to the conclusion, she followed the story back to the beginning. And that's what I have to do when I talk to Abel.

35

Sawyer

I KNOW THAT ABEL lives in a house in the woods, set back from the cutoff where the dirt roads intersect. But still, it's not easy to find the house. I park in a clearing off the road, knowing I can't drive any closer, but I can't find a footpath either.

Anticipating the lack of cell service, I snapped a screenshot from Google Maps earlier. I pull it up to study the aerial shot. A few hundred feet from the corner sits a gray blur that may be a house. There are three more blurry objects in the bird's-eye view. I zoom in as far as I can, but the pixels blur. One takes the shape of a trailer, one might be a marooned boat in the middle of the forest, and the last is an indistinguishable boxy object near the house. I look to the dusty corner and try to measure the distance, scaling it with the pixelated aerial map.

Winding through the dense woods, I find that there are no snapped branches, no bare ground, and no obvious path to the house. It smells like pine and sap and wet leaves, but there's no hint of the damp, heavy lake scent here. On foot, it might take a good thirty minutes to make it to the lake.

Before I saw the woods, I thought distance alone prohibited Abel, a man with no car, from kidnapping Melody so swiftly that summer afternoon in 1992. But now, as I paw my way through the thicket, I reconsider. It would be easy to get swallowed up by this endless forest.

Finally, I see it through the trees. A two-story wooden farmhouse, weather-beaten and faded to a tired gray. Some of the wooden panels, stained green where leafy branches have rubbed against the house for decades, are starting to tear away from the house, and it looks as if the glass is missing in all of the upstairs windows. Standing near the house feels like I'm being enveloped by a decaying cancer; even the air feels polluted, malignant, on my skin.

I step out from the canopy of trees into a clearing with knee-high grass. It's eerily still. There are no houses or farms in sight. I know I'm on the edge of the sixty acres that belong to the Bowens, but I feel as if I've disappeared into the deepest part of the property.

I take a deep breath, eyeing the house and the trees and the grass all at once. I'm not sure if I should be scared of Abel, a wild animal, or a snake, so I settle on a jittery nervousness about all three. Somehow I know that Abel is the key to solving Willa's death. Standing here, before this rotting, dying house, I'm certain Willa uncovered something, possibly concrete evidence tying Abel to Melody Wynne's disappearance, when she interviewed him, and it led to her murder, which was disguised as a suicide. So why do I creep closer to the house?

The porch is in danger of collapsing. Not just the floorboards, but the wooden columns and the roof too. I step lightly at first, testing my weight, before moving forward. A forgotten piece of fencing, scraps of wood, an overflowing garbage can, and an empty milk carton litter the porch. An old straw broom is propped beside the door, which looks like it lost its glass long ago. I knock on the boarded-up window. I bite my lip as I wait for a response or even foot-steps. It's quiet. I turn to scan the woods again. Is Abel out there, watching me? At the edge of the tall grass I see a rusted ax leaning against a thick log. I don't know how to swing an ax to chop wood, but I will use it as a weapon if Abel attacks me.

I knock again. I gnaw on my thumbnail as I wait. Then I hear it: the thunder of footsteps on hollow stairs, the creak of old floors, and the groan of a heavy door opening.

His face is flaccid and uncomprehending when he opens the door.

"Mr. Bowen? Do you have a moment to speak?" I use my most professional voice, but it comes out as little more than a squeak.

"Who are you?"

"My name is Sawyer," I say, giving up the lie and the fake name.

He blinks. His eyes are unfocused and hazy, like a drug addict, but I don't think that's it. He probably doesn't get many visitors.

"Sawyer," he says slowly, dragging my name across two syllables, testing it on his tongue. "I knew you were okay. You were resurrected, just like me."

I frown. Does he think I'm Willa? Between our height, weight, and hair differences, we never got mistaken for each other.

"Can I talk to you about what happened before?" I ask vaguely.

He starts to nod and doesn't stop. He turns and retreats into the dark house, nodding his head so vigorously I won-der if it's a spasm. I glance back at the woods outside and the light filtering through the trees. I close the door lightly behind me so it doesn't latch. I follow him as he shuffles through the house, dodging cans and newspapers and dry leaves and garbage. I want him to be big, stocky, and full of bravado to convey the larger-than-life menace he's become to me, but he has a folded way of walking. The walls are lined with religious paintings and crosses. Relics from his mother, Dorrie. I recall that Roberta said she was extremely devout.

He leads me to the kitchen, where there's a table buried below fur pelts. My eyes snap around the room, looking for signs of dismembered animals. Lochlyn said he hunts for food, not sport. Every surface is crowded, but I don't see any meat or hunting knives sitting out. The oven is a gaping black hole; the door has been removed. I think of Justine's story about Dorrie's punishment spot for the boys and wonder now if it may be true. I take a seat on the chair nearest the hallway for a quick exit.

"I'm here to talk about before," I say again. "Can you tell me what happened before?"

"They found that baby, you know. Is that why you're here?"

"What baby?"

"The songbird baby. They found her. She didn't turn out like they wanted, so they got rid of her."

Songbird baby? The embroidered bluebird flashes through my mind. Melody.

"What do you mean, didn't turn out?"

My mind constructs a whole new story: a baby with a disease, a disability, a problem. She was just learning to walk and talk. Maybe the Wynnes saw something they didn't like. I shiver.

"They rejected her," he says. "Abandoned her. Hated her." He slams the table with his fist, and the fur absorbs the impact. His voice starts out rapid and agitated at the beginning of his sentences but slows and quiets toward the end. The cadence puts me on edge. Fury fades to resignation with each sentence. His lips keep moving as if in a silent prayer. *Hated her, hated her, hated her.*

It's Lochlyn, I realize. He thinks Melody returned as Lochlyn and the Wynnes turned her away. I lean back in my chair, scared of his intensity and instability. He's a killer, I tell myself, which doesn't help my nerves. His impulsivity got the best of him, and he killed a driver with a rock. He could turn on a dime and kill me too.

"What about what happened before that?"

"Before that?"

"Yeah, before all the stuff with the baby. Like, when you were younger."

He shrugs. "Everyone left."

"Who left?"

"Mother and Father and Leroy."

"Did they leave you alone?"

"Sometimes."

"Did they leave you for good?" I try again.

"Sometimes."

"Did they die?"

His throat saws the words before spitting them out. "Leroy shot Dad, and then Leroy shot himself. Mother left after Leroy."

The skin prickles on my arms, and I look around the kitchen. Did his mother actually die? I can't remember what Roberta said about her death. Abel says she left, but what if she's still here?

What is it about this place that makes me question if people I was certain were dead are actually alive? Reality feels suspended out here, like everything I once believed to be true is an open question. How easy it would be to become disconnected from reality out here. How easy to go mad.

My eyes catch on the fridge. There, beside a magnet that reads *Beacon Hill Ministry: A church alive is worth the drive*, are photos. The door is a wall of family photos, just like the Wynnes' living room, but all the faces have been blacked out in hatred. They're old Polaroids, bearing the faded yellowish-orange tint of photos from the sixties and seventies. Among them, there's one photo taped to the fridge that doesn't fit in with the others. It's a young woman holding a newborn baby. It's the only photo without blackened faces.

"Do you ever see your mother since she left?"

"I hear her. She yells. *Bad, bad, bad, bad.*" His shoulders fold in, and he crumples until his head rests on the table. The table shakes as he thunders on about his mother. "*Bad, bad, bad.*"

I have to get out of here. I don't want to take my eyes off him. His wild, rapid mood swings are terrifying. He's too unpredictable. I shouldn't be here alone.

"I don't want to be alone," he wails, echoing my thoughts.

He looks up from the table. A scar cuts his brow in two, and his eyes are unseeing. "The only way to guarantee Mother's devotion is to die," he says.

My breath catches in my throat.

"Dad died, and she worshiped him. Then Leroy died, and she worshiped him too. I thought I'd finally be the only one left for her to love, but she loved them even more once they died. Then she died like everyone else. Mothers only love you once you die. Why did she abandon me?"

"She didn't abandon you," I stammer. "She loved you, I'm sure."

His head snaps to the side as if his name has been called. He stares at a crucifix on the wall.

"I am the last son," he says. "I die for the sins."

My breath quickens. I stand just slightly, hovering over the chair. With my eyes on him, I back up, careful not to rise to my full height.

The Lord's Prayer tumbles from his mouth. "*Forgive us our trespasses . . .*"

I grope at the photo on the fridge. It's taped, but the adhesive is as old as the photo, because it comes off easily. I tuck it into my back pocket as he drops to his knees like a penitent.

"*Lead us not into temptation . . .*"

I calculate the distance down the hall and note the debris in the way.

"*Deliver us from evil . . .*"

I run.

CHAPTER

36

Willa

Six months before

IT WASN'T A house Willa wanted to be in after the sun went down. Or in the winter, for that matter. She shivered. The kitchen was drafty and dim, with the final fractured rays of sunlight casting shadows on the crucifix above the table.

Time felt endless in this house, but Willa knew from the waning daylight that she would have to wrap up the interview soon. They'd recorded fourteen hours of tape so far—not all today, but over the week. She'd thought she'd have to fight harder for an interview with Abel.

"You look different," he said after she introduced herself.

"How so?" Willa prodded, steeling herself for the tangents and nonsense he was sure to spout as she interviewed him.

He studied her, letting his eyes travel the length of her body slowly. She was past the indignant self-respect of her early twenties, so she let his eyes linger. She was tired.

"You don't have Mother's eyes or Leroy's nose. But maybe you never did. I have trouble remembering sometimes."

It wasn't until Willa pressed him on his mother and brother and his past that she realized it: in stressful times, Abel believed in things that weren't real and heard things that weren't there. She couldn't pinpoint how old he was when the delusions and hallucinations started, only that they'd filtered into his reality more and more often the older he became. Medication might have helped, but it was probably too late for that.

Abel hesitated at the door until she said, "I'm going to write about you, about this, either way." And then he pushed the windowless door open wider, revealing his burnt forearms—scarred from a stint as a line cook while in jail, not a fabled childhood punishment in the oven—and led her to the kitchen, where they sat for the duration of their conversation.

The battery on her phone was about to die, and she knew the house didn't have power. Abel used the trailer with an old generator farther out on the property when he wanted the comforts of electricity. But most days he spent his time in the house, shrouded in memories of Dorrie and Leroy and what he could remember of his father.

Willa scribbled a note on the page. Her notebook rested on an uneven, patchy rabbit pelt. It was probably a by-product of slaughtering one for its gamy meat. Her former self would have been indignant at the thought of burrowing her notebook into the fur of a hunted animal. Now she was still tempted to protest sometimes, but frankly, she didn't have the energy anymore.

"So you felt powerless in your house. That feeling of impotence led to depression and frustration and rage," she summarized. Her diction and syntax were above his education level; she could see it in the way his eyes remained unfocused as she spoke. "Tell me about how you took control again after your mother's death."

Her pen was poised above the notebook, ready to highlight the best quotes, the ones she'd feature in her book. They'd been through this before: the rock on the overpass and the girl. His disciple. She asked the question in different ways each time to see if he'd say something new, something more quotable. Best sellers were made on controversial quotes from convicted killers.

After he finished, Willa nodded sagely. "It's understandable," she said. "Your mother was religious to the point of puritanical."

Willa didn't believe that even Dorrie, flawed from a tragic childhood and molded by fanatical religious principles, had given Abel the impression that he was Jesus. There was no question she had been a bad mother to her sons, but Willa suspected that Abel's diseased mind didn't need much help creating an intensely distorted self-image.

That was enough to set Abel off on one of his prayer chains. His rapid breath sent tiny puffs into the cold air as he gestured with the impassioned mannerisms of a zealot. Willa wondered how much of the recording would end up being mumbled strings of prayers when she replayed it later. While he carried on, she glanced around the kitchen. Her eyes settled on the collage of defiled photos on the refrigerator.

She could picture Sawyer, still pudgy with baby weight on her cheeks at twelve, as she sat on her bed with her knees pulled to her chest. Sawyer's eyes narrowed with uncharacteristic focus as she studied a photo in her hand. It was a man with feathered brown hair, an easy smile, and a striped shirt lounging on a couch backed up against a wood-paneled wall. He had a strong, square jaw and kind eyes. He was a man you'd love to imagine was your absent father if you lived with a mercurial mother. Sawyer generously offered Willa his cheekbones as she parsed out his features.

But Willa was almost seventeen then and didn't need the man in the picture to tuck her in at night or to teach her how to drive. She knew he wouldn't come anyway; she knew where the photo came from. She had seen Claudia turn the page in her library book to find a dog-eared, glossy photograph of a smiling man tucked between chapters. Saw her study it for a long time, just like Sawyer liked to do. Saw her turn it over, write a name and date on the back, and pass it off as their father. That handsome stranger who probably lived close enough to be in the same library district.

And so Willa fought back the words she really wanted to say as Sawyer studied the photo. *He's not our father. He's a lost shopping list, a forgotten recipe. He's a bookmark.*

She'd kept her mouth shut back then, as she always did, and as Abel continued to talk, she continued to keep her mouth shut. Soon it would be time to break her silence. She buried her fingers in the coarse rabbit fur for warmth. She let him talk about Dorrie, his favorite subject, and how he'd once hid under her bed and seen her paint herself in thick, theatrical makeup just to sob in front of her mirrored vanity. He saw her naked breasts that day, but he thought that was inconsequential.

Willa continued to nod and write the occasional note. Her forearm rested on the rabbit fur between notes. She started to chronicle Abel's history, writing and editing and swapping out better words in her mind. She wasn't eager to do it, but she had enough to tell his story.

Cry of the Cicadas: The True Story of Melody Wynne's Disappearance

Part 4: The History

Abel Bowen's childhood follows a complicated narrative.

Born in 1957 to Doris May Bowen (née Gorman) and Raymond Dale Bowen, Abel was the second child of these extremely devout Christians.

When Abel was only four years old, his father, Raymond, was killed in a hunting accident during a weekend getaway with Abel's brother, Leroy, who was nine years old at the time. Leroy accidentally shot their father with a Savage Model 99 rifle.

Following the accident, Dorrie, now a widow, developed an unbending hostility, and gripped her deeply held religious beliefs even more firmly. The Bowens were an insular family even before Raymond's death; they didn't have many relationships outside the Beacon Hill Ministry. But after Raymond's death, Dorrie and her sons became more isolated. She was domineering and overly protective, often refusing to let Abel and Leroy play with other children or leave their home. The boys became misfits.

Dorrie instilled the fear of God in her sons. Abel grew up in the church with near-constant anxiety about the arrival of the rapture if he didn't repent of his sins. It wasn't uncommon for Dorrie to administer beatings with wooden spoons, belts, broomsticks, and other household objects for what she perceived to be wrongdoing. She was known as a strict disciplinarian, and locals still recall the way she shrieked at the boys in public. Only Abel and Leroy know the extent of Dorrie's abuse.

Abel had a lonely childhood. Leroy was his only ally. When Dorrie would allow them to leave the home, the brothers spent their time in the woods near Lake Chicora. The Bowens owned sixty acres, mostly wooded, from the lake to where the paved road becomes gravel. Undeterred by their father's accident, Abel and Leroy enjoyed hunting small game in the woods to pass the time.

In the late sixties, Abel began to inflict self-harm. He experienced rapid and intense mood swings, followed by chronic feelings of emptiness and abandonment. It was during this time that he began to form an extremely close bond with Dorrie. He idealized their relationship and rationalized her physical abuse.

A reliable diagnosis would have pointed to the onset of borderline personality disorder. It's difficult to say if Abel's disorder was a result of family history or environmental factors—instability, abuse, and adversity during childhood are risk factors. It's likely that Leroy would have been diagnosed with BPD as well.

In 1970, when Abel was thirteen years old, Leroy killed himself in the basement of the Bowen's farmhouse using his late father's hunting rifle. He had steadfastly blamed himself for his father's death. Leroy was eighteen at the time.

After the suicide, Abel became an even bigger target for classmates who liked to torment the outcasts. Bullied relentlessly, Abel engaged in frequent impulsive behavior as he coped with the loss of his brother. Following a minor infraction resulting from marijuana possession, Dorrie encouraged Abel to remain home from school to protect him from his peers and the police. She confined him to the basement of their farmhouse.

In 1972, a truancy officer from Mapleton Union High School showed up to check on Abel and found Dorrie was dead, with Abel locked in the basement. An autopsy showed Dorrie had died of a stroke. Abel denied that he was kept captive by his mother, saying he could leave the basement whenever he wanted. He refused to reveal how he could escape, and it led to speculation that he moved behind the walls of the old farmhouse.

His loneliness was overwhelming when Dorrie died. He felt that Dorrie had intentionally abandoned him. She was the only person who loved him, if you could call her dominance love. It was after her death that Abel began to experience feelings of disassociation and unreality, hallmark symptoms of BPD. Unsurprisingly, he had difficulty trusting others and developed an irrational fear of other people's intentions.

Estranged from the Bowens following her brother Raymond's hunting accident, Abel's aunt Ruth, a widowed schoolmarm, moved in with the troubled minor following Dorrie's death. Ruth insisted on homeschooling Abel, and he became more isolated than ever before.

One year after Dorrie's death, Abel was convicted of throwing a rock off an M-90 overpass that killed a passing driver. When faced with a stressful situation, Abel had a tendency to believe things that were not true—delusions—and to see and hear things that did not exist—hallucinations. It's impossible to know if a delusion or hallucination caused him to drop the rock off the overpass or if it was simply a by-product of his impulsivity and destructive behavior.

Charged with second-degree murder and a felony count of malicious destruction of property, the judge in his case handed down a sentence of twenty-five years. Abel served only twelve.

While Abel served his time in prison, Abel's aunt Ruth received a "pauper's funeral" when she passed away with no known surviving relatives besides Abel. Though Ruth was a recluse and rarely left the farmhouse, her death would only further isolate Abel after his release from prison.

Melody Wynne went missing in 1992, and thirty-five-year-old Abel Bowen was no stranger to murder when the investigation turned to him.

CHAPTER

37

Sawyer

SCRATCHES FROM SNAPPING branches cover my arms. I'm breathless when I reach the car. I look over my shoulder. He hasn't chased me, but he still could. I scramble with the key. The door is barely closed before I turn the ignition and pound on the gas. The car spins its tires as it tries to gain traction over the grassy clearing. The car juts into the rutted road.

I fumble with the seat belt to quiet the insistent dinging from the car. I'm going in the wrong direction. I drove straight north, but I need to go back to the cut-off to begin angling west, toward Lake Michigan. But by now he might be hiding in the brush again. I keep driving north as I pull my phone from my purse. I'll take any route as long as I don't have to drive past Abel again.

Once rerouted, I dial Leo.

"I met Abel," I say by way of greeting. I've been in the car for nearly ten minutes, but I still sound winded.

"And?"

"Well, I told you I talked to Willa's publisher, right? She said Willa found a conclusion to this case. And I think she found it in him."

"Why? What happened? Are you okay, Sawyer?"

"I'm okay. I took this photo," I say, swerving the car as I lean to reach into my back pocket, "and I think it proves something. I don't know what yet."

"What's in the photo? Is it Melody?"

I pin the photo to the steering wheel with my left hand. I glance down at it, then back at the road. "I can't say for sure, but I don't think so. There's a woman and a baby. The woman doesn't look like Grace, but the baby looks like any baby. The baby is younger than Melody was when she was kidnapped, so it's definitely not taken after."

"So what does it prove?"

"Maybe that he has a long-standing unnatural interest in baby girls. It's an old photo, taken in the eighties, judging from the woman's hairstyle. Maybe that's why he would kidnap Melody—because he was obsessed with this baby in the photo and decided to steal a baby for himself. I don't know, Leo. He's a psychopath."

"I doubt he's a psychopath," Leo says reasonably, almost affably.

"I met him. He is insane."

The road curves ahead, so I pin the phone between my ear and shoulder as I grip the steering wheel. I recognize the silo and sunflower field ahead, and I know my detour has taken me back to my usual route.

"Well, I haven't met him, and I'm not a forensic psychologist, but I've observed some of Dr. Ito's classes, and once I listened to her speak at a trial. She talked about how killers are usually pretty ordinary."

"He's not ordinary. He's insane, Leo," I repeat. "If you saw the way he recited prayers and freaked out about his dead mother, you'd believe me. I think he actually thinks he hears her too. The dead mother."

"Okay, well, he could be emotionally disturbed, sure. But probably not legally insane, and probably not a psychopath. Did he seem empathetic or charming?"

"He's the farthest thing from charming. I'm pretty sure he left a drowned cat in a bag in my trunk last night."

"What?" He can't keep the alarm from his voice.

"I'll tell you later," I say with a sigh. "Look, Leo. If I can figure out why he might have done it, maybe I can figure out what Willa knew. So why would he take this eighteen-month-old baby girl?"

A horn honks. I whip my head to look for an offending car, but there's no one in sight. I wonder if Leo is sitting outside on a bench at the university right now.

"Let's first answer this: Was it premeditated? Did he plan to take Melody?" he asks.

I consider it. "Honestly, probably not," I say. "He doesn't seem like a planner. He seems like the kind of guy who could snap, though."

"This is contrary to what people tend to think these days, because so many people have seen that show *Snapped*, but that's not how most crimes are committed. That's not most criminals."

"Leo, we already know he's impulsive," I interrupt. "He threw a goddamn rock off a bridge and killed someone."

"Right. Even that was probably not a moment of Abel 'snapping.'"

"Something pushed him over the edge."

"Anger and hostility can simmer under the surface. He could have been nursing rejection and abandonment issues for years. It could have been a slow build until he was dominated by these feelings. Maybe he was contemplating this for a while," Leo says.

"Maybe. He's unstable. I think it's more likely that he had an overdose of emotion than that he planned to take her."

"Then what does the photo you stole have to do with anything?"

I look down again. The edge of the photo is curled under the steering wheel as I grip it.

"Could he have been jealous or resentful of the baby? Of the attention she took away from him somehow?" Leo continues. "Obviously, the victim didn't knowingly trigger him, but from what you've told me, he might be the kind of person who's intensely jealous when someone displays interest in another person. He could have been frantic to avoid abandonment. Maybe the presence of the baby triggered something dormant, and it festered in him until he took her."

"You don't think it was a crime of passion. Even though he's obviously impulsive."

"I think you can't disregard everything else. Everything that comprises him. Fear of being alone is powerful. He's got mother issues. I just think there's more at play here and that you're oversimplifying."

I sigh noisily into the phone. I pass a speedboat marooned in an empty field and grain bins that seem to rival the tallest skyscrapers in Chicago, signaling that my exit is only a few sprawling farmhouses and an apple orchard away.

"He thought Melody was still alive. This girl, Lochlyn, impersonated her a few years ago. He was convinced that she was really Melody."

"He could have been in a dissociative state when he took her. Psychologically, he wasn't where he was physically. He might not even remember what happened."

"So you won't allow me to say he's a psychopath, but you'll suggest he has amnesia?"

"He could be in denial, or by now he could believe the lies he's told himself over the past how many years? Thirty?"

"Twenty-six," I correct. "So you think it was premeditated or not?"

A truck pulls out of a turnoff for Apple Blossom Barn and Cider Mill, though a handmade sign shouts that visitors have missed their chance at the season's cherries and peaches. I slow as a Yellow Delicious bounces from a bushel in the truck bed and rolls into the road without a bounce. A gray field is dotted with orange pumpkins. My first fall without my sister, I realize. At first, waves of grief slowed down and scrambled time, but now, six weeks after Willa was found dead, the stopped-clock sensation hits me sporadically, most predictably when I realize that time is marching on without her.

"I really can't say, Sawyer. I'm only playing devil's advocate to help you think of all the possibilities. I haven't met this guy; I don't know him. I don't even know if he had anything to do with this kid's disappearance."

"So you're basically no help. Tossing ideas at me, that's all. Don't you think I have enough alternatives in my mind already? I've thought through a dozen different options. He did, he didn't. The parents. The psychic. I don't even know if this missing girl is connected to Willa in any way, other than that she wrote about the case. I know nothing concrete, which is why I've considered a million possibilities already. I don't need more, Leo," I snap, pressing down on the gas pedal in frustration.

"Then let me help with something real. Where are you now? Will you meet me at Willa's apartment today? I can pick up her laptop and bring it to the forensic tech."

"I'm driving, but I'll be home in about three hours."

"That's fine. If you're looking for absolutes, focus on what you can find out. This kidnapping is a cold case, but Willa's is still active, right?"

"No. They closed it."

"Oh."

The cell phone crackles as we sit in silence, considering the weight of her case closure. It takes me back into the moment after trying so hard to dissect the unknowable past for the last few weeks.

We don't have more to say to each other after Leo realizes Willa's case is closed. It's as if hearing that the police consider her dead of suicide kills her all over again in his mind. His voice wavers as he stammers a good-bye.

When we disconnect, I'm nearing my highway exit. I drive through a quaint coastal town, stopping at each crosswalk to let straggling tourists wander to tiny shops. I pass an ice cream shop with a giant cow statue on the roof, and I hit my turn signal. I pull over in front of the busy parking lot filled with picnic tables.

The car idles while I put it in park. I smooth the edge of the photo in my hand as I examine it. The baby's face is turned to its mother's chest. I can't tell if it's Melody, or even if it's a girl. The woman, though: she is familiar. Her cheeks are plump, and her eyes droop at the corners. She has a mess of wildly permed hair. I peer closer. Nothing about the room they're in is recognizable. A couch, a window, a white wall. Then I see something peeking out from behind the woman's perm. It's the wooden shake-style roof of a well. The well at the house next door to the Wynnes.

The woman in the picture is my mother.

I flip it over. December 1990.

This must be me, I realize. Melody wasn't born until February of the following year. We would have been so close in age. We probably would have been best friends, growing up next door to each other and only a few months apart in age.

So why would Abel have this photo?

The longer I hold it, the more certain I become that he got this photo from Willa's apartment. She once took Claudia's old photo albums. Willa loved traditions, was driven by her memories, and sometimes dwelled in the past more than I thought was normal. I was always more future minded than her, even though she was the one with ambitions and goals and plans.

My cell phone is down to 28 percent of its battery life when I pick it up and dial Officer Curry. She answers on the second ring.

"Officer, it's Sawyer Stannard," I say quickly. The phone's battery drains as it connects. "I know you told my mother you were closing Willa's case. But can you do one more thing for me first?"

"Ms. Stannard," Curry says, her voice full of resignation. She must receive phone calls like this, from those who survived when crime touched their family, all the time. "How can I help you?"

"That unidentified DNA you found at Willa's apartment. I need to know if it matches this man. His name is Abel Bowen. He's . . . it's hard to explain." The words tumble out of me in a rush. "He killed someone a long time ago, and he's been a suspect in this other case in Michigan since the early nineties. Willa talked to him for this story she was working on. I think he might have hurt her, killed her, when she found out something about him that tied him to the case." Out the window, kids smear their faces with cloudy blue ice cream, and parents chuckle. They're steps away, but they couldn't be farther from me.

"We ran the unidentified DNA through CODIS, which is a national database coordinated by the FBI. DNA from convicted felons and from unsolved cases are put in the system. There were no linkages."

"But . . . that's relatively new, right? DNA testing isn't that old. When was that created?"

"CODIS was piloted in the early nineties and fully operational by 1998."

"Oh! There. See," I say, jabbing the air in front of me as if it could help Curry see my point. "This crime, the one he was convicted for, happened long before that." I rack my brain. "In, uh, 1972 or 1973."

Officer Curry makes a patient "hmm" into the phone, as if she's contemplating this angle. I jump on her silence.

"Can you please get a sample from the police? Call Detective Corbin Campbell. He's part of the Mapleton Sheriff's Office. Trowbridge Township in Michigan. Please, please just look at the samples side by side. I really think he could be responsible for Willa's death."

"I'll see what I can do," Curry says. "Ms. Stannard? If this doesn't turn up any results, this is it. The case is closed. I have to do this off the record as it is. I'm not formally reopening the case to request this information."

"Thank you," I breathe. I'm about to promise that I won't bother her anymore after this, but I know that's not true. I'll continue to call her until I'm satisfied she's found the right answer and not just any answer.

When Curry disconnects, I glance out the window and see two little girls—sisters, probably—in overalls and bright shoes, bumping shoulders as they peer at the ice cream behind the counter. My heart clenches. I ignore the low-battery warning and navigate to my favorite contacts. I hit Willa's name and wait for her husky voice to greet me and invite me to leave a message like nothing is wrong.

"Hello?"

"Uh," I grunt. I look at my phone. Willa's name is on the screen. "Hello?"

"Yeah?"

"Who is this?"

"You called me."

"This is my sister's phone number."

"I guess she forgot to pay her bill, then, because this is my new number."

I'm not sure if the person on the other end hangs up on me or if my phone finally dies, but when silence blankets the warm interior of the car, I begin to cry. My breath hitches, my shoulders heave, and I release a leaden sob.

38

Sawyer

MY CHEEKS ARE tight and itchy from tears when I pull up to Willa's apartment.

Blue and red halos of light pulse from a police car parked out front. My fingers tighten around the leather steering wheel until I remember that the worst has already happened to Willa; these lights can't mean anything as bad as what I've already experienced.

Leo stands by the steps leading down to Willa's garden apartment, talking to an officer I recognize. It's the young cop, the *uniform*, and he's alone. Whatever it is, it can't be too bad if they let him come here alone. As I cross the street, I wonder if he's here about the stolen plates.

"Sawyer! I tried to call, but your phone must be dead," Leo says, and I think of the charger dangling uselessly beside my dead phone on the drive. After the man answered when I dialed Willa, I couldn't bring myself to plug it in and allow the outside world back to the cocoon of the car.

"I didn't want you to freak out when you got here," he continues. He must be thinking of the way I fainted when I saw him at my door.

"Ma'am," the uniform says with a nod of his head. "It's nice to see you again."

Self-consciously I rub at the skin under my eyes, trying to wipe away any smears of mascara left over from my teary drive. I steal a glance at his name badge. Lackey. Right. "Is it?"

Lackey and Leo exchange looks.

Leo is the first to speak. "I got here about twenty minutes ago and saw that the door was open. I figured it was a break-in, so I called the police."

"Is anything gone?"

"We've been waiting for you to take a look, ma'am. I did do a security check when I arrived, but the perp is long gone," Officer Lackey says, looking proud with his police slang. He's younger than I am, but the way he calls me *ma'am* stings. I think about correcting him but don't want to witness the conspiratorial way he and Leo exchanged looks when I arrived again, as if they were colluding and communicating my instability with their eyes.

I peer past them to the dark apartment. The door is open only a crack, and I can't see inside. The lock has been jimmied open and hangs from the door at a useless angle. The gashes on the wooden door remind me of the gouges I found on the car just this morning. Could this have been the same person?

"You could have gone inside," I say. "I'm sure Leo knows better than I do what might be missing. I've only been here since her death."

"You're the most recent visitor, though," Lackey argues.

"Fine. Well, I'm here now." I straighten my shoulders and step down into the apartment. I'm cautious even though Lackey said no one is inside. I lead him and Leo in, feeling like a bitter hostess as I sweep my arm wide. "Here it is," I say dismally.

The living room looks undisturbed. Same stark couch, same book-lined shelves, same lack of coziness. Willa's possessions are so firmly placed that it shouldn't be difficult to tell what's missing or moved.

I see it immediately: the empty surface of her desk. Her laptop and cell phone, placed neatly side by side even after I used them, are missing. The only thing that remains is the photo of her as a little girl, and that's been placed facedown.

"In here," I call.

Lackey shoulders past Leo in the narrow hallway. He's at my side in a moment, his hawk eyes trying to place what could be missing from the flawless room. The downturned frame is the only thing out of place.

I point to the laptop charger behind the desk. "Her computer is missing. And her cell phone."

"The small electronics," Lackey says knowingly. "Easiest to pawn."

I glance down the hall. Leo is still standing beside the bathroom door. I skirt around Lackey and lean against the wall next to Leo.

"I think it might be haunted," I say. He doesn't look up. His eyes are fixed on the tub as if he's conjured her and can't blink for fear she'll disappear.

I place a hand on his back and feel his shoulders curve as he lets out a deep exhale.

"I think you're right. My mom always told me to hold my breath when I pass a graveyard so the spirit of evil can't enter. She's notoriously superstitious. It's a wonder she raised an academic. I was doing it, holding my breath, just now. I didn't even realize it."

"There's no evil here."

Leo exhales deeply again. "Are you sure about that?"

"Ma'am? Would you mind filling out a report?" Lackey calls from the bedroom.

I squeeze Leo's arm and ask him to look around the apartment more to see if anything else is missing. An hour later, after Lackey leaves and a locksmith has been called, Leo drops onto the couch looking visibly drained.

"Who do you think did this?" I rummage through my bag for a snack, knowing better than to hurt myself by checking the empty kitchen cabinets for a remnant of food.

Leo shrugs as he pulls off his glasses and sets them on the springy sofa. He massages the bridge of his nose with his fingers. With a voice muffled by his hand, he says, "Could be anyone, really. Willa's death is in the public eye. Anyone who watches the news would know her apartment is going to be empty."

I shake my head. "It's not just anyone. It's someone who knew her."

"Why do you say that?" Leo stretches, and his shirt becomes untucked from his pants. He looks more disheveled than I've ever seen him, but he also looks . . . comfortable. At home. He sits on the least accommodating couch on the planet under crackling fluorescent lights and the insistent trample of steps overhead, but he looks like he fits into this apartment, amid what's left of Willa's belongings.

"The picture. It was facedown. That's purposeful. Whoever did that knew her."

"It could have just been someone who was ashamed of breaking into a dead woman's home."

We sit in silence, thinking. I wonder if a death and a break-in in less than two months make this the most dangerous apartment or the safest—what's the likelihood that more could go wrong in this tiny space?

"Can I use your phone?" I ask Leo.

He tosses it to me, and I dial a number I know by heart.

"Momma? It's me," I say.

"Sawyer? What's wrong? Whose number is this?" Her voice is craggy, as if I've woken her, but she seems instantly alert.

"Well, everything's okay now, but there was a break-in at Willa's apartment."

"Oh God. What happened?"

"You tell me. Have you seen Oz tonight?"

"Oz? What does he have to do with this?"

"Your *boyfriend*," I spit, "has a history of stealing. I know that he broke in and stole Willa's laptop to pawn it for money."

"He did not."

"How do you know? Were you with him?"

"Yes."

"When?"

"What?"

"When, Momma? When were you with him?"

"Today. And yesterday."

"What time?"

"What is this, Sawyer?"

"This is you blindly lying to cover for Oz. You don't even know when to say he was with you, because you don't know when it happened yet. You're lying. I need her laptop back. I will buy Oz a goddamn new laptop if I can get Willa's back."

"Sawyer—"

"Her laptop was supposed to be given to a tech today. He was going to uncover her deleted files. I was going to have answers finally. I need it to read her manuscript so I can see what she sent to her publisher."

"Oz didn't take it, baby."

"Then who did? You?"

"Why would I break into my own daughter's home?"

I seethe through my teeth and punch the red button to end the call.

"Whoa," Leo says when I toss the phone on the couch beside him. "And I thought you were the good daughter."

We laugh, and it feels good.

Later, Leo orders a pizza and insists we sit on the couch to eat each gooey, cheesy slice.

"Willa never let me eat on this couch," he says through a mouthful of crust and pepperoni.

It feels wrong to disobey her and tease about her fastidiousness when she's not around to defend herself. But it's also kind of freeing. Leo, I realize, lived under the shadow of her rules just like I did.

"You're going to need to spend some time here to close out Willa's estate, you know. I can help with her finances if you want," he says.

"I know," I say, nodding. "I know that. I've just been so busy."

"Yeah, about that. You need to stop going to Michigan too. For your safety."

I roll my eyes.

"It's not safe, Sawyer. Seriously."

"Leo, I am so close," I say, squeezing my fingers together. "I can feel it. I'm going to get to the end of this."

"You may get to the end, but you might not have any more answers than you had when you started. You might even have more questions."

We're quiet for a moment.

"Listen," I whisper. I point to the ceiling. "No footsteps. Finally." I glance at a clock on the wall. "Two in the morning before it stops. That guy must be nocturnal."

Leo smiles ruefully and rubs his greasy fingers on his jeans. "Willa always had to wait until the middle of the night for it to be quiet enough to write. I think it caused her insomnia, actually."

He stands and heads to the door. "So tonight, I learned not only how insanely fast a locksmith works, but also to not answer the phone if your mom tries to call back to yell at you," he says with a laugh. "I can come by next weekend, if you want. To help you pack up all these books she left behind. Let me know."

I nod weakly. I don't want to think about dismantling Willa's carefully curated life.

He points to a package by the door. "And don't forget to cancel Willa's mail."

"Got it," I say. "Hey, Leo?"

He pauses with his hand on the shiny new doorknob.

"Did you know . . ." I swallow, willing myself not to cry. "Did you know Willa's phone number has been reassigned? Some guy answered today."

His eyes go soft above the dark circles shadowed below his glasses.

"I know. I spoke to him the other day."

"You do that too?"

"Every day since she died," he admits. "I couldn't believe her phone number was reassigned so quickly. I found out her area code was considered high demand. Her number got recycled faster than usual."

"Recycled," I huff.

"Their word, not mine," he says. "I've been watching clips of her newscasts on YouTube just to hear her voice. I've never watched the one with the panic attack, though. It comes up as the first twenty search results, at least, but she'd never forgive me if I gave it any more views."

"You're a good guy, Leo," I whisper.

He hangs his head. When he looks up, I can see in his face that he knows that, in the end, it doesn't matter if you're good or not.

CHAPTER

39

Sawyer

AFTER LEO LEAVES, I flick off the buzzing fluorescent lights, casting the room in the shadowy glow of the table lamps. The smell of pizza has settled in, obliterating the acerbic scent of bleach and cleaning products that's lingered after Willa's death.

Finally alone, I tug the box labeled *Sawyer, Keep* from the bedroom closet. I lift the lid to see that this box holds the memories of Willa's childhood. The awards, the ribbons, the high school newspaper clippings bearing Willa's byline: it's all there. There's the stuff I expect, like concert stubs and movie tickets, yearbooks and old birthday cards. But there's other stuff too. A threadbare stuffed animal that was loved until its fur rubbed off. A Ziploc bag filled with many years' worth of colorful friendship bracelets I braided for Willa. An empty perfume bottle is zipped in a plastic bag. I open it and take a whiff. It's fruity and floral, but it means nothing to me. What moment did it take Willa back to?

At the bottom of the box, I find it. A stack of photos is held together with a brittle rubber band. I sort through them once, twice, three times. I set aside every photo with our mother, even those showing just her back, an arm, or a face obscured. From my pocket I retrieve the now-creased picture I took from Abel's fridge. I arrange the photos below a desk lamp and train the bulb to shine on the glossy surfaces.

Willa's photos cover her earliest years, and I'm in none of them. It's as if she curated a life that ended at five or six; she has no photos from after my birth. In the pictures, our mother doesn't exactly look vibrant or happy, but she does look younger. If I pencil in deeply grooved lines and erase the eyebrows, I can see how the woman aged into Claudia as I know her now. But is she the woman in Abel's picture?

After I examine each photo for the slope of her nose, the width of her brow, the droopiness of her eyes, I'm certain it's the same woman. I can almost smell the powdery scent of the Love's Baby Soft perfume she wore on special occasions.

I gather the photos into a pile, with Abel's on top. I need to confront my mother again. But this time, it might be about more than just Willa and Melody, if that weren't enough. I think of the photo I have, the only one Willa let me keep: the photo of our father. There's no way his sandy-brown hair and smiling eyes are those of Abel Bowen, but our family seems to have more ties to Abel than to any other man. I think of his proximity to my mother and how this photo of her is the only one on his fridge without a black-ened face. Could Abel Bowen be our biological father?

With a glance at the clock, I see it's past four o'clock. If I head home now, I could get three, maybe four hours of sleep before my morning spin class. More if I stay at Willa's overnight.

No. I'd have to put fresh sheets on her bed and use the cursed bathroom.

Balancing the leftover pizza box on my hip, I head to the doorway. I remember the package Leo brought inside.

What could Willa have ordered that would arrive so long, more than a month, after her death? I set the pizza box down and, with Willa's keys, tear open the package.

Inside, there's a book: *Cry of the Cicadas: The True Story of Melody Wynne's Disappearance*. By Willa Stannard.

This is it. Willa's book. The full story. I flip to the first page and see the word PROOF stamped on the inside cover. With a closer look at the box's return label, I see it's from Privet Publishing Agency. Inside the box is a slip of paper. It reads, *Once you have completed proofing your book and have confirmed that it meets your expectations for print publication, please select "Approve Proof" on your Privet self-publishing account. Upon approval of your proof, digital and physical copies of your book will be available for order.*

This didn't come from Gemma Matthews. Willa went through the channels to self-publish. She must have decided to circulate the story in whatever way possible, sensing she didn't have enough time to jump through the hurdles of traditional publishing. Maybe she knew her agent would dispute the factuality of the ending.

The book is my biggest break yet. I tuck it under my arm, feeling as if I'm carrying a briefcase with a million dollars across the street to Willa's car. I no longer need the missing laptop. The book is more valuable.

I haven't slept in twenty hours. I can barely keep my eyes open to drive home, let alone speed-read Willa's book. I ease my tired, aching body into the driver's seat with the satisfaction of knowing I'm closer than ever to finding out the answer to every unresolved question surrounding Willa's death.

But first, I need to know if Abel Bowen is our father.

CHAPTER

40

Sawyer

I WAKE WITH THE kind of buzzy excitement I feel when I have a morning flight to vacation. It's ironic, really: Willa always thought I lacked ambition, but the thing I'm most committed to is finding out why she died. I have to find an explanation for everything that's been left unexplained.

Keeping up with eight classes a week has been nearly impossible since Willa died, but I have to make up for my absence or I'll lose my coveted spot to a relentlessly perky girl itching to hound riders into tapping into their inner strength. I avoid Kelly's judgmental gaze as I totter from the bright-white locker room into the steamy studio in my narrow cycling shoes.

My inspirational maxims are more rousing today. I relish the burn in my thighs and my calves and pedal faster as I think about how close I'm getting to settling this mystery.

"Persistence always gets results," I cry. "Feed the activities that bring you power and purpose. Eyes closed, hearts open!"

Push harder, faster. Willa would be proud to see how hard I'm working, to see how close I am to figuring out why she died.

What if she didn't want you to find out? The thought creeps into my mind.

"This isn't a gym. This is a sanctuary," I call out, more for myself than the riders, who are in the grueling arm-weight sequence.

Of course she wanted me to find out, I argue with myself. She wanted me to know what happened the moment she wrote my name in her suicide note.

We're about to enter our soulful jog. "I want you to go into a trance right now. I want you to disappear inside yourself."

I bear down on the bike as the sweat pours into my eyes. A few weeks ago, I would have welcomed this as a means to mask my unprompted tears over Willa. But today, I feel as if she's given me what she berated me about for so long: purpose.

I can't get to the end and not know what happened. I pedal harder.

*   *   *

When I pull into my mother's driveway, she has dirt stains on her flabby arms and holes in the knees of her faded jeans. She's kneeling beside rosebushes to prune them of dead wood, humming as the bagpipes play their familiar funeral march at St. Cyril across the street. I'm relieved to see Oz's truck isn't here.

"Sawyer!" she says, startled. She stands and sways on her feet, as if she's debating scampering into the house, away from me. A weed hangs from her hand. She gave up on gardening gloves long ago, saying she liked the feeling of earth in her fingers. I always thought it might be because she didn't have a wedding ring or an accompanying manicure to protect. "I'm cleaning up the perennials before the first frost. It comes sooner than you'd think every year."

I peel away the wrinkles and the years; I tighten the skin around her mouth and volumize her hair. Those sad, searching, apologetic eyes—did an abusive uncle really cause them? Were all the years of inauthentic reactions, the parenting flaw that Willa railed against, bred from years of my mother being who her abuser wanted her to be?

"Momma," I say, my voice barely above a whisper. I want to slide under her arm and let her forgive me for yelling at her so late last night, for accusing her of helping Oz steal Willa's laptop. But in my tote bag, Willa's book burns against my body, giving me strength I didn't know I had. "I need you to come with me."

Claudia looks from my face to Willa's car with fearful eyes. "Where?"

I swallow. "Willa's home."

Her face is stricken. She hasn't been to Willa's apartment; she probably fears that the bathroom is covered in bloodstains, just like I did. But I'm not taking her to the apartment. I'm taking her to Willa's *first* home, the tiny cottage on Lake Chicora. The place I suspect started it all, and changed it all. I need to know what happened at the lake, why Abel Bowen had her photo on his refrigerator, and what it all has to do with the kidnapping of Melody Wynne.

"I don't like to drive," Claudia says. "I don't like to leave home."

"It'll be safe, I promise. I need you to come with me."

It takes cajoling, and I have to get her purse from the house and lure her into the car, but she finally joins me. As soon as she sits down, her eyes turn wild, like a caged animal. She grips the door handle so tightly that her knuckles are white before we've even left Hillside. As I merge onto the expressway, I engage the locks, fearful that she'll try something crazy when she realizes we're bypassing Chicago.

She stares straight ahead and, after a while, crosses her arms to avoid shaking. She's teetering on the edge of panic,

I realize. The harder she tries to avoid her anxiety, the more intrusive and forceful it becomes. It reminds me of the effort I've put in to avoid fat, just to be consumed by thoughts of weight gain. She's concentrating so hard on her thoughts—whether she's scared to be in a car or to see Willa's apartment, I don't know—that she doesn't say anything when we pass the sign announcing Indiana's border.

My phone rings, startling both of us. I look at the display: Officer Curry.

"Hello, this is Sawyer," I say, putting a false note of cheer into my voice.

"Ms. Stannard, good morning. I ran the results of the DNA comparison at your request."

"And you have that already?" I try to keep my words neutral as I move the phone to my left ear, farther from my mother so she won't overhear. I glance at her out of the corner of my eye. She's rocking in the passenger seat, eyes trained straight ahead, unblinking.

"This request is off the record, so I didn't want this to make its way into the public domain. Freedom of information and all," Officer Curry says curtly. "Abel Bowen of Cheshire, Michigan, is not a match to the unidentified DNA sample found in Willa's apartment. The sample remains unidentified."

"I understand." My heart falls in my chest. I thought I was onto something.

"There's more, though."

Something in her tone makes me punch the volume down even lower and fiddle with the controls to turn on the radio to mask the sound of the call.

"The sequencing between Willa and Abel Bowen is too similar to be a coincidence," she continues. "I believe that Willa and Abel were related."

I swallow. My palms feel instantly sweaty on the steering wheel. "I understand," I say again.

"Do you know what this relationship may be?" Curry prompts.

"I am driving with my mother at the moment, so I will need to give you a call back later. Thanks for letting me know," I say, trying to hide my shaking voice.

A click tells me Officer Curry has hung up without another word. I set the phone down in my lap.

"Who was that?" My mother's first words since she settled heavily into the passenger's seat. By now she must realize we're not going to Willa's apartment. Or her sense of direction and mileage are so off from years of refusing to drive anyplace that she remains unaware.

"It was Leo," I lie.

She accepts it at face value. A mile later, I exhale deeply and mask it by letting a car cut in front of us.

"Traffic," I say to explain away my shaking hand, which probably doesn't help to calm my mother's nerves.

My sunglasses hide my reaction as I absorb Curry's words. Abel and Willa may be related. He's our father, I realize. Is there any other option? A cousin, a brother, the sickening uncle? It's hard to tell Abel's age through his sloped posture and untamed appearance, but I wouldn't peg his age as more than a few years older than my mother.

Static overtakes the radio, fuzzy interference, then silence as it searches for a local station.

"WUOM, Michigan," the announcer says in a strident voice. "Up next is a song from a hot new artist . . ."

"Michigan?" my mother asks, suddenly alert. She grips the door handle again. "I can't go to Michigan."

41

Sawyer

"SAWYER, PLEASE," MY mother cries. "Pull over. Pull over now. I have to get out." Her voice is high, and broken by the sound of her gulping for air. Her chest heaves as she struggles to catch her breath. She exhales noisily through her mouth. She lifts her arms over her head and clasps them behind her neck, bowing her head.

I glance at her nervously as she drops a hand to her chest, covering her heart, and continues to breathe heavily. Her breaths are coming in quick bursts, and tears form at the corners of her eyes.

"I think I'm having a heart attack," she croaks, her hand still pressed against her chest. A sheen of sweat forms on her upper lip and forehead.

She folds at the waist until her head nearly touches the glove compartment.

"Momma, stop!" I shout, gripping the steering wheel tighter and involuntarily pressing down on the gas pedal. "We're in the middle of the expressway. We're not pulling over."

"I can't breathe," she gasps as she straightens. Tears stream down her cheeks. She shakes her limp hands in front of her, as if she's lost all feeling in them. "I'm dying."

"You're overreacting," I snap.

The road widens for our exit. I press harder on the gas instead of slowing and yank the steering wheel to veer right, onto the road that leads past the taxidermy shop and the stands selling fresh blueberries. My mother continues to moan and cry. She holds one hand to her head as if she's fighting a wave of dizziness while the other presses into her chest.

I try to breathe steadily to counteract her gasping, wheezing breaths. I bite my lip because I know what's happening to her. Leo might have promised Willa he'd never watch the video of her on-air panic attack, but I didn't make that promise. I saw in her eyes that she thought she was dying. I know she died naked, slowly, in her bathtub as she floated out of consciousness from the alcohol and the loss of blood, but when I think about her dying, I see her face as she sat in front of the camera that morning. Terror at the loss of control, certainty that she was facing her death. It's the same look my mother has now.

We pass the field of sunflowers, but they've been harvested, and in their place giant blackbirds feast on leftover seeds. The cutoff where the dirt road begins appears ahead. For what seems like the first time since we got in the car, I begin to slow.

I don't have a plan. I'm going to pull up to the little cottage on the lake with the overgrown oak crowding the window and see what happens. I have the photo from Abel's fridge tucked into my back pocket. I'll show it to her if she doesn't admit to living here, if she doesn't tell me the truth. I don't know what I'm looking for from her: Confirmation? Confession?

It's nearly sundown, but it seems darker as the car bounces over the rutted road and becomes sheltered by the trees. They haven't lost their leaves or even changed color yet though it's mid-October; the warm fall has tricked nature's cycle.

We roll past the bullet-ridden stop sign as a fox darts in the road. My mother has mostly quieted, but now she begins to moan and rock in her seat. It's an inhumane, guttural sound. She grips the door handle with both hands.

"Ooh," she moans. "I'm going to be sick."

I stamp on the brake. She fumbles with the door and swings it open, letting her purse spill to the ground as she staggers out.

In the car, I wait, listening to her retch into the brush. Finally she falls silent, and the sound of the wind whipping through the trees takes over. There's a jingling as she gathers the items from her purse. She climbs back into the car and closes the door gingerly behind her. She doesn't reattach her seat belt. We're only driving a short way, a half mile more, to the cottage, and she must know that. But she's so terrified of driving in vehicles that the gesture surprises me.

I ease the car back into drive and haven't gone more than two hundred feet when there's a loud pop. I slam on the brake again. What was it? A gunshot?

I glance at my mother, but she's staring straight ahead, holding her body perfectly still. I wait for another crack. It's silent. Even my mother's breathing has quieted, as if she's afraid to make a sound now.

Slowly I open the door. Crowded trees lord over the dirt road. There are no cars, no animals, no people. I creep around the vehicle slowly. As I round the back of the car and pass the gouges on the trunk, I stop. I place my hand on the side of the car to steady myself.

A knife is wedged in the tire. The tip is angled upward in the sidewall. Did I run over it on the road? I peer into the thick brush again. There's no one there.

Fear stabs at my heart.

CHAPTER

42

Sawyer

MY EYES TRAVEL to the side-view mirror, where they lock with my mother's direct, unblinking gaze. She's eerily still as we stare at each other. She doesn't crane her neck or lean out the window to see what's happening.

I imagine that the knife isn't plunged very deep in the sidewall of the tire, but I don't know if it's safe to take it out. I remind myself of all the times I've heard how people who try to use knives in self-defense often get injured when it's forced from their hand.

I swallow hard and cast another look into the woods and the road behind me. The wind whips my hair across my face. A few raindrops spatter on my arms. I step away from the vehicle, distancing myself from the knifed tire. I pass back around the trunk while keeping my hand on the car to steady myself. I feel short of breath.

As I slide back into the driver's seat, my mother opens her door, and the wind catches it, flinging it wide open. She stumbles out. I almost miss her words, but the wind carries them back to me: "I can't do this."

Dumbstruck, I watch her as she clumsily angles her thick body through the roadside brush and disappears into the forest.

"Oh my God. Oh my God," I repeat frantically. I scramble across the seat, catching my foot on the gearshift. I tumble out the open passenger door and land heavily on the gravel road. Bits of rock dig into my knees. I cry out in pain. I grab at the door and pull myself to my feet.

She's not fast, but she has a head start. We're still a good ten-, fifteen-minute walk down the road to the lakeside cottages. Here, you wouldn't know there's a lake at the end of the road unless you'd been here before. I'm too far away to smell the stagnant water or hear the bullfrogs croak their evening song.

The headlights strain to illuminate the shrouded road. Darkness is falling fast. I wonder if she's heading to her old house. Why would she pitch herself into the woods instead of running straight ahead? She's running east, not north to the lake. Where could she go? The RVs, the campground store, and the Tiny Giant grocery mart: they're all on the other side of the lake.

I don't know where she's going, but I know I need to follow her. I look to the car. It's emitting a low dinging sound to remind me the door is open. I heave myself back into the car, throw it into drive, and punch the gas pedal, wincing as branches scrape at the paint as I pull as far off the road as I can. If someone comes flying down this road too fast, there's no way they won't sideswipe the car, at the very least. The road is narrow and veiled by thick branches.

I stumble out again and cast myself into the trees while calling my mother's name. At first I feel agile as I lithely dart between trees and overgrowth. But it gets thicker, harder to see, quickly. The forest becomes more impenetrable the farther in I go. Thorny spruce needles swipe at my face, and branches snap loudly. Leaves crunch under my feet, and the footing is uneven. I trip on an exposed root more than once and each time catch myself on the rough bark of a tree.

I pause and hold one hand to my chest as I try to catch my breath. I prop myself against an angled tree that has started to lean toward its fair share of sunlight. I listen.

Branches seem to snap from all directions. My mother is out here, but I can't follow her trail when it sounds like there are footsteps all around me. It's the wind: it's picked up, stronger now, and it's cracking dead branches off trees with force.

"Momma," I call again, my voice becoming hoarse and questioning.

The forest welcomes the enveloping darkness like an old friend. I regret leaving my cell in the car; I could have used its flashlight feature even while the phone is useless without a signal.

I take a few steps forward. The ground starts to slant, and my feet scramble for purchase in the mucky, wet terrain. I lose my balance. I fall, landing heavily on my wrist in knee-high water. I sputter as silty water splashes into my face. I try to stand, but my feet sink deeper. I'm in the creek. It's about four feet wide, and the current is fast and shallow. The water's cold. I shuffle across the width of the creek, praying the muck doesn't suck my sneakers into it. The creek bed is firmer on the other side, and the incline of the bank is less severe.

Wet leaves stick to my palms, knees, and shoes as I crawl out of the creek. I crouch on the bank as I try to catch my breath. The wind tackles a limb to the ground with a loud crack, and I jump.

I pull myself to my feet and begin to follow the creek as it winds through the woods and heads north to the lake. If I follow the creek, I know I won't get lost or turned around. But now the last reaches of daylight have disappeared. I take small, tentative steps, my arms stretched in front of me as I feel my way through the trees, careful to hold branches out of my path so they don't snap back and scratch my cheeks. Still, some do, and I wince but keep going.

The creek starts to turn, and I follow it. Up ahead, something wide and silver shines through the trees. I squint, but I can't tell what it is. I move faster.

Then pain sears my outstretched hand. I cry out and pull away, but not before my other hand drags across it too. I lose balance and fall backward. I cry out again. My palm is stinging and, as I draw it closer, it's dripping blood. The sleeve of my sweatshirt is torn, and my right arm has a long, bloody scratch. But my left palm, it's punctured deeply.

I look up and let my eyes adjust to the darkness on the forest floor. I see the parallel lines and the jagged points every few inches. A barbed-wire fence.

I moan again and hold my palm to my chest. It's probably an old farm fence erected at the edge of the Bowens' property. Angry, rusty steel. Dangerous enough, I decide, even without electricity running through the wired barbs.

Just beyond the fence, the silvery thing reflects moonlight. It's a roof, I realize. A tin roof. Shelter in the middle of the maze of trees.

Overhead, the wind snaps another tree limb; it drops into the creek close enough that I feel the splash. The water is higher here, the current faster. It's enough to send me toward the fence. I position my hands between the barbs and strain to pull the wires as far apart as I can. I cry out as the wire presses into my injured palm, and I lose my agility—just for a moment, but long enough to scrape my ankle across another barb as I shimmy between the wires.

I crawl out of the brush into a clearing around the tiny building. It's as small as a shed. I'll break a window if it's locked, I think, but the door swings open easily.

Inside it's empty but for two easels, paint, and a bucket of water. A few paintbrushes have been set to dry on the windowsill. I can see they're stiff and brittle. It smells deeply of cedar wood.

The night bubbles with the threat of rain. A few drops hit the tin roof at first, then a branch lands as loudly as a thunderclap. When the sky opens and rain bullets onto the roof, I start to cry. I cower in the corner of the painting studio, nursing my still-bleeding palm. The wound feels hot, and I wonder if it's already infected. I don't know what I was thinking, running after my mother like this. I should have driven Willa's car down the road as planned and waited for my mother to arrive. She can't sleep in the woods all night, I reason now. She would have shown up to the cottage eventually.

Unless she was heading somewhere else. Not to the cottages or the campground stores or even to the wool farm three miles away. Maybe she was crashing her way indelicately through the woods to Abel Bowen.

As I sit in the corner and let the possibilities run through my mind, I remember something Lochlyn said. She mentioned a girl—Corinne—and her father, who'd built this painting studio for her. But she refused to spend time here after Abel crept around too much.

I glance at the large window facing a clearing. I picture Corinne tying a horse to the post and arranging her paints for a peaceful afternoon. It isn't hard to imagine Abel's dead eyes peering back at her through the window.

I shudder. I'm shaking and wet. Blood hasn't stopped flowing from my palm. I don't know if I've ever been so scared in my life. I'll take cover from the storm in the studio for the night and return to the car after sunrise.

Oh no.

I pulled the car off the road, but I didn't take the keys. The wind swallowed up the open door chime so fast that I didn't have time to realize what it meant. I left it running. The battery will be dead by morning.

Then I'll follow the creek to the lake and wait for my mother outside the abandoned cottage. If she doesn't show up, I'll call Detective Campbell from the Wynnes' house.

There's a flash of light outside the window. Lightning, I think, but it's not expansive enough. It sweeps across the window again. The rain has stopped for the moment, but the wind still howls, forcing its way through the simple construction. The light slows and steadies. It's narrowing in on the studio window.

Branches crack at a methodical pace. Footsteps, slow and steady. I pray it's my mother, using the flashlight on her cell phone to find me. I picture her purse spilled on the floorboard of the passenger seat and her cell phone among the clutter. I know it's not her, but still I pray.

I crawl to the opposite wall and huddle in the corner, below the window. If someone looks through the window, they won't see me at this angle. My muscles are taut with panic. There's nowhere to hide in this tiny room. I watch the doorknob. It gleams even in the dark room, and I see the turning of the knob so many times I can't be sure what's real.

If the door opens, I'll grab the wooden easel and whack the intruder over the head with it. I keep one hand on one of the easel's legs, even though it makes me feel even more vulnerable to stretch my arm away from my body.

The roving beam flashes through the studio again, sweeping across the cedar planks.

The door was unlocked, I realize. Is there a lock I can engage? I squint at the polished nickel handle. The beam has disappeared, so I decide to crawl closer to take a look.

I'm halfway across the floor when the rock comes through the window. Glass ricochets around the tiny space. The rock hits my calf as glass showers over me. I let out a howling cry of surprise and pain. My foot kicks out and knocks over the easel. It's not heavy, but it lands squarely on top of me. The lower front beam on the easel strikes the soft skin by my eye. I see stars.

I'm on my back, tangled in the limbs of the easel, when I look out the window, expecting to see Abel's scarred face staring at me. It's the only moment I've taken my eyes off the door.

The door hits my thigh as it swings open. Abel stands above me, in the same stained work shirt he wore when I talked to him in his kitchen. I try to kick out from under the easel, knowing I'm strong enough to tackle him at the knees and take him down. But the open door pins the easel in place; the room is too small to maneuver it. I try to lift it but it's heavy from this angle, and it bangs down on me.

Abel is silent and still. His eyes seem unfocused. I thrash below the easel, screaming when I put pressure on my wounded palm as I grapple with the wooden legs.

His back is so folded that I barely notice when he drops down at the waist. But I see his fingertips graze the rock he pitched through the window. His motion is quick, faster than I'd expect him to move. He brings the rock down on my kneecap, and I scream.

I'm still screaming when he brings it down again on my head.

43

Sawyer

WHEN I COME TO, I can't decide what hurts most.

My back is flat against the hard floor. A piercing headache thunders through my brain. My hot palm thuds with a dull ache. I hear voices, and I try to sit up. Bending my knee sends a howling pain through my body. My vision is dark and starry as I raise my head.

My fingers graze the dry, pebbly floor. A dirt floor. I wince as pain throbs at the corner of my eye. It's swollen shut. My vision is blurry, and I blink my other eye rapidly, trying to clear it.

I'm in a damp, unfinished space. A root cellar or a basement, maybe. I put both hands on the ground to steady my spinning head and blackening vision. I peer through slatted bars. Not a cage. I'm in the shadowy place beneath the stairs. The wooden planks are bowed and warped. A few are cracked. There aren't many stairs. The ceiling is so low. There's a five-, maybe six-foot clearance from the dirt floor to the wooden-beamed ceiling. There are wide gaps between hanging bulbs, casting the light in dim halos with dark edges. I wonder if this is where Abel's brother Leroy shot himself all those years ago.

Most of the items are pushed up against the stone and wooden walls to avoid a swampy pit in the center of the basement, where the dirt floor slopes downward and standing water pools. The cut by my swollen-shut eye stings as the scent of the stagnant water sends tears to my eyes.

There's a rickety ironing board, a wire kennel, and crates of glass bottles and newspapers visible below the glow of a single bulb. Below another, leaning against a wall, is a three-tined pitchfork with a handle that looks like it's made from bone.

And across the room, below what might be meat hooks hanging from the low ceiling, is a cot with two figures on it. I know Abel hunts, but I can't picture anything besides human bodies being speared with the hooks and strung up by the feet or the hands or the torso.

I'm outnumbered. I know I'll die in this basement, just like Leroy and probably Melody. He'll kill me for digging into his past, just like he probably killed Willa too.

The figures come into focus in the shadowy space. Abel Bowen sits on the cot with a hunched back and clasped hands. Beside him is a woman. I recognize her heavy breasts and bad haircut.

It's Claudia. My mother.

44

Sawyer

I GAPE AT THE way they sit shoulder to shoulder, endlessly comfortable with each other. My mother speaks to him in a low, soothing voice. Abel nods to her words and stares at his clasped hands. Is she trying to distract him to save me? They look too intimate and self-contained. She doesn't glance my way once.

"I never thought I'd see you again," Abel says.

"I told you we'd be together. I told you to wait for me," Claudia says, her hand reaching to cover his. "I wrote you. Didn't you get the letters?"

Abel nods feverishly. "I walked to the Outpost to get them every week."

"Then you know," she says, "that I was always thinking of you, even when we couldn't be together."

I peer at them in the dim light. I've never seen Momma like this before. Is she manipulating him so I can get away?

I bend my knees again as a test. Pain sears through my left leg, but I think I can walk. I won't be able to kneel or crouch. I can't sneak up on them. I'll have to make a run for it up the rickety wooden stairs, but from this angle I can't tell if there's a locked door at the top. If I distract them, I may have enough time to run before they can make it across the watery basement and up the stairs after me.

As I shift, my fingers brush against a cigarette package. It looks old: the red packaging is faded to pink, and the font reminds me of something from the sixties. I picture my mother and Abel down here, sneaking cigarettes as teenagers, huddled together the way they are now. But with all the woods stretched out before them, why would they hide in the house, where they could get caught by Dorrie? The package must have been left behind by Abel's brother, Leroy. Leroy, who shot himself in this very basement.

And I have an idea.

Abel didn't seem sure what was reality or memory or a hallucination when I talked to him. I wonder if I can trigger that in him now, just long enough to steal up the stairs and out of the house.

I pat the ground beside me. Half buried in the dirt is a rock. I dig with my uninjured hand while I hold my other palm, aching and crusty with dried blood, to my chest.

"Mother warned me about an impure temptress," I hear Abel say. "She told me your blood is not pure."

"I gave you a sin offering to cleanse my blood. Besides," Claudia says, "your mother is dead."

"She ascended into heaven."

I watch them through one eye as I scrape at the hardened dirt and try to dislodge the stone. Claudia pats him on the back as he shakes with a tic. She doesn't question his religious rants. She feeds them, even when he points out her impurity. I wonder how much that would have scarred her when she was younger, after years of abuse at her uncle's hand.

"No, Abel," Claudia coos as she strokes his back. "No."

Abel looks up to study her face. I wonder if he sees her at a younger age, when they met. If, in his mind, he's still an abused, unworthy teenager desperate for love after his family's deaths. And my mother, does she look at Abel and see a man who loved her while he was safely locked up in jail, the only man to profess to care for her who didn't force himself on her in the night as she slept?

I free the rock from the packed dirt. I rise, careful to stay in the shadowy spot by the stairs. My sneakers squish with water from being submerged in the creek. I freeze, sure I can be heard across the basement. But my mother and Abel don't look in my direction. I heave the rock as far across the basement as I can, aiming for the opposite corner, which is shrouded in darkness where the arc of light from the dangling bulb doesn't reach. It hits the stone wall with a sharp thud.

It's enough to send Abel flying from the cot.

"Leroy!" he screams in a guttural voice. He shakes his head and starts to choke out erratic groans and yelps and moans. Claudia grabs his arm and pulls him to her chest.

I race around the banister and bound up the stairs. The stairwell is shallow, only a few steps to the top, but there's a door. I paw at the surface as Abel's cries deepen and Claudia's voice becomes high-pitched and frantic as she tries to soothe him.

There's no doorknob. There are no visible locks, but there's no doorknob to get out. I slide my fingers in the narrow space below the door and shake it. It's wedged shut. I sink into the corner of the doorway. What kind of door doesn't have a knob?

The kind that's designed to be accessed from the outside only.

I'm trapped down here with my mother and Abel.

I push at the heavy door with my shoulder from my spot on the stairs. It doesn't budge. I look over to see my mother shaking Abel by the shoulders.

"You can't go to jail, not after all this time," Claudia shouts.

His head snaps back to face her. He looks confused. "I already did. The rock."

"No, for Melody this time. For Sawyer."

45

Willa

Twenty-six years before

I T WAS ALREADY hot when Willa woke. It had never cooled; it stayed hot all night. Sawyer had cried most of the night and finally fallen asleep in Momma's bed. She wasn't supposed to do that anymore; Momma said she was too big now that she'd be two years old in a few months. But if it stopped Sawyer from crying so loud in their tiny bedroom, Willa was happy about it.

The day stretched before her like it could only for a seven-year-old. She wanted to catch a toad, and maybe Momma would let her go swimming after lunch. Papa had told her toads loved heat, but also that they could be poisonous. Willa had gotten a butterfly net for her birthday in June, so she wouldn't have to touch the toad's dry, warty skin if she caught one.

In the morning, Willa tied one end of a string to a stick and another end to a rotini noodle. She tried to fish for toads in the wishing well out front with the noodle but didn't catch anything. She hoped Momma would make hot dogs for lunch, because she bet she could catch a toad with a hot dog better than she could a noodle.

She peered into the well and tried to see if she could spot a toad or a frog or even a water snake moving down there, but it was too deep to see. Behind her, Papa yanked on the screen door and sent it banging open so hard that the shiny glass on the wind chimes nearly ripped through the screen.

Willa knew enough to stay out of the house when he got like that. It was the reason Momma insisted they live separate from him and not talk to him when the neighbors were looking. It was unusual to see him during the day. So she brought her doll with her as she explored the boathouse next door. She accidentally caught her doll's dress on a loose nail and it ripped, leaving a little pink flag drooping from a beam. She was happy it wasn't her shirt, because Momma would have gotten mad. She left her doll in the dry grass beside the front door and set off to pick wildflowers from the side of the road. Momma had taught her the names of the flowers when they tossed the seeds, and Willa was excited to bring home a handful of red poppies and white baby's breath. She held the bouquet in her sweaty palm and ran down the road as fast as she could once she saw the blooms had started to wilt in the afternoon heat.

Inside, she called for Momma and shouted that she needed water for the flowers. But Momma didn't come. Instead Willa heard her crying in the same noisy way that Sawyer did when she had a temper tantrum. She peeked around the corner of the kitchen and saw Papa wipe sweat off his forehead with his sleeve as he muttered to Momma.

Willa crept closer, trying to see around Papa in the doorway. Momma's bedroom was even smaller than the one Willa shared with Sawyer, and she had a very tall bed that took up most of the room. Momma was standing in the skinny aisle between the wall and the bed, and she was crying. Tears dripped down her cheeks onto her checkered blouse, giving it polka dots.

"You didn't mean to," Momma said.

Papa cursed and slammed his hand against the wall.

Willa's little body seized. It scared her when he swore. He went from quiet to loud, nice to mean, so fast.

Momma grabbed his arm. "Your life was already ruined for something I did. I will cover for you like you covered for me. I won't ever tell anyone you did this."

What did Papa do? Willa wondered. She craned her neck around the doorframe and tried to see what Momma was looking at. Something on the ground. Willa dropped to her knees, wildflowers still in hand, and lay her head on the threadbare carpet to see better.

And then she was level with Sawyer. Her eyes were open, staring right at her, and her pudgy fists were clenched. She wore only a diaper, and her chest looked funny. Like someone had scooped out a part of her without breaking the skin. She looked caved in. Cratered.

But her baby sister didn't move when Willa waved at her from the floor in front of the bedroom.

"They'll find out, Claudia. When they find out Sawyer's dead, they'll look at me."

"They won't ever know she died today."

"They will," Papa moaned.

"No, they won't," Momma argued. "They didn't know it was me that threw the rock, just the same as they won't know it was you who hit the baby."

Willa couldn't tell what was wrong with her sister. She tried to whisper to her, thinking that Sawyer could hear her despite the yelling. Willa was on her stomach, whispering Sawyer's name, when Papa stepped backward, and his heel jammed into Willa's ribs. The pain sent stars to her eyes, but she knew better than to cry out. His foot smashed the flowers and sent little crumbles of red and white petals into the carpet.

Papa swore more and stomped into the kitchen while Momma turned to her and pulled her to her feet.

"Willa. I need you to do something," Momma said as she gripped Willa's thin shoulders. "I need you to go next door."

46

Sawyer

"I TOLD YOU I'D never let you go to jail for this, the same way you wouldn't let me when I threw the rock. If you go down, I do too."

Momma threw the rock? I shudder at the way they say those two words—*the rock*—without emotion. They don't equate the phrase with violence, a person's death.

"We didn't take that girl," Abel thunders. "Willa did. She became a believer that day. You were my disciple, and she was our follower. I suffered for your sins when you picked up that rock for me. I was crucified. But I achieved atonement. And Willa did our bidding just the same. We do not have to die for her, because she's already dead." Abel's voice rises, fast and loud, and falls as he finishes, almost as if he loses his sense of urgency and gives up before he's done speaking. His mania and depression ebb and flow so dramatically that they manifest in his speech cadence.

"We might not have taken Melody from the house, but we knew. And we hid Sawyer," my mother says in her quivery, victimized voice.

At the sound of my name, my muscles tense. What are they saying? That they hid me? That it was Willa who took Melody Wynne? I try to make sense of it, but my head throbs with pain, and I can't focus long enough to figure it out.

My mother threw the rock that killed a passing driver, but Abel took the blame and went to jail. What does that have to do with the missing girl and Willa? Willa was just a little girl when Melody went missing. Are they saying that Willa lured Melody from her bedroom? Why? And where is Melody now?

I think of what Lochlyn said when we met: how she believed Melody would be found in the walls of this basement. That Dorrie used to lock Abel down here as a boy. And I wonder if there's another way out, not through the door his mother kept locked from the outside.

Scanning the basement, I see a row of rusted-out empty cans of food lined up against a wall. A wooden wall. I think of the rock I tossed in the corner just a few minutes ago, how it rang out as it hit stone. One wall, the one alongside the stairs, is the only one made of wooden paneling.

Willing the boards not to creak, I slide down the stairs, staying close to the edges where the wood is strongest. My heartbeat thuds in my ears. My vision is a little narrower than it was when I woke. I wonder if I have two black eyes, if the other will swell shut before I can find a way out. I lower myself into the dark spot where I woke, but my knee convulses in pain as I bend, and my toe scuffs in the dirt, sending me flying. I land hard on my punctured palm and cry out.

Claudia stands, sloshes across the standing water in the center of the basement, and is at the stairs in moments. Abel comes to her side with a revelatory gleam in his eyes. I scramble backward and bang into the wooden wall behind me.

"I never thought I'd feel the unspeakable grief of losing another daughter. Sawyer has been dead for twenty-six years. And now Willa's dead too," Claudia says, shaking her head, sending her sagging, jowly cheeks flapping.

Her words send my remaining vision into a tailspin. I'm dead? I press my palms into the dirt, hard. The pain and the solidity ground me. My head stops spinning, but I can't grasp what she's saying. I try to wade through muddy thoughts, but they don't make sense.

"Everyone already thinks you're dead," Claudia says. "They gave up looking for you long ago. But our lives are over if this comes out. I loved you as if you were my own, but I begged you to leave this alone."

Everyone thinks I'm dead? They've been looking for me?

"Who . . . who am I?"

"You're the songbird baby," Abel croaks. "I told everyone I didn't take you. And then you came back."

The room shifts.

"Momma, did you kill Willa when she found out you kidnapped Melody . . . me?"

"I'd never kill my own daughter, and I'd never steal someone else's. Besides, Willa already knew. She did it. She woke you from your nap." Claudia casts a sidelong glance at Abel. "Willa killed herself, just like her uncle did. Suicide runs in families."

With my back to the wall, I run my hand along the surface lightly, wincing as a splinter embeds into my finger. The wall is warped and wavy from the damp basement. I pat at it discreetly, feeling for some sign that the paneling can be broken to reveal an exit, while I keep my swelling eye on my mother.

She turns to Abel. "I promised I'd always protect you. Now . . . I need you to do one last thing for me."

47

Sawyer

"THE POLICE HAVE wanted to pin the kidnapping on you for almost thirty years now," Claudia continues, her eyes boring into Abel. He stares at her with reverence. "We have to get rid of her, but not here. If she's ever found on your property, everyone will think you had her here all along. They'll think they were right," she spits.

I clench my fists, and pain shoots through my body. My breath is hitching in my throat, coming faster and faster. My own mother is going to kill me, I realize. My mind races, trying to think of something reasonable to say to free me from this basement and their conspiratorial whispers.

Claudia starts to move, hunting through the debris lying around. "She can't be recognizable, at least not in any way that ties her to me. Do you still have it?" she asks as she rummages through a cardboard box. "The gun, Abel. The one your brother used. You said you couldn't see his face after, right? That's what you need to do."

Abel turns to follow her. "I threw it in the lake."

My hands start to shake so hard I can barely move my fingertips. I start to paw at the wooden wall behind me, feeling for a gap or a break in the paneling. Sweat pours into the cut by my swollen eye and stings. Behind me, I hear Abel sloshing through the standing water. I don't turn to see if he's approaching me. I grope along the wall as my brain screams at me to hurry. Hurry, hurry, hurry.

I grab the bottom edge of a wide wooden panel and tug on it, hard. It creaks loudly but doesn't break.

"Did you hear that?" Abel shrieks. I stop, but he doesn't look at me. He races to the stairs. "Is she leaving? If it's Sunday, she'll be at services all day."

He thinks it's the floorboards. I yank at the panel again. Nothing. I yank at another, and another. The wood creaks again, and Abel scrambles farther up the stairs.

"Mother, don't leave me!" he howls.

I grab hold of another panel. The wood is rotted at the bottom. The panel is damp. I wrench it as hard as I can. It tears off the wall with a thundering crack.

Abel screams. It's a terrifying throaty bark of a scream. It doesn't stop. He screams so hard he loses his balance and lands heavily on the stairs.

"The shotgun! The shotgun!" he wails.

Claudia pounds through the water. "You're hallucinating! Dorrie's dead! Leroy's dead! You know this!"

She's at his side, pulling on his shirt, shaking him. He's throwing his head from side to side, screaming. My mother kneels in front of him, pulling him to her chest. Seeing them together shakes my core: the way she cradles his body, the dirt on her knees—she looks like the mother I've known my whole life. How many times has she held me like that?

But she'll still kill me to keep her secret.

48

Sawyer

M Y BREATH IS coming shallow and fast. My heart beats so hard in my chest I feel like I'll go into cardiac arrest. I grope at the wall. I'm frantic and jerky, leaving bloody streaks on the panels. Abel screams. And screams. Louder, wilder.

"I'm sorry, I'm sorry. Tell me you're okay," my mother begs.

I can barely see anymore. My left eye is swelling shut, fast. My knee screams in pain. Abel screams louder the more my mother apologizes.

And then I hear it through the screams: "Do you have another gun in the house?"

She's still holding his head. "Dorrie's asking. She needs it." Her voice is a whisper with a chiding, manipulative edge.

At the sound of his mother's name, Abel quiets. He stops writhing. He stops screaming. His face goes slack, but his body tenses. A vicious mood swing rumbles through him. With a grunt, he swings his fist, striking hard, landing a blow on Claudia's jaw. It sends her to the floor. She twitches, and a trickle of blood appears at the corner of her lip. It settles into the deep groove of her sagging cheek and pools in the dirt.

Abel's eyes latch on to mine. It's the same dull, unseeing look that transfixed his face that day in the kitchen. I don't know who he thinks I am. I eye the pitchfork. I imagine raking it across his face and blinding him with howling pain. But he and a pool of sitting water block me from making a dash for it.

He stands, swaying on unsteady feet, and lets my mother's unconscious body roll away from him. I backpedal on shaky legs and stumble. My knee won't hold my weight. My ankle hits something solid, something that sends another wave of pain through my leg. I look down. It's an old cast-iron teakettle.

I grab the handle and swing at the paneled wall. The kettle is at least ten pounds, maybe more. The spout tears through a weak spot in the rotted wood. I swing again, harder, in another spot. Another tear. I drop it and begin to rip at the holes with my hands, widening them. Wood punctures my fingers. I kick. The wood gives way with a loud crack. Behind the paneling, it's hollow. I clamber through the hole and squeeze into the space between the paneling and the stone wall. Abel's at the hole in a moment, peering through, tearing through.

I'm in the passageway where he hid as a kid. My toe kicks cans and garbage as I shoulder through the narrow opening. I'm inside the walls of the old farmhouse. It stinks of death. Moldy food, but probably dead animals too. Light from the dim bulbs doesn't penetrate the hole in the paneling. It's dark and suffocating. My shirt snags on a nail, and I feel it puncture my shoulder, but I keep moving.

He hacks at the wall. He's inside the passage now. He's angling through sideways, his shoulder leading the way. His breathing is as calm as mine is ragged.

My shoulder strikes something. I grabble for it in the dark. Bars. A ladder, I realize. I grab above my head and try to pull myself up. I wail in pain at the pressure on my palm. My shoulders scream from the exertion. He's getting closer. His feet crunch across the same garbage I passed. He grunts.

I'm backed up against the ladder. He jabs a hand toward me. I turn to him. My voice comes out rough, strangled.

"Bad, bad, bad, bad, bad!"

He stops. His face becomes wooden. While he's dazed by Dorrie's old mantra, I kick him in the gut. He loses his footing and stumbles backward, twisting in the tiny spot. As he falls, I reach for the nearest rung again and hoist myself up.

Bending my knee is excruciating. I howl in pain. My toes slide on the stone wall as I haul my body up the ladder. When my sneaker touches the lowest rung, I scramble the rest of the way, banging into the ceiling as hard as I can. A wooden cover panel pops up. I heave myself through the opening and wail as my knee—probably shattered, maybe irreparable—touches the floor.

It's even darker up here, out of the passage. I put the cover back over the opening and feel along the wall. Where am I?

My fingers slide along what feels like a shelf. Something falls to the floor and shatters at my feet, sending a sickly sweet smell into the space. I picture dead animals. Dead people. My fingers touch a smooth surface, and I push. It gives way. The pantry door opens, and I go flying into the kitchen. I crash into the table that's still littered with animal pelts. It's dark, but moonlight filters weakly through the window.

I bound through the hallway and thrust open the door. My footsteps are heavy and loud as I stagger over the porch and into the woods.

Cry of the Cicadas: The True Story of Melody Wynne's Disappearance

Epilogue

Abel Bowen's crimes were galvanized by love.

A perfect storm of dysfunction bonded Abel and Claudia as teenagers and formed the base of their codependent relationship. Exposure to violence, shaming, and abandonment as a child left Abel, who suffered from symptoms of borderline personality disorder, with a dizzying lack of self-worth and the inability to tame his impulses. Claudia, only fourteen when she met Abel, felt unbearable shame and humiliation at her history of sexual abuse at the hands of her uncle Morris.

Together, their feelings of worthlessness receded momentarily. Their emotional dependencies grew until they held the romanticized illusion of an unbreakable bond. They became coconspirators, dreaming of any way to regain control after feeling powerless their whole lives.

When they decided to throw the rock off the M-90 overpass, killing thirty-year-old wife and mother Martina Grabbel, it wasn't an accident. It was a way for them to feel invulnerable. An opportunity to victimize. Entangled with misguided religious beliefs, the rock was power for the powerless.

And so solidified their toxic connection.

Maybe they initiated their relationship believing in authentic love. Instead, the romanticized illusion of passion became the means to justify violence. The thrill of an unbreakable bond and a solemn oath to never tell the truth both cemented and strengthened their relationship, even when Abel went to prison for their crime.

Claudia could justify that she suggested the abduction of Melody Wynne out of love for Abel— to protect him from spending the rest of his life in prison for an accident. After all, criminal couples have lied, robbed, embezzled, kidnapped, and even killed for each other—all in the name of love.

Claudia could even claim she feared for her own safety if she revealed Abel's violent attack. But it wasn't love or safety she was protecting when she suggested Melody's kidnapping. She was protecting herself, for if Abel's crime were revealed, he could implicate her in the overpass death.

Self-preservation is natural. It's basic, instinctual. And it's also the root of countless crimes.

49

Willa

The night of

THE WORDS DANCED on the screen like a moth batting at a light. Willa rubbed her eyes. She knew it wasn't because she'd been staring at the screen for hours in the dark. She took another sip from the bottle and set it on the floor so it wouldn't leave a ring on her wooden desk. Wasn't it Hemingway who suggested writing drunk? She dismissed the thought as she hit save.

Willa squinted at the screen as she attached the file to an email to Gemma, and, for good measure, clicked *Submit* on the self-publishing website too. She imagined her story soaring through the internet as if through the pneumatic tubes at a bank. She wondered if Gemma, in New York, would check her email this late, and how long it'd take her to get to the author's note at the end. Willa felt a mixture of regret and relief at knowing she'd never see her name on the cover of this book. She reminded herself that she'd seen her byline on enough articles to validate her career as a writer. With a few practiced keystrokes, she typed a command and dragged and dropped files until her notes and manuscript were hidden from view in a virtual vault.

As she stood, she ran a hand over the end of her bed. She'd neglected to wash the sheets for a few weeks, maybe longer, and they still held telltale crusty stains from a series of hookups. There were some things she just couldn't muster the energy to do and other habits she just couldn't shake.

Willa picked up her phone and thumbed through the contacts until she found her sister's name. With a limp wrist she dangled the phone near her ear, listening until the dull ring was replaced by Sawyer's chirpy voice imploring her to leave a message. She asked Sawyer to return her call, but she knew she wouldn't—not fast enough, at least—so she set her phone beside her laptop.

She finished off the bottle and walked into the bathroom, unleashing a pool of tepid water into the tub as she undressed. She stepped into the bath.

Placed neatly beside the tub was a razor blade.

Cry of the Cicadas: The True Story of Melody Wynne's Disappearance

Author's Note

"Where do you get your ideas?"

It's a perennial question that every author should be ready to answer. My answer is one I've wrestled with for nearly thirty years.

At my best, I could consider myself an investigative journalist. Researching and revealing systemic flaws is fascinating to me. Every journalist hopes that change may arise from their story. It's my sincere hope that, in telling this story, I've helped bring closure to many people, most of all Grace and Jack Wynne.

In a nonfiction book, it's essential to gather input from those who lived through the event. The perspectives of the perpetrators, victims, and survivors are crucial to retelling the crime.

I am all three.

It would not be fair of me to reveal Claudia and Abel's crimes if I didn't also admit to my own complicity in these unfortunate events. In the spirit of transparency, I am compelled to confess that, when I wrote the first pages of this book and posed questions about Melody Wynne's whereabouts, I knew exactly where to find her.

I knew she was teaching her Tuesday morning cycling class, using her most energetic voice to motivate toned suburban mothers. I knew just how she'd tuck her buttery-blond hair behind her ear when she doubled down for the final cardio push. I knew what she didn't know—who she really was.

She trusted me implicitly, and that was the root of the problem. Melody trusted me when I walked into her bedroom in 1992, found her napping, and told her to come with me—"Quietly, like a mouse." She continued to nap beside me, dressed in the clothes of my poor dead sister, when the police came to our cottage to ask if we knew anything about her kidnapping. She trusted me when I told her not to cry and when I told her we were her family now. She was too young for doubt ever to cross her tiny face, too young to know she used to have a different name. She grew up believing I was her sister, not the monster who lured her out of her home.

Now these revelations will break that trust, irreparably, I'm sure. She'd never forgive me if I were alive.

If I could go back, I'd be the girl with the dead sister. Instead, poetically, I am the dead sister. I hope that in my death, healing can begin.

Willa Stannard

50

Sawyer

B Y SPRING, NEARLY half the trees on campus are deci-
mated by Dutch elm disease. Most of the faculty and
the sisters mourn the loss as the chain saws buzz and whip-
skinny trees are planted, but Leo reports that it feels new for
the first time since he arrived at the university. That death
has brought some life back.

He convinces me to speak to his SOC 365: Sociology of
Deviant Behavior class before finals begin. Nothing I say
will be on the test, he assures me, but I know that the students might actually pay attention when I share the story.

Leo introduces me by saying that I have firsthand experience in understanding the psychology of criminal couples.
He tries to hide his sudden, jittery doubt when I walk to the
front of the classroom. He avoids eye contact and crosses his
ankle over his knee to quiet his anxious muscles. It reminds
me of the hyper, restless way he jiggled his foot as he sat
with me in the hospital room after I got away from Abel's
house.

A few hours after the Wynnes found me in their boathouse and Roberta drove me to the hospital when they were

too shaky to do it themselves, Leo showed up. He was rattled, and his eyes carried a quiet dread, as if he'd realized I didn't have any family sooner than I did.

But I did have family. A DNA test confirmed it, and the *Trowbridge Gazette* almost ignored the story, recalling the Lochlyn Farmer hoax. And Leo was there, in Cheshire, staying on Roberta's couch, for it all.

And now his face is choked with the same shivery worry he had when he looked at me in those early days. Before he shook it off and helped me clean out Willa's apartment and hire a lawyer and swap my state ID for an official driver's license. Before he confronted Oz about the missing laptop, the dead cat, and the stolen license plates—all commissioned by Claudia to slow my progress and scare me off Willa's trail. Before he realized I'd be okay, even if no one else was.

So I steel myself to tell the class what I told the *Gazette* and Frenchie at *TruthShout* and Gemma, to relay to her fact-checkers, and even KZTV's Brooke Conroy. I told them how Abel and Claudia's love didn't transcend the interrogation. When caught and separated, their delusional codependent bond disappeared. Self-preservation took over. At least it did for Claudia. Ever the victim, she claimed she'd been battered and abused and went along with Abel because she feared for her life. To avoid being charged as an accessory in her daughter's murder, she copped a plea deal to reveal that Abel wrapped the twenty-five-pound body of baby Sawyer in chicken wire before disposing of her in the unattended manure pit of a nearby dairy farm before the search for Melody expanded past Lake Chicora. When an officer from the Mapleton Sheriff's office relayed Claudia's story for the evening news, they ran a clip of him agreeing that a concentrated blow to the chest can stop the heart when delivered just right—"That's why you've got to keep an eye out at baseball games," he said—nodding at the camera, almost bored, as if he knew it all along. But the police didn't know, because they never found her tiny bones in the manure pit, not even when it was emptied to fertilize the fields a few times a year. Did the farmers find traces of her when they pumped the pit all those years ago? If they did, they aren't revealing it now.

Because Claudia was a sexual abuse survivor, a supposed witness to the crime on the overpass, and a terrified mother of two dead daughters, no one questioned her claims. But Abel said he'd never leave her, that he'd never turn on her, and that he'd never live in a world without her. So instead of implicating Claudia in a forty-five-year-old death or a kidnapping, he hung himself in his cell at the county jail.

Suicide does have familial bonds.

But now I know they're not my family. I never have to look at that photo I thought was my father again, redrawing his eyes or chin onto my face. Now I know that Jack is my father. After a lifetime of cherry-picking men's facial features and aligning them to my own, I finally know who gave me my rosacea-stained cheeks and round face. While our reunion has been slow and cautious, he gifted me a rescue dog from his clinic, and somehow I can tell that the scruffy mutt is his way of saying he can still love me after all this time apart.

Grace, of course, isn't nearly as guarded as Jack. Her voice takes on a motherly, instructional tone as she shows me how to mix watercolors to achieve the perfect blue of the lake. She cried when I helped her dismantle her wall of children's photos. I visit most weekends, and she wavers between relief and sorrow until Jack sternly reminds her to be grateful for the present moment.

Too often, Grace says she's sorry—for the lost time, for humming so loudly that day in the garden that she didn't hear Willa sneak into her house—but she's no Claudia.

I can't call that woman Momma anymore. We haven't spoken since the night in Abel's basement, but I did drive by her house once. With Claudia in prison, convicted of kidnapping, it was my house, briefly, before I put it on the market. A young couple calls it home now. As I drove by, two deer munched mindlessly on her long-stem tea roses in the front yard. I hit the gas pedal too hard, squealed around the corner, and pulled over to cry. I cried because I knew how proud she was of those roses, and then I cried for the pain she made Willa carry for so many years.

A heavy rock settles in my heart when I think about Momma and Willa. At first, without them, I felt like a little girl lost in a grocery store: confused, overwhelmed, abandoned. It was Leo who helped me reorient myself. He insisted I meet with a career adviser at the university—a pretty woman with a gentle voice whom he asked to dinner recently—and she enrolled me in courses to become a counselor. My shattered knee forced me to quit my job at the cycling studio and find something more permanent. More fulfilling. When my program ends, I'd like to get a job at an eating disorders clinic for teenagers in the north suburbs.

Claudia's worry about Willa's insurance money was valid; since she committed suicide so soon after taking out the policy, there was no payout. While the money would have been helpful toward my education, I find I don't miss something I never expected to have.

I'm waiting to be furious with Willa. Everywhere I go, a chorus of voices asks me if I blame her. The assumption makes me feel guilty, because I can't shake the feeling that the blame still belongs to me, for not saving her. The burden of responsibility didn't die along with Willa; it simply shifted to me. Just as I grew up both envying and admiring her, I have mixed feelings about her now, but my little-sister loyalty is muffling my anger.

"It raises the question: How much do you trust your partner? And what happens when you put your life in their hands?" I give a half smile and bow my head slightly as I step away from the center of the classroom.

As I finish, I know I'm not done telling the story. On every anniversary, there'll be calls for quotes and memories. There'll be questions about the criminals and the victims, and forever the question of how you tell the difference between the two in this story. And I'll look back. I'll point to what came first.

But I won't lose sight of what comes next.

ACKNOWLEDGMENTS

First, I'd like to extend my warmest gratitude to my agent, Amy Moore-Benson. Thank you, Amy, for your insightful guidance, hard work, motivation, and enthusiastic belief in not only this manuscript but my future as an author.

The sharp eye of my editor, Terri Bischoff, helped shape this book into what it is today. Thank you for this opportunity.

I'm grateful for the help of everyone at Crooked Lane Books who helped bring this book to life.

Thank you to my family for encouraging my creativity and determination, and for instilling in me a love of reading and writing.

Finally, thank you to my husband, Darren, who firmly believed in me at every stage of this publishing journey. Your support, encouragement, and celebration of each milestone helped me realize my dream.